SCARLETT FINN

Also by Scarlett Finn

GO NOVELS
GO WITH IT
GO IT ALONE
GO ALL OUT
GO ALL IN
GO FULL CIRCLE

EXILE
HIDE & SEEK
KISS CHASE

WRECK & RUIN
RUIN ME
RUIN HIM

THE BRANDED SERIES
BRANDED
SCARRED
MARKED

FORBIDDEN PREQUEL DUET
ALL. ONLY.
ONLY YOURS

TO DIE FOR...
TO DIE FOR TRUTH
TO DIE FOR HONOR
TO DIE FOR VIRTUE
TO DIE FOR DUTY
TO DIE FOR LOVE

LOVE AGAINST THE ODDS STANDALONE COLLECTION
SWEET SEAS
HEIR'S AFFAIR
RESCUED
MAESTRO'S MUSE
GETTING TRICKY
THIRTEEN
REMEMBER WHEN...
RELUCTANT SUSPICION
XY FACTOR

NOTHING TO...
NOTHING TO HIDE
NOTHING TO LOSE
NOTHING TO DECLARE
NOTHING TO US
NOTHING TO SAY
NOTHING TO GAIN
NOTHING TO YOU
NOTHING TO THIS

THE FORBIDDEN NOVELS
FORBIDDEN DESIRE
FORBIDDEN WANT
FORBIDDEN WISH
FORBIDDEN NEED

KINDRED SERIES
RAVEN
SWALLOW
CUCKOO
SWIFT
FALCON
FINCH

THE EXPLICIT SERIES
EXPLICIT INSTRUCTION
EXPLICIT DETAIL
EXPLICIT MEMORY

MISTAKE DUET
MISTAKE ME NOT
SLEIGHT MISTAKE

RISQUÉ & HARROW INTERTWINED
TAKE A RISK
FIGHTING FATE
RISK IT ALL
FIGHTING BACK
GAME OF RISK

LOST & FOUND
LOST
FOUND

PROLOGUE

'I DON'T WANT TO TALK.' Darcy turned to see that the dark-haired man looming behind her was not the one she'd been expecting. 'Who are you?' she asked, taking a step backward bringing her back abruptly against the tree she had been using for cover.

'This is my party, who are you?'

'I'm with Lottie,' Darcy said, allowing herself to lean forward. 'You're Johnny Sloan?'

'The one and only, Cookie… Aren't you a little young to be hanging here?'

Her attention was drawn to the dimple that formed in one of his cheeks as his lips ever so slowly curled upward in one corner. Mostly he was in shadow; the woods around the community hall had been used by generations of manic teenagers for clandestine activities, as demonstrated by the cigarette his long-fingered hand was bringing to his mouth when the dimple disappeared.

'I wanted to be alone.'

'You're never alone in these woods, haven't you heard the stories?' he asked.

Stories of the un-dead, scorned lovers taking revenge, and the dangers of drugs were passed from generation to generation. If all the tall tales were to be believed, the forest was more heavily populated than the town.

'Why are you leaving town?' she asked and took a step toward him. 'Is it true your mother killed herself? Is it true you had sex with Mrs Taylor in the art cupboard?'

'You're a curious little thing, aren't you?'

'I heard your dad was sending you to rehab for heroin addiction… Did you really beat Sawyer for buying Josie that Pepsi last summer?'

'Man,' Sloan said on an exhale. 'And you wonder why I'm getting out of this town?'

'You're a legend around here. I heard that Josie was admitted to hospital for a mental breakdown when you told her you were leaving… Did your dad really stab you?'

'Where do you get these stories?'

Darcy's hands trembled as she brought herself ever closer to his static figure that still loomed in shadow. Illumination cut through the trees from the community hall security light, the harsh yellow sliced his cheek, showing the harsh angle of that chiselled jaw and the bulk in that infamous shoulder.

'Lottie says that your father kicked you out for driving your mother to drink… Is that what happened?'

'You're practically salivating there, Cookie. Don't you have some drama of your own?'

His tone was as she would have expected: un-rattled. She was nobody and chances were he had heard all of the rumours about himself and then some. Her wide eyes relaxed, her fingers stretched out of the fists that had gathered her skirt against her legs. When she realised she was leaning forward, she straightened and tried to do what any other self-respecting teenager would do in this situation: act cool.

'My drama isn't driving me out of town,' she said and moved back to her original position against the tree. This time she let the tension go from her shoulders and lounged, except the tree wasn't that wide and the roots had broken ground. Sliding from the bark, her shoulder stung, and she lost her footing, hooking her heel on a gnarled root that took pleasure in sending her backward into the compacted mud with a thud.

'You okay there, Cookie?' His attempt to hide his humour was pathetic.

Growling, Darcy pulled her shoes from her feet and threw them to the ground, she flopped her elbows to her knees and dropped her forehead to her wrists. 'Oh, laugh it up, Sloan… You'd hardly be the first.'

A sharp inhale followed a low exhale and then his burning cigarette appeared on the ground in her peripheral vision. His heavy black boot ground it out and then before she could wave him off, he appeared at her side, landing on the earth much more gracefully than she had.

'What's your name, Tyke?' he asked.

'Darcy Holmes,' she grumbled, trying not to watch as he took off his leather jacket.

'Ah,' he said as if understanding something. Without a word he hooked his jacket over her shoulders.

Rolling her head on her arm she looked up at him through her rapidly curling hair, the straightening irons never kept it under control for long, even with a whole can of hairspray. 'What?'

'You smell like, cakes and cookies,' he said. 'You're Hayley Holmes kid.'

'Grandkid,' Darcy said.

Her mother had died when she was just a few months old, so Darcy was used to the mistake. She and her father had lived with her grandmother ever since, Darcy had no memory of her mother. Although living in a small town, she had heard all the stories about how wonderful her mother was. Those stories gave her a lot to live up to.

'She owns that bakery, on Main Street, right?' Darcy nodded. 'It must be great to have access to all of those free baked goods, whenever you want.'

'It means I learned the importance of exercise young.'

When he conceded a smile so did she. The charm in that dimple alone would be enough to bring girls running Darcy realised. Her breath stopped in her throat when he leaned closer, his hair flopping in wide fingers over his long-lashed coal eyes.

'What are you doing at a party like this, Darcy? You hardly seem the type.'

'For drink, drugs, and rock 'n roll… no,' she admitted. 'You're probably right… Ricky said he would get Lottie in, and she didn't want to come alone.'

'My cousin Ricky?' Sloan asked.

Darcy nodded. 'He's been trying to get into Lottie's underwear for like two years.'

'Lottie who? Is she even legal?' Darcy snorted a laugh, her hand flew to cover her mouth, but his relaxed smile goaded her on. 'Got something to say, Tyke?'

'You and Josie were caught having sex at school when you were fourteen.'

'That was different,' he said. 'That was then, no one cared about that shit then.'

'You just turned nineteen,' she said, hiding her smile that seemed glued in place. He wasn't breaking eye contact, and neither was she. 'It wasn't that long ago.'

'Half a decade,' he said then his smile disappeared. 'Jesus that makes me sound old.'

Falling back onto her elbows, she let herself

laugh. 'You're still a teenager.'

'Just,' he said. 'You know a lot about me.'

'You're a legend around here.'

'So you've said,' he said.

Darcy was sure there was an edge of irritation in his tone. It occurred to her for the first time that maybe being cool and popular wasn't all it was cracked up to be. Anytime anything went wrong in the town everyone automatically assumed it was perpetrated by Johnny Sloan and his crew of renegades. Darcy – having never known any of them personally – always assumed the gang enjoyed the notoriety and, like everyone else, she assumed the reputation was accurate. But if the way he scuffed his boot against the tree root while he muttered under a lowered brow was anything to go by, maybe all the stories about him weren't true.

Suddenly her back straightened as she considered the opposite, what if all the stores were true? What if his mother did kill herself? What if his father did kick him out because he blamed Sloan? What if his girlfriend really was mentally unbalanced?

'Johnny,' she murmured, her hand sliding onto his forearm. Her touch caused him to recoil as though she had burned him. His head snapped around and he pinned her with such a fierce glare that it made her physically shiver.

'What about you, Cookie?' he asked. The glare relaxed a little, but she could still see anger burning behind his eyes.

'What about me?'

'Are you legal?'

His deep voice rumbled now as he twisted his body and brought himself closer to her. Tension flooded through her. As much as she tried to tell herself it was fear that made her eyes round and her breathing quicken, she couldn't help but notice his heat radiating to her own.

His nicotine-laced breath warmed her lips and filled her nose, the aroma of his leather jacket and deodorant joined in a heady mix that made her mind fog.

'In six weeks,' she managed to croak.

'Close enough,' he muttered, his lips only a hairs breadth from hers. His fingers combed her hair from her face until his hand cupped her base of her skull and he angled her mouth toward his.

Squeezing her eyes closed she waited for the unthinkable, Johnny Sloan, *the* Johnny Sloan was going to kiss her! Darcy Holmes was about to be kissed by Johnny Sloan!

His hand relaxed and before his mouth made contact with her the heat of his breath cooled. When Darcy opened her eyes, she saw him frowning at her.

'What?' she asked still unable to control her breathing.

'Rocks?'

Oh no! Darcy wanted to curl into a ball and die. 'I didn't... Was I singing?'

'Aye,' he said his frown relaxing as his eyebrows inched closer to his hairline. 'You were.'

Darcy swallowed down her embarrassment. 'It's a nervous habit.'

'What is?'

'I sing,' she said. 'At least you got Primal Scream, when Tom Welsh kissed me for the first time, he got Prince.'

'What?' Sloan was definitely backing off now. His hand left her hair and she wanted to scream in frustration.

'I said he wasn't beautiful,' she said, sitting up as he did. 'You know, Kiss.'

'I know the song,' Sloan said running his hand into his hair. 'You weren't attracted to him... and you think I'm a drug dealer or a thief... maybe both.'

'It's not like that,' Darcy said. 'I just… I've done it since I was a child. I don't know I'm doing it… really. Usually it stays in my head.'

Sloan ventured a look over his shoulder and she managed an awkward smile. Just as he returned it her body slackened in relief. The moment didn't last long, a twig snapped, and Darcy sprang to alert when she heard her name.

'Darcy!'

'Someone is looking for you,' Sloan said. 'And it doesn't sound like a girl named Lottie.'

'No,' Darcy hissed and pounced to her feet. 'It's Tom.'

'Boyfriend Tom?'

'He dumped me tonight,' she said. 'Rather I caught him snogging Lottie's face off.'

'Nice of her to invite you to the party,' Sloan said retrieving her shoes from the dirt.

'Generous to a fault is our Lottie,' Darcy said wiping the earth from her skirt. 'I better go… It was nice to meet you.'

'Ditto, Tyke, take care.'

'Darcy!'

Tom's voice grew louder but as Sloan got to his feet he held Darcy's attention and for just a second, one second, the intensity of those vortex eyes made her heart stop in her chest.

'You too, Johnny. Good luck in the big bad world.'

'I think I might need it.'

A smile spread to her mouth. 'No, Johnny, I think it's the big bad world that needs to look out.'

Darcy barely caught the wink he sent her way because she was momentarily mesmerised by his dimple again. The sound of Tom coming ever closer made her spin on her bare feet and rush away from the happiest happenstance of her teenage years. One that she would never speak of to anyone, because who would ever believe her anyway. The only evidence she had of him was his leather jacket that still to this day hung at the back of her wardrobe.

Sloan was a legend and through the years became a myth, a cautionary tale told to youngsters seen to be heading onto a similar path. Life went on in Inverquay after Sloan left. Those who knew him personally spoke of him fondly, but he had his share of enemies, most notably his father. As such, Sloan didn't come back to Inverquay and through time, the stories became fable. Darcy wondered if he had really ever existed at all, and if he did, would he remember the serendipitous few minutes when their lives collided, and they were the only two people in the world.

ONE

'I'LL KILL HIM,' Sloan muttered, shuffling from foot to foot as he watched the fog of his breath curl out into the night air. 'Here I am, busting my balls; I'm a fucking idiot… Yeah, Sloan, I'll be there Sloan, don't worry, I'll be right on time… bastard.'

On an almost deserted side street in the centre of the city, Sloan dug his hands into the pockets of his zipper and pinned his arms to his body. Backing into the secluded residential doorway he leant on the scarred wooden door and closed his eyes thinking of the most effective ways to murder Doug with the least amount of mess and the most amount of pain.

The time had to be after midnight now, but in these Baltic conditions Sloan wasn't about to take his hand from his pocket to look at his watch. 'The story of a lifetime,' Sloan groaned again and banged his head back on the door; he was an idiot who got everything he deserved. Since when had Doug ever been reliable? He screwed his best friend's sister; his best friends married sister for goodness' sake.

A rush of air and what sounded like a pant made him crack open one eye. Ready to scream bloody murder at Doug he was surprised to see a waif of a woman sharing his doorway. Not only was she short and skinny but her wild curly hair almost covered her face as it cascaded to her more than ample chest. He could make that observation because she was also barely clothed. Clutching a pair of platform spike heels to her cleavage the rest of her chest was covered by what appeared to be nothing more than a bikini top that tied in a neat bow between her breasts. His eyes travelled down across her flat abs and to the skintight siren red micro miniskirt that started at her hips and ended, well a few inches below that. Short she might be but as his gaze moved further south, he noted she was all leg, long, slender, shapely—

'Hold these,' she barked and thrust her shoes against him.

His choice to take them was not his own but his curiosity was piqued. She had to be a working girl, this naked, this deep in the city, had to be.

'Are you okay?' he asked, hazarding a closer look.

'Oh, just dandy, pal, thanks.'

Her obvious note of sarcasm was aimed at him, but her attention slid out of the doorway to peer up the street the way she had come. Scooping her hair from her face she came back into the doorway and took a hair band from her slender wrist with her teeth. Shaking her head back, Sloan became fixated on the line of her neck. Taming her hair took her a few seconds but she deftly secured it back and peeked out of the entryway again.

Only now, when the line of her neck and her cleavage was out of his sight did he realise she was talking, muttering to herself… No, he thought and found himself going slack jawed; those weren't words, they were lyrics.

'You're singing,' he said.

Her attention snapped back to him. 'What? Who are you? Please don't tell them you saw me.'

Narrowing his eyes, he stared into those fathomless green eyes. Eyes filled with such innocence that he couldn't help but recognise them. 'Darcy,' he breathed and found himself smiling at her.

Something in the way her innocent pleading melted told him she recognised him too. When her hand went to his face and her thumb traced his dimple, he saw nothing but wonder in her eyes. Their quiet appreciation of each other was abruptly ended when he saw the vibration in her chin, and he realised her lips were blue.

'What the fuck are you doing out here like that?'

He unzipped his hooded sweatshirt, dropping her shoes to the concrete he stood on, and pulled it off to wrap around her. She didn't hesitate, which he took as a sign she was grateful. Shaking fingers failed to do up the zip so he swiped her manicured nails away and did it up for her then took his time rubbing her arms through the cotton.

Heavy make-up tried to hide the girl she once was, but her body betrayed the woman she had become, and his own body found himself all too aware of the fact when he pulled her into his arms and began to rub her back.

Though shivers wracked her whole body she forced her hands between them and pushed herself away. Just at that he heard what sounded like voices, a lot of voices, and stampeding feet. He watched as her eyes slowly closed, her lips were moving again but the lyrics were silent this time.

Bouncing on her bare feet he saw her pull his hood up over her hair and pull the strings tight. 'Good to see you again, Sloan,' she whispered.

Before he could open his mouth, she slid out of the doorway and bolted down the street. Nimble on her tiptoes he thought, but realised the concrete would be like ice under her toes. The voices grew louder, as did the footsteps. Actually it was more like thunder now, Sloan looked over his shoulder and he realised the voices were shouting after her. Ducking back into his doorway to avoid the stampede, his jaw fell again when he absorbed the scene. These voices, the thundering feet running belonged to dozens of men and women, most with camera's, some with notebooks or smartphones and some with pictures just waiting to be autographed and they were all shouting for Darcy. Darcy Holmes from Inverquay, a girl he hadn't thought about for ten years and yet somehow the world knew her, better than he did apparently.

***

DOUG DIDN'T BOTHER to phone. But it wouldn't have mattered because as soon as the rowdy mob turned the corner and disappeared out of sight Sloan remembered his phone was in his hoody pocket, as was his wallet, and his house keys. Cursing at himself he fell back into the doorway, this time thumping his forehead against the door. When his eyes opened, he saw her shoes scattered at his feet. A smile threatened his lips as he realised this was the second pair of her shoes he had been left holding. He had just lifted the silver sequined straps when he heard footsteps behind him, heavy footsteps, soled footsteps, no chance she had returned.

'Did you see her?'

Sloan turned to see Doug's usual exuberant grin. 'Her?' Sloan asked but knew already whom his friend was referring to.

'Darcy! The hottest thing on two legs! I went to see her for the floorshow, but I got way more than tits and ass! The girl is… Shit! I don't even know how to describe her, the voice is one thing, the body… don't even get me started but wow, I don't think anyone was expecting tonight.'

'What are you talking about?'

'Buy me a drink and I'll fill you in,' Doug said, slapping Sloan on the back and bringing him out onto the street.

'Buy you a drink? I've been stood here freezing my balls off for half an hour.'

'No one was betting on waiting for the emergency services… I guess that's why they call them the "emergency" services though, right? They're not the "expected" services, are they?'

'I have no idea what you're talking about,' Sloan said, noting the way Doug was looking at the shoes in his hand.

'Something you want to tell me, mate?'

'How about you first?' Sloan asked, pushing his way into the bar that Doug pointed at.

Doug took his usual time buying the drinks, ensuring to stop and flirt with anything that smiled his way. When he put the pints on the table Sloan had found, Doug's eyes were still on the bar. 'You want the blonde or the brunette?'

Sloan glanced over his shoulder to see the pair at the bar smiling at them. Containing his growl, he snatched up his pint and slurped it down. 'Neither. Tell me about Darcy.'

'Hidden talent,' Doug said, gulping his own pint and putting down the glass to wipe his palm on his jeans. 'New reality thing on some satellite channel… Anyway, the producers tour the country looking for talent, no auditions malarkey; they just find people who actually use their talents to earn a bit of income. The Darcy girl apparently applied for some cooking show and got the knock back but one of the producers remembers her, catches up with her singing in some local dive.'

'Singing?'

'Whatever,' Doug said. 'Back story is boring… No one expected anything, the producers put the talent they like in front of six agents, each agent picks three acts and spend a few months trying to make their acts the next big thing. It's all about turnover, whichever agent pulls in the least money each week gets one of their acts evicted by the public. It's bullshit, money making scheme. Tonight was the big reveal of the acts. Each of them got to sing a number at the Winter Hall round the corner.'

'You were there?' Sloan asked. Not that he had any interest in reality TV, but if he had known Darcy was going to be there he would have had Doug take him along.

'Aye,' Doug said, sampling his pint again. 'It's a gimmick; they don't do big studio shows. The agents have to work with their acts to get them doing shows in standard venues, the bigger the venue, the bigger the crowd, the bigger the turnover, blah, blah, blah.'

'Hence the Winter Hall.'

'Exactly,' Doug said. 'It's the introduction to the acts and the only venue the studio ponies up for. They invite a few media pundits to get the ball rolling.'

'So, what was special about tonight? You get invited to loads of crappy events by people who want exposure.'

'Aye,' Doug agreed, shoving his pint aside and practically bouncing into Sloan's lap. 'That's what I thought. Bit of a laugh, good view, nothing serious.'

'So?'

'So! This Darcy chick starts singing, the crowd is like stunned into immediate silence, she is that good.'

'Great,' Sloan said. 'Good for her—'

'No,' Doug said actually grabbing Sloan's wrist as

he sprang to the edge of his seat. 'This girl is so good that Paulie Hayes, who is front row, literally drops down dead.'

'What? She killed him?'

'That's not even the best bit!' Doug was, vibrating with excitement now. 'Paulie falls to his knees, clutching his chest.' Doug fell to his knees next to Sloan doing a dramatic reconstruction. 'Gasping for breath, his life is slipping away, the room in suspended in silence as his heart stutters to a stop…'

Sloan found himself caught in the moment too, leaning toward Doug as his voice lowered in a typical croaking, near death fashion.

'And?' Sloan prompted as his friend's eyes closed.

'Darcy!' Doug called, his eyes snapping open and his face glowing in a renewed grin. 'Leaps from the stage, like a ninja, freaking superwoman or something! She starts barking orders, "everyone back off! Someone call an ambulance!" she's loosening his tie, undoing his shirt and then get this! She starts mouth to mouth! The babe has got skills, serious skills! No panic, no hesitation, complete calm. A room full of people, probably even a first aider on site and this girl with the incredible set of lungs is using them to resuscitate the media's most shrewd, calculating bastard! And! And! She keeps it up for twenty minutes! The fucker is still hanging onto life when the paramedics appear and take over!'

'Wow,' Sloan breathed, slumping back in his chair while Doug climbed back into his.

'You're telling me,' Doug said, moistening his throat. 'This girl has this competition locked on night one. She's a media sweetheart. The woman saved the most influential man in print and music media north of the border.'

Sloan could see it now; the paramedics come in

and start their work as Darcy backs off then the questions start. She's in a room full or reporters, full of camera's… the first night of a reality show, she's not used to the media, she's alone, she panics and somehow escapes. That explained the outfit, the hair, and the shoes.

'Why didn't you follow her?' Sloan asked Doug.

He shrugged, downing another mouthful. 'I thought I was getting laid tonight, I didn't take any equipment. I didn't think it would be that entertaining.'

Doug was a photographer for the Daily National, a newspaper they both worked for. 'Toby will have your behind in a sling.'

'We'll get something,' Doug said. 'We always get something. She was doing CPR for twenty minutes; there will be dozens of pictures. Toby will be more interested in the story.'

'I thought backstory was boring,' Sloan said relying on his trusty facade to hide his own awkwardness.

None of his colleagues knew he was from Inverquay but if anyone started asking questions around the village his name could come up. Okay, so he couldn't claim to have history with her exactly, but if Darcy had told anyone about the few minutes they'd shared, chances were someone would tell the media the story.

'You want it?' Doug asked. 'Toby owes me a favour, wouldn't be much of a hardship to tail her for a few weeks.'

'No,' Sloan said, trying to think if there would be anything worse than having to tell Darcy's story.

Yes, he could omit facts about his own connection, but he would bet his boots that the whole village would read that story and with his name on it… he could kiss a happy welcome home goodbye. Not that he was sure there would ever be one on the cards for him.

***

DOUG BARTERED WITH HIM to stay for another two pints. In exchange for Doug buying them, Sloan worked his magic with the women at the bar, ensuring Doug got his wish for the evening. Doug also gave Sloan taxi fare and his house key. Sloan only let Doug move into his flat after Nick – another reporter at the paper – vouched for him; or rather begged him. The two had only been flat sharing for a few weeks but already Sloan was missing his seclusion.

Ready for bed, Sloan rubbed his hand across his eyes as he slid Doug's key in the lock. Frowning when it didn't turn, Sloan made note to tell Doug off for leaving the door unlocked. Except when he opened the door and heard the boom of music – that he had assumed was coming from elsewhere – he realised the flat was not vacant.

Much to his surprise when he rounded the wall that separated entranceway from open plan kitchen, living area, he saw a woman swaying her hips and grinding her body to the music as she looked up at the CDs on the shelving unit in front of her. Her hair was damp and draped to her waist; she was wearing what appeared to be his tee shirt, and not much else. His jaw once again hung loose as his feet sloped slowly toward her. At a crescendo of the music, she spun around and froze, blinking at him as he too stopped in the middle of the room.

To her credit, she turned and flipped off the music immediately before spinning to grin at him. 'Hi, Johnny.'

'Tyke.'

The word had come out of its own volition but the pet name caused her grin to widen further.

She leapt toward him, snatching his hand from his side. 'You are going to laugh when you hear this story.'

From the way her teeth pressed into her lower lip, he could tell she wasn't sure of that herself. But he had to give her what she was due because she confidently held eye contact with him and had the decency to appear contrite.

'What are you doing here?'

'I know we don't know each other very well—'

'At all.'

'No,' she said with a shrug. 'I suppose we don't but see… I don't know anyone in the city. I don't know anyone away from the village and I—'

'Why aren't you in the village?'

'It's a long story.'

'I thought you were running Hayley's bakery.'

'How would you know that?' she frowned. 'You haven't been back, not since… your party.'

'I still talk to Glo sometimes.'

Gloria was his father's sister; she was the only one who had been in contact since he had left town. She persisted in asking him to come home, but Sloan knew the blood between him and his father had long been putrid.

'You asked about me?'

'What are you doing here, Darcy?' he asked again this time not allowing the emerald of her eyes to mesmerise him into forgetting himself like he had done in that doorway.

The false grin fell from her face and for a second, he saw the truth.

'I need help, Sloan. I'm alone here and I… I think the bottom just fell out of my world.'

Allowing her words to hang in the air between them he drew in a long breath and dropped his hands to her shoulders. 'What is a girl like you doing in a place like this?' he sighed.

'I,' she started and wriggled under his palms. He squeezed to hold her still, the last thing he needed was for her to start squirming and reminding him of the body she possessed under that tee shirt, his tee shirt, that currently had the pleasure of skimming those lush curves. 'I needed money.'

'Money,' he said surprised by the answer.

Most people on reality shows wanted fame, exposure and yes, the lifestyle but she didn't strike him as an attention-seeking party girl.

'I signed up to do this reality show, it's silly really, but it's temporary… I didn't think for a second I would ever have to deal with… what happened tonight… I need somewhere to stay, just for tonight. I couldn't go back to my hotel the place is swarming with reporters… I don't have any money, nothing so—'

'So you stole my wallet?'

'It's in your room,' she said. 'I didn't take anything I swear. When I realised your wallet was in there, I was already a mile away. I'd lost most of the reporters and I was going to return it, so I checked your address. I got here and you weren't home, I left the door unlocked so you could get in… Then once I got here I… well I was cold and I… I thought I would get a shower and… I'm sorry I, I don't have anywhere else to go.'

When he saw the moisture glisten on those long dark lashes of hers, he couldn't stop himself from pulling her against him and burying his face in her hair. What he hadn't been expecting was for her to wrap her arms so tightly around his waist and cling to him wholehearted. As they stood holding each other in the middle of his living room he was struck by how natural it felt and yet, he had never held this woman before in his life, not properly. But they held each other without thinking, their bodies obedient to each other, both locked in automatic trust without question.

'I could be a complete bastard,' he muttered into her hair. 'Do you know that? We don't know each other.'

'Are you kidding,' she said into his chest. 'You're Johnny Sloan. I already know you're a bastard… But right now, you're my only hope.'

***

THERE WAS SOMETHING oddly comforting about settling her in the middle of his big bed. No further questions were asked; she used his toothbrush, washed her face, and lay down in his sheets – the whole time smiling at him as if he had just given her an answer to the meaning of life.

'Stop looking at me like that, Tyke,' he said as he pulled the curtains closed.

'Why didn't you come home, Johnny? Are you married?'

'If I was married, I doubt my wife would be happy with a woman like you in our bed.'

Finding himself watching her as she smoothed his duvet down on her waist, he forced himself to take a step toward her and reach for the light. 'A woman like me, what does that mean?'

Oddly when he paused with his hand halfway to the light, he could see that she genuinely meant it. The women he had experienced over the years knew just what affect they had on men and just how to use that to their advantage. Yet, Darcy Holmes, perhaps the most luscious of any woman he had the pleasure of seeing in his sheets was smiling at him, her head tipped slightly to the side, blinking at him as innocently as a child.

'Go to sleep, Tyke, we'll talk in the morning.'

Managing to avoid the question, he reached for

the light and clicked it off. Before he could remove himself from the bedside, he found his hand snatched into hers. Both of her tiny, delicate hands cradled his, pulling it closer to her and before his eyes adjusted to the new darkness around them the petal soft skin of her cheek was under his palm.

'Thank you, Johnny,' she said turning her head back and forth against his touch as though she were a stray kitten grateful of a dry bed.

Frozen against her caress he supposed the thought wasn't so inaccurate. Then, just as his body relented to her presumptuous act and began to react in a typically raw male fashion her warm skin was gone. His vision adjusted to see her lying in the centre of his bed, eyes closed, slight smile on her lips and the gentle rise and fall of that chest beneath the stark white of his quilt.

TWO

FINDING HIMSELF on his own couch was no hardship. Somehow knowing Darcy was safe provided major consolation. Although when he woke up with a crick in his neck, he was ready to curse. Jumping into the shower he stood under the hot, hard jets for twenty minutes trying to relieve the ache. That was until the pounding started on the bathroom door. Panic hit him, he worried that Darcy had woken to reporters, maybe they were on the phone, or maybe they were crowded under his bedroom window. He couldn't work out how anyone could have known she was here. It took him only seconds to jump from the shower and wrap the towel around his waist.

On opening the door, he was prepared to see the nymph he had tucked into his bed last night. Instead, he found his reluctant roommate grinning like a clown.

'There's a woman in your bed!' Doug exclaimed.

'What the hell are you doing going into my room?'

'I was looking for you,' Doug said, all innocence.

'I wanted to tell you about my night.'

Sloan looked at the wall clock. 'Can't have been that good, it's eight a.m. and you're home.'

'It's proper to duck out before breakfast. Breakfast means commitment.'

'You're insane,' Sloan said, ignoring his personal disgust at his friend's intrusion. Fixing the towel tight around his waist he knew his only clean clothes were in his bedroom. 'Future reference, you go nowhere near my room, ever… And I have no interest in the details of your sordid sex life.'

'My sordid sex life?' Doug said, trotting along behind Sloan as he headed to his room. 'You're the one with the naked babe in his bed.' Sloan stopped. 'When the hell did that happen between the taxi and the flat?'

'You saw her naked?'

Doug took a step back and held up his hands in surrender. 'I got a boner at a flash of thigh anything more I think I'd have come in my pants. She's a little cracker.'

Sloan found himself frowning at his friend. Friend – that was a loose term. Doug was a great laugh when nothing had to be taken seriously. That said, Nick had told him that Doug was instrumental in getting him with the girl of his dreams: Sloan found it hard to believe. It was easier to believe Doug had nearly caused Nick to lose the girl in the first place, which, apparently, he'd also done.

Taking the last couple of steps to his bedroom Sloan paused with his hand on the door and pinned Doug with a glare. 'Stay,' he commanded and noted the flicker of disappointment in Doug's eyes.

Sloan entered the room, careful to keep his attention away from the bed as he closed the door. Keeping his eyes front, he crossed the room to the built in wardrobe on the opposite wall. Although aware of the figure slumbering stretched out in the centre of his bed the white lump remained static. Deliberately blurring his eyes, he reached the wardrobe and opened it silently. Inside was a set of drawers, he slid open the top one and began to retrieve his clothes.

'Johnny?'

The quiet, husky voice had him squeezing his eyes closed and cursing. He wondered if he was worse than Doug because her voice could provoke the same reaction in him that Doug achieved through sight.

'Sorry.' His reflex apology wasn't heard or at least wasn't acknowledged by her. Her hands reached for his ceiling, and he vaguely heard an Amy Winehouse lyric as her body followed her hands.

Something in him clicked, literally, he heard the snap. Mindlessly he turned to stare at the figure bathed in white cotton and the sunlight that streamed through his muslin curtains. Truly, in that moment his breath caught, and he witnessed an angel liberated from her purpose.

'I haven't slept this late in years,' she said, her eyes on the clock by his bed. Only then did he notice the way her hands had moved to her chest. 'Your bed is really comfy.'

'Uh.'

'But boy does it get warm in here.'

'We're above a pizza place,' he said. 'The oven is on all night, it's right under us.'

She nodded and sighed as she flopped back against his pillows. 'It's like sleeping in a cloud,' she giggled.

The number of pillows at the head of the bed was to support him as he sat up into the small hours writing. Usually he didn't sleep with them; usually he stuffed them all to one side. But now as she lay back with the duvet pulled to her chin, the smile on her face and her drowsy gaze locked onto him. Just then he realised while she smiled, he stared without a word.

'Sorry,' he said again, turning his attention back to the drawers.

'That's twice you've said that,' she said with a hum in her voice. 'Shouldn't I be apologising to you for kicking you out of your bed?' Sloan opened his mouth, but he needn't have. 'Which you didn't have to do by the way, but I suppose it's just a little late to be saying that now. Although I can just imagine the kick Lottie will get out of hearing I slept in Johnny Sloan's bed… Not that she'd believe me… Everyone in town is pretty sure you're dead.'

'People really think that?'

'That or in jail,' she answered, smoothing his duvet down over her chest to her hips. The rhythmic motion had him mesmerised and her words were lost. At least until her hands brought attention to her smooth, creamy shoulders… Smooth creamy bare shoulders.

'You're naked,' he said.

'I told you I was hot,' Darcy said. 'Besides, so are you.'

Finding himself looking down at himself he realised she was right. Yes, his towel was still in place but the rivulets dropping from his hair ran down his chest to then be absorbed by the tucked in towel.

'Lottie will definitely get a kick out of that,' she said pointing her toe out of the bottom of his duvet and rotating her foot. The smooth shin that followed had him once again struggling to follow the conversation. 'Come here.' She sat upright again, holding the duvet to her cleavage.

'What?' he asked, snapping back to reality.

'Here,' she said, reaching for him and gesturing to bring him closer. 'Come here.'

'Why?'

'Just sit down with me, would you?'

The coquettish smile on her face as she shifted over the bed made the bounce in her hair seem so innocent… not innocent, naive. Those round eyes were so pleased when he rolled his eyes and perched on the edge of the bed she had cleared for him.

'Now what?'

Again, she giggled and this time she dropped her hands to his shoulders, her hair caressed his neck as her head fell forward. 'Now I can tell her we were in bed together naked.'

Naive was right, Sloan thought to himself. Wondering just how much of a kick it would give her if he turned and stripped her security blanket from her chest and showed her just how much Johnny Sloan would do with her if given half a chance.

The cushion of her hair remained against the back of his neck, it warmed his shoulders as her hands slid around him and his very own duvet became the only thing between his back and her chest.

'What am I doing here, Johnny?' she whispered, the heat of her breath bringing him out in goose bumps.

'You are a dark horse.'

Sloan's attention snapped around to see Doug loitering just inside the doorway, hands in his pockets he rocked back on his heels. 'I told you to get,' Sloan groaned.

As quickly as she had been against him, she was gone. Pulling the duvet over herself as much as was able, her eyes peeked over the top when she scurried back onto the pillows. Like a terrified rabbit facing down the farmer she blinked and cowered in a ball surrounded by his bedding.

'Who are you?' she asked, her voice quivering.

'I am your ticket to ride, Gorgeous.'

'Oh my God,' she breathed.

Sloan leapt to his feet. 'Ignore him, Tyke… You,'

he demanded, marching toward his friend. 'Out!'

Snatching Doug's shoulder, Sloan gave his friend a hearty shove out of the room and slammed the door behind them. 'That was… that was—'

'Nothing,' Sloan said. 'No one.'

'You got her into bed! How the fuck—'

'Keep your voice down,' Sloan hissed, shoving Doug toward the kitchen.

'All I saw were curls and those legs this morning. I never thought to look at her face. I never thought—'

'Nothing,' Sloan growled. 'You saw nothing.'

'How can I do that? This is unbelievable! This is incredible.' Doug paced away, his face glowing as his hands gripped his hair. 'You… You are my hero! How the fuck did—'

'It's nothing.'

'It's not nothing,' Doug said. 'No way! How can you even pretend—'

'I'm not pretending. You need to forget you saw her.'

Doug marched up close. 'You have got to be shitting me,' Doug hissed. 'She is *the* hottest property this side of the Atlantic… If we get the story, we can kiss goodbye to national… We're talking international! One interview and we could retire; the market is hot for that babe!'

'I don't care,' Sloan said. 'You forget you saw her, or so help me—'

'What?' Doug asked. 'What are you threatening me with?'

'I am not a man to cross, trust me.'

Something in his eyes must have conveyed his sincerity to Doug because the man took a step back. Before another word could be said his bedroom door opened and closed in a second.

'Thanks for everything, Johnny.'

Her head was tucked down. She wore the same skirt she had on last night but was again barefoot. He had forgotten to tell her about her shoes that he had dumped by the front door. He assumed she was wearing her top too, but she had on his zipper again, the one she had worn last night. Only now it was tied in a double knot just beneath her naval.

'Get out of here,' Sloan grumbled at Doug who stood frozen for a second before leaping into action.

'I've got to get going,' Doug said.

The men exchanged a look. Doug gnashed his teeth and nodded before rushing to the front door, beating Darcy to the punch.

'Don't run out of here like this,' Sloan said to Darcy who was reaching for the door Doug had just used.

'I really appreciate your hospitality last night,' she said, turning to him then she pulled up his hood to cover her restrained locks. 'Where's the best place to get a taxi from here?'

'You're not getting a taxi,' Sloan said, crossing the room to her. When he got there, he instinctively curled his fingers around her wrist, holding her in place.

'If I can get back to the hotel, I can get my bank card and—'

'Darc,' he said his thumb drawing lazy circles on her wrist. He might not even have noticed he was doing it if her eyes hadn't moved to the action. 'You're not getting a taxi.'

'I can't hang around here very long, if your friend—'

'He won't.'

'But if he—'

'He won't.'

'It's for the best, Sloan,' she said and the naive playful woman from his bed this morning became staunch and stubborn. Leaning on his forearm, she pushed herself upward to press her lips to his cheek. To his surprise, she moved higher caressing his cheek with her own. 'A kiss for luck and we're on our way,' she sung softly against him. Whether she was aware of the words or not, he didn't know.

Lowering herself she offered a smile and turned again for the door. This time she got as far as opening it. In that minute he learned she wasn't the only one who could do things without being aware because when he heard the thud, he almost looked for the source but straight ahead there was his hand flat against the painted wood of his front door which was firmly in the door frame again. Beneath him she shrank in alarm, blinking up with those glistening, round eyes.

'You've forgotten who you're dealing with,' he said, surprised by the depth of his own tone.

'Is that a threat, Sloan?'

'If I tell him not to talk, he won't talk.'

'And will you?'

'Already have, Tyke.'

'Thank you but I'm not your responsibility... I have to go, now.'

'I'm going to get dressed. Then you and me are going to sit down and work this out.'

'Why?' she asked. 'Why would you take time out of your life to help me?'

'Us Quayers stick together,' he said, offering her a wink before he walked away from her. He might have been desperate to turn and check that she wasn't going to leave but he held firm. Johnny Sloan was nothing if not confident... apparently.

***

'COCKY BASTARD, aren't you?'

Sloan had to give her that. She sat in the middle of his couch, her hands on the seats at her sides and her feet up on the coffee table. 'Worked, didn't it?' he said, taking the seat at the head of the table.

'Truth is I don't have anywhere else to be,' she said. 'After last night I'm not sure I'll have anywhere to be for quite a while.'

'It can't have been that bad.'

Her eyes rolled to him. 'No, maybe not. But I didn't come here for… fame.'

'What did you come here for?' he asked and then immediately regretted the question.

Truth was, he wasn't sure he wanted to know anything about her. Plausible deniability would work best with Doug and with his boss. He didn't want to compromise his loyalties, except this thought got him wondering where his loyalties were.

'It's a long story,' she said, leaning forward, running her hands down the front of her legs. 'Why did you never come home, Johnny? I don't think you've been back a day since you left.'

He shook his head. 'That's a longer story.'

'Josie's still single,' Darcy smiled. 'At least she was when I left.'

'Josie,' Sloan said as if remembering a distant dream and he supposed he was.

The first girl to give him her virtue or maybe more aptly the girl he gave his virtue to. He'd never met a woman since who got off on things so morally wrong. Now, looking back he was shocked at some of the things he, his girl, and his gang got away with. As kids it all seemed so cool and exciting, he wouldn't dream of chancing anything so stupid and dangerous now.

'She nearly married Ritchie a few years back,' Darcy said. 'Very messy affair I have to say, it caused quite the scandal at the time.'

The sound of her voice was an enchanting ode. From the sweet melodies she could conjure at almost inaudible volume through to her right now, teasing him and somehow taking the piss out of their heritage at the same time. Apparently, she took the rumour mill as seriously as he had.

'What about you? Did you marry that guy?'

'Guy?'

'The one you caught kissing your friend?'

Her brow lowered and Sloan was shocked. She had recalled him in the doorway last night, but she didn't remember her ex-boyfriend. 'Tom!'

'Right.'

Her body folded to curl her fingers around her ankles. Sloan found himself transfixed on her cleavage proudly peeking from his zipper, which was pressed into her knees. 'No,' she said, broadening her smile. 'His father went to jail for fraud and… something else. His mother trucked the family out of town the day after he was arrested.'

'For real?' Sloan asked and she nodded. 'And people thought I was a rebel.'

'Tom wasn't a rebel,' she said. 'His father was greedy and that's the end of it really. But you know what small towns are like.'

'I used to,' he said. 'I try my hardest to leave that part of my past firmly there.'

'You can't deny who you are,' she said, and that tiny groove appeared between her brows again. 'You might not like it, but you come from the Quay, you grew up there, your family are there, it's where you went to school, it's part of your history.'

'Aye,' he said. 'And I like it there.'

Getting up to head for the kitchen, he thought making coffee might give him the chance to change the subject.

'You're very lucky you know.'

Reaching for the coffee grounds, he looked back to see her hanging over the back of the couch, her chin on her wrist which rested on the fabric. 'Lucky?'

'Yeah,' she said. 'You grew up never wanting for anything. You were popular, you were smart, and you got the respect of your peers. I don't know any boy who didn't want to be you or any girl who didn't want to be with you. You were a legend… You still are.'

'So what? I'm supposed to bask in my local celebrity and be whatever anyone wants me to be, what anyone imagines me to be? It's bullshit, all that false bravado… My life was as fucked up as anyone else's, but no one ever wanted to look that deep.'

'You were fearless.'

'I was reckless,' he said. 'Aye, I did stupid things, and most of it was for attention but I never got it, not from those I was aiming for.'

'When was the last time you spoke to your dad?' she asked.

'How did we get onto this?' he asked, retrieving the milk from the fridge. 'That shit is all in the past. It's done with; I want to forget it, all of it.'

Waiting for the coffee to percolate was driving him mad, so he poured each of them half a cup. 'Just milk for me,' she said, and he was aware she was off the couch coming toward him. 'I'm part of your past… A teeny, wee part.' She accepted the mug and perching on the counter next to him while he spooned two sugars into his black liquid. 'Do you want to forget me?'

He paused with his hand on his mug and wondered for a fleeting second how women could always manage to turn anything into an insult or a compliment depending on their mood.

'You're present,' he said, letting the steam warm his lip before he drank.

'I'm not,' she said. 'Running into you last night was a complete coincidence. If you hadn't given me this…' She lifted the hoodie in two pinched fingers and giving him a glimpse inside confirming to him that she wasn't wearing the top from last night, he saw no strings. 'We would never have crossed paths again.'

'Are you saying it was fate?'

To his surprise she snorted in laughter. 'No, I said it was coincidence.'

'You don't believe in fate?' he asked although he had no idea why, he wasn't a big believer in anything like that himself.

'No,' she said, looking down into the mug she rolled between her palms. 'I think if there was any higher power out there it would have a pretty sick sense of humour to put us through a life like this.'

Again, he reacted. Without thought process, his hand moved toward her, and he had his finger under her chin drawing her eyes up to his. She looked sad, he'd never seen this side of her, concern etched on his face, and he knew it. It had to be deeper than he thought though because he saw her try to force a smile.

'You're not religious either,' she said, unhooking her face from his finger and strolling as casually as she could back into the living room, but he knew she was creating distance, for her own reasons. 'You were caught with a bong in the rectory. I remember the assembly called at school about drugs after that. They made an example of you.'

She was good at deflecting, and she had an excellent memory, most of these things he hadn't thought about in years. Then again, to him they were childhood games and pranks but in a small town these trivial acts became tall tales.

'When did you leave town?' he asked.

'Just last weekend,' she said. 'I can't wait to get

back.'

Seating herself at the coffee table again Sloan joined her.

'You like everyone knowing your business?'

'There is more to Inverquay than gossip,' she said. 'Granted, not a whole lot, but my friends are there. I have a business to run and a life, a life I like… for the most part.'

'A business? Hayley's bakery?'

'It's my bakery now,' she said. 'Hayley helped for a while, but the pace was getting too much for her. At least that's what she said but in fairness she's in her eighties now.'

'Wow,' Sloan said, running a hand through his hair then he put his mug down.

'Funny how life carries on without you,' she said.

'Is that what you're worried about? Life carrying on without you?'

'No,' she said. 'But there are other considerations.'

'You have family then?'

'Just my dad and Hayley,' she said. 'Same as always.'

'No husband?'

'You're obsessed with my love life; no, I'm not married.'

'Engaged?' he asked.

'You're teasing me,' she said, watching his smile grow.

'No,' he said. 'I want to ask you to dinner.'

'No, you don't,' she said. 'You're Johnny Sloan.'

'Aye,' he said seeing the flush in her cheeks. 'And I'm asking you to have dinner with me.'

'Johnny, I don't think I'll be in the city long. Last night freaked me out I'm not ashamed to admit it. I think I want to go home.'

'If you "think" that means you're not sure. You might not want to tell me why you left the Quay, but you did and you didn't do it lightly, did you?' Again, those tentative eyes met his and he almost groaned when he saw her pearly whites drag against her plump lower lip. She shook her head. 'No funny business, I just want to know you're alright.'

'You want to know I'm alright?'

'While you're in town, you might need a friend, and I'm offering my services… You said it yourself we're both small town kids in the big, bad city… How could I live with myself if something happened to you?'

She laughed and moved along the couch toward him. 'You want to be my big brother? I've never had a brother.'

Brotherly thoughts couldn't be further from his mind, but that glowing smile made him nod. 'Whatever you need, Tyke.'

'This place has been a pretty good refuge,' she said. 'If your friend can keep a secret?'

'I guarantee it,' he said but as soon as the words were out of his mouth, he regretted them.

Darcy moved closer still and he found himself holding her. She wrapped her arms around him, rested her head on his chest. Her curls caught on his stubble, but she didn't move.

Whether it was a friendly hug, or something more, he followed suit, encircling her in his arms and pressing his mouth to her berry scented curls. As his hand thought about moving downward of its own accord, she bounced away from him again. This woman was hard to anticipate.

'If I make you a list, will you go to the shop for me?'

'Sure,' he said. 'What do you need?'

'I want to make my famous bramble and oatmeal

cookies, to thank you for last night.' Mentally Sloan began to run through all the ways he would accept her gratitude when she snatched his hand. 'Baking relaxes me, but if there is something you would prefer?'

Now it was his turn to force a smile. 'Cookies sound great.'

THREE

'I DON'T WANT TO HEAR IT,' Sloan said as he marched through the newsroom looking through a stack of faxes.

Doug was hot on his heels. 'You can't keep her all to yourself. I'll keep your name out of it. Just give me her number.'

'She's working tonight,' Sloan said. But he knew that didn't matter, he wasn't giving Doug anything.

'I know that,' Doug said. 'You don't think I know that? The world will be on the edge of their seats waiting to see her perform tonight.'

Sloan dragged his eyes to his friend and wondered at Doug's easy exaggeration. 'Aye and she's nervous enough about it without you hounding her.'

'She's nervous, did she tell you that?'

'It's no surprise. Last time she performed to an audience someone was removed in an ambulance. I think that would give anyone stage fright.'

'But did she say that?'

'What are you trying to do? Get a quote out of

me?' he asked with his hand on the door to the briefing room. Doug didn't say a word and Sloan shook his head. 'What were you going to say, anonymous sources? Do you think Toby would let you run with that?'

'Sources close to,' Doug said.

'We're not close,' Sloan said, pushing into the briefing room and finding a place near the back of the room. Dozens of reporters were in this afternoon, far more than was normal for a Saturday. Toby had called a special meeting of anyone even remotely related to the lifestyle and entertainment section, Oh, and the features staff.

'You're fucking her,' Doug hissed at Sloan when he slumped into the seat next to him. 'How much closer do you want to get?'

Sloan had given up denying that he and Darcy's relationship was physical. When he did it only seemed to whet Doug's appetite for details. Instead, Sloan had taken to just ignoring Doug and letting him make up his own ideas.

After the morning they had spent together the previous Sunday, Sloan had given her his number and told her to phone if she needed anything. Much to his surprise, she had. Part of him hadn't expected to hear from her again after he dropped her off at the back entrance to the hotel she was staying in. The press had still been camped out at the front, but he managed to sneak her in the service entrance and through the kitchens. Darcy was staggered by how much he knew about the press and their methods. He brushed her comments off with a joke but couldn't shake the feeling he was lying to her.

That very night she had called him to thank him again although the cookies she had left him were tribute enough to that and he had to wonder if the woman's skills had any limit. Finding himself genuinely concerned for her wellbeing he quizzed her on her agent, what his recommendations were, and then offered his own advice. Much as Darcy Holmes looked like a fully-grown woman, her roots were firmly in the naive.

After that she had called at least once a day and he looked forward to every single call. Two nights ago, he had been surprised to open his door to her at eleven thirty. She told him that they had finished early, and she had snuck out to make him more cookies, again to thank him, this time for answering her calls. Welcoming her in he had received a kiss on his cheek and a prolonged hug, which ended in him consciously keeping his hips away from her body.

Doug had been out that night but when he got home to more cookies, he knew immediately that she had been there, and the questions started again. Sloan knew then exactly where his loyalties were. Listening to Darcy talk as she cooked and sipped the wine he poured; he was spellbound. She moved so efficiently through his kitchen when she had only cooked in there once before. This time she made several batches of cookies, of different flavours and varieties. Somehow, she had managed to gather the ingredients herself and had brought them to him. When she was finished, he realised that she had washed and tidied as she went. His kitchen was in better shape than it had been when she started.

Then, she had made him leave the room with his cookies of choice. When she joined him in the front room, she brought him the most delectable mug of hot chocolate that he had ever tasted. It was so sumptuous, like sipping luxury liquid velvet. His compliments only made her laugh and shrug him off. Although she did invite him to the bakery back in the Quay, she said her efforts would be better with her own ingredients and equipment. Sloan silently thought there was no way she could make the experience any better, unless of course she had served him in the nude.

'If Toby gets wind of this, you're finished, you know that?' Doug said, bringing Sloan's attention back to the briefing room.

Sloan understood his boss wouldn't be happy with him if he knew of his relationship with Darcy. Truth be told he didn't really care, this career choice was never his first, and being stuck writing a column, giving his opinion on sporting matters that only vaguely interested him was fun enough, except he spent more time editing than writing which was what he really wanted to do. Working with the junior staff put him in a position of authority but herding upstart, know-it-all, fanatics made him feel more like a boring school professor than a real down to earth journalist.

The side door opened and the roar of voices, died to a rumble. Toby entered with three others behind him, one of which Sloan knew was Nick Bracken, Doug's best friend. Toby stormed to the front of the room, looking as frazzled and pissed off as usual, his cohorts all filtered into the audience.

'Right, you all know why you're here,' Toby declared. The rumble of voices started again. Toby lifted his hands and the room quieted. 'Put it this way: if you don't, you're shit at your jobs.'

'The girl!' a bodiless voice called out.

'Right,' Toby said, perching himself on the corner of the desk. 'You all got an assignment this week and you were all told to keep your eyes and ears open about the girl… and what do I have? Fuck all!'

'Boss—'

'No excuses! We have nothing! No one has anything! It's pathetic! The woman saved the life of Paulie Hayes! He will make her famous! We need this!'

Sloan shouldn't have been surprised at his boss's fervour, but he was, the room was too if the shocked silence was anything to go by. 'Does anyone know what she is singing tonight?'

'They do three numbers,' someone up front said. 'I think tonight they are starting with Queen.'

'And what is she singing?'

Sloan thought it odd that no one had yet referred to her by name but maybe that was how the piranhas distanced themselves. Sloan closed his eyes and shook his head again; he had never thought of his colleagues as piranhas before.

'Hazarding a guess,' someone shouted. 'Another one bites the dust?'

'No,' another voice piped up. 'Killer Queen!'

'Save me!'

As the room laughed along Toby looked about as peeved as Sloan felt. Here they all were taking the piss out of a woman who saved a life the previous week. Trying to maintain his composure he blocked out the noise around him and focused on doodling on his pad.

'The show must go on!' a voice hollered from beside him.

Sloan's attention snapped up to Doug, the owner of that voice. Luckily his voice was as inconsequential as the others in the room, and no one paid much heed. Only when Sloan increased his glare did Doug shrug and nod down to his notepad. Sloan had to give Doug his due, without realising it Sloan had been doodling the name of the song she had told him earlier in the week she was perfecting.

'Do you have any idea the points you could be scoring?' Doug muttered, taking his mouth behind his hand while his eyes moved back to the front. 'You have to let go of this, whatever it is. She's going to be famous, huge! Do you know what Hayes has planned for her? Tell me you've at least read the paper? When he's out of hospital—'

'I get it,' Sloan snapped.

'You better,' Doug said. 'You're a dick if you think she's going to keep you along for the ride. She'll up and hang you out to dry without a second thought.'

'You don't know her.'

Doug sniggered. 'Oh, and I suppose you do? You think a week of shagging lets you in on her character. You've seen what she wants you to see. She's a woman, mate, like all the rest of them; just the same.'

Toby carried on. 'Press is limited tonight. I'm guessing the other venues for the other agents' acts will be effectively deserted because this has become the hottest ticket in town. I'm sending our best in with what we've been given. But it's only studio cameras allowed backstage or into rehearsals. I'm telling you now. Anyone who can beg, borrow, or steal their way into that show will be in tomorrow's paper... I'll print anything that's not libel... But I'll go as damn close as I can.'

Toby had just given open invitation for anyone in the room to hound Darcy as though she was an animal. Plenty of people in this room would be more than happy to take him up on that offer. Honour among thieves there may be, between journalists... not so much; not when their careers were at stake.

Doug's elbow pushed Sloan's from the arm of his chair when his phone silently vibrated in his pocket. 'No,' Sloan said without looking at Doug, he didn't need to, he knew just what the man wanted.

Sloan took his phone from his pocket and pressed the icon telling him he had a new message. A smile quirked his lips when he read Darcy's name. The subject line brought a whisper of laugh. "What are you wearing?"

Considering his answer, the message opened. A picture took just a few seconds to load. As soon as he saw it, his free hand went to the arm of his chair, and he sat bolt upright. There, on the screen in front of him was Darcy, much as he knew she was smiling he couldn't take his eyes from the outfit, or rather the body. It had to be leather, a black waistcoat that barely reached her waist and the smallest hot pants he had ever seen. The view was incredible. Black leather was quite eighties, but the length of her legs encased in those high heel boots was enough to parch his throat.

'What the hell are you looking at?' Doug asked and leaned closer, but Sloan locked the phone, sending it black.

'Nothing.'

'Nothing my ass, I've never seen you move like that and… Are you…? Are you blushing?'

Sloan slapped Doug's hand away when he reached for Sloan's phone again. 'Mind your own.'

'It's her, isn't it?' Doug ribbed. 'Is she naked? Oh, can you imagine that front page?'

Sloan didn't grace his friend's exuberance with a response. Toby was still rambling on about what he wanted or rather expected of his staff. Being here was pointless; nothing that Toby could say that would move Sloan to want to betray Darcy. Doug's drooling and eager pant was driving him close to violence. To save face and his criminal record Sloan left his seat and went straight for the exit.

As soon as the door clicked closed behind him Sloan suppressed the urge to punch through the wall and instead looked at his new favourite picture. That shot would be a worthy screensaver, if she had been any other female. Just as he took in her features again the phone vibrated and blackened only to start flashing "Tyke."

'You're trying to get me fired,' he said when he brought the phone to his ear.

'It's too much,' she said. 'I don't get it, is my voice that bad?'

'Your voice? Your voice is amazing, and you know it, or else you wouldn't be there.'

'So why do I have to be naked on stage?'

'Naked?'

'You know what I mean. Last week I couldn't really say no, I can't say no this week either, it's in my contract. I wear what they put me in—'

'Breathe, Tyke,' he said. 'If you are uncomfortable tell them. It won't help much if the star is self-conscious.'

'I don't have the body for clothes like this, Johnny,' she murmured.

It took him a minute to understand what she was implying. 'Are you fishing for a compliment? 'Cause you got it, babe. I was in a meeting with my boss, and I had to get up and leave the room when I saw you. Literally, I was speechless. You left me dumbstruck.'

'Johnny,' she laughed. 'I'm not fishing for anything. I just don't, I don't usually dress like this.'

'Sure,' he said. 'The Quay is permanently twenty below, that's why.'

'It is not,' she protested. 'Don't you dis' my town.'

'Our town, Tyke,' he said.

'Oh, now you're claiming birth rights.'

'A town that produces babes like you is a place worth coming from.'

'Stop hitting on me, Johnny,' she laughed.

'Why? Am I embarrassing myself?'

'Only a coward's seduction takes place over the phone,' she said.

The lightness in her voice made him think she was teasing but a spark in him wondered if she was goading him to try it on with her in person. 'Are you calling me a coward?'

'I'm the coward,' she said. 'The crowd will be so

much bigger tonight. What if I forget the words and fall on my face?'

'You won't.'

'Did you see how high these heels are?'

'Darc,' he said in his most soothing tone. 'You're incredible. You can sing and you look unbelievable. You'll have them all eating out of your hand, and you will win this.'

'They say he's getting out of hospital on Wednesday.'

'Who?' Sloan asked but he knew the answer.

'The man from last week, Hayes.'

'You did a good thing,' he said.

While she was baking the first time, she had given him her own account of the story, much less dramatic than Doug's rendition.

'I did what anyone would do,' she sighed.

'You reacted,' he said. 'Everyone else froze, it's commendable.'

'He says he wants to make me famous… Did you read the paper?'

'I saw it,' he said not yet willing to tell her that one of those articles was in his very own paper. Leaning back against the wall he stared into the newsroom behind the glass door at the end of the corridor.

'I don't want to be famous,' she said. 'No one would ever understand it, but I—'

'I understand it,' he said and strangely, he did. By his own reasoning, that was why he had left Inverquay. Maybe it wasn't international stardom, but it was infamy, and unwelcome infamy at that. Not all notoriety was welcome or sought.

'Do you remember the burn that runs along the viewpoint path?'

'That splits off to the Witches Lock?'

She laughed; he was a step ahead of her. 'Aye,'

she said. 'Just up the valley from the Lock there's this cave, when it rains the water falls right over the top of it and cascades into the valley.'

'Creating the fountain of youth… I know it.'

'Of course you do,' she teased. 'Bet you deflowered many a girl up there.'

True that location was the teenagers choice for mischief but once again she was relying on his unfounded reputation… well, mostly unfounded. 'I'll have you know I was pretty faithful to Josie.'

She laughed again. 'Only a man would think that "pretty faithful" was something to be proud of or a defence for anything.'

'I was a kid, what do you want from me?' he asked, feeling his own smile grow. 'I'd be faithful to a lass like you.'

'Careful, you're bordering on that coward's route again.'

'I'll save it for when we see each other then,' he said.

In actuality, they didn't flirt much when they were together. Maybe she was right; maybe it was easier to flirt on the phone when there was no need to prove his salt.

'You are coming tonight, aren't you?'

That made his smile fall. 'You want me to come?'

'You don't have to,' she said but he heard the tremble in her voice.

'Just how scared are you?'

'I'm not scared,' she said.

He could almost hear her thrust her chin upwards. 'Right, which was why you called me to ask if you're that bad a singer?'

'I just figured that if they wanted to me flashing the flesh it must be because I don't have much substance… you know?'

'They want the women wishing they could sing like you, and the men wishing they could make you sing… you get me?'

She laughed again and his smile once again found his lips. Clearing her laugh, her tone lowered, and her voice became all husky. 'I'd sing for a man like you,' she taunted.

'Is that right?' he asked, trying to ignore the shivers that racked his body at her smoky intonation.

'Plenty of songs about bad boys,' she teased.

His eye roll became his laugh. 'Aye, okay.'

'Sorry,' she laughed. 'You don't have to come tonight. I understand, it's date night after all. But I get two tickets every week apparently, and you're the only person I know here so… they'll be at the box office if you want them.'

'Darc—'

'Just tell them my name and—'

'There will be many people going to the box office saying your name, Tyke, believe me.'

'No, silly,' she said on another laugh. 'No one dubs me as you do.'

FOUR

SHE WOULD NEVER UNDERSTAND Sloan thought to himself as he pressed his elbows into the bar and lifted his pint to his lips. Here he was clock watching at a bar on the same street as the woman who had plagued his thoughts all day. But he wasn't moving, he was here, alone, watching the clock, counting the minutes until the show started.

He couldn't, there was no way… if he sat in the audience, if she saw him… if she didn't… But if Toby did, or any of the other Daily National staff, how could he explain to them how he got there, and how he did it at such short notice. He was hardly a TV buff of any kind, Toby had put him in the TV entertainment section before and he had failed miserably, it just held no interest for him. And yet, he had chosen this bar because it was advertising Hidden Talent outside. They were screening the programme tonight, the obscure talent show had really pulled in the punters, but with the amount of press coverage this week it was no surprise. Next season there would be a bidding war for the format by all the major channels. Except next season, there would be no Darcy.

Again, he searched his pocket for his phone and tried to phone her, voicemail, again. If he didn't show up, she would be disappointed, he knew that and what possible reason could he give for not being there, other than the truth… But if he told her the truth, she might never trust him again.

Sloan watched the gaudily dressed groups on their way to the venue she was performing in traipsing and singing past the windows of the bar. Mostly the groups were women with only a few men interspersed. If he had to hazard a guess, he would suppose that the majority of men were gay. He couldn't imagine many straight men forking out for a reality show like this, unless they were forced to go with girlfriends or sisters; not with the kind of music they played. Sloan had seen the other acts in the paper that week and watched them on the internet. He fancied Darcy's chances. He'd already put his bet on at the bookies earlier in the week, but she was the favourite, so his odds were awful, but he wanted to show his support.

Show his support, he thought as he slurped his pint again and observed the crowds thin out to just a few stragglers. How could he claim to be supportive when he wasn't going to show up? He couldn't show up but how could he explain it to her? Never had he tied himself in knots over a woman like this and he'd stood up his share of women in the past without a second thought. Why was this girl any different? How could she ever understand when he couldn't make sense of it?

***

DARCY LET THE WOMAN in front of her brush the powder on her cheeks while she looked upward. As soon as the brush was gone Darcy looked straight at the wide black door that separated this large hair and make-up area from front stage.

'Come on,' she muttered to herself. 'Don't prove them right. Please.'

Why she was deluding herself, she didn't know. Truth be told she knew he wasn't going to show. Why should he? In the last week, they had spent a lot of time on the phone, but she had been selfish, just like Donnie had told her. She looked down at the blood red metallic polish on her false nails and had the urge to rip them all off. Who was she kidding really? Darcy Holmes was nothing more than a blip on the Inverquay radar. Darcy didn't cause drama, Darcy did as she was told, Darcy never appeared on the gossip train. She heard everything, being that the tearoom in the bakery was the main social hub of the town, during daylight hours at least.

Staring at the point on her stiletto heeled boot she let herself sink into a dwam. It didn't take much for her to conjure up the image of her long ovens and floured workspace or feel the heat in the kitchens on her powdered cheeks. The sweet scent of caramel and chocolate overtook the permanent smell of fresh baked bread rolls that had followed her since she was in preschool.

All her life the only thing she ever wanted to do was work in that kitchen. From the moment she could say the word 'bake' she was groomed into the ways of the family business. Darcy remembered being too small to reach the counters, and too weak to cream the sugar and the butter but it didn't deter her. Her father gifted a step stool and a bigger spoon to her, and she persevered, just like she had always been taught to do.

He wasn't as lucky, Darcy knew. Johnny Sloan was a legend in Inverquay to be sure, but it was only now she began to think about what that was like for him. There was no way for her to know what, if any, of the rumours were true. But if even half of them were then he was right about the attention seeking. His father had been a tyrant; everyone knew that of Sloan Senior. Everyone knew that he shacked up with a woman half his age not six months after his wife, Johnny's mother, had died.

Had Johnny deserved the beatings the town whispered about? Did he want to hurt his family with his actions? Did he really have anything to do with his mother's death? Was Josie really a focus of his rage? How could Darcy ever make sense of any of this without talking to Sloan…? But would he talk to her?

She had spent all week talking about herself and she knew nothing about him now. In her own selfish way, she was disappointed that he wasn't here, but maybe he worked nights, maybe he had a girlfriend. There could be a million reasons, but she hadn't bothered to find out.

Maybe not showing up was his way of trying to gain her attention, did he really still act in that way? Did he ever act that way? The image she always had of him in his black leather jacket, smoking a cigarette while perched on the back of that huge black motorcycle always inspired ideas of a rebel, a bad boy with an attitude who would hit first and ask questions later – who would look out for number one and screw everyone over eventually. Trouble was, that didn't play with the image she had of the man welcoming her into his home and into his bed without question even though she was practically a stranger. It didn't match with the image she had of him sipping her hot chocolate and smiling at her like a child in a sweet shop.

No, nothing matched, and she hadn't made any effort to put the pieces together. He had said he wanted to be her friend and that they should look out for each other. It was time she held up her end of the deal.

***

'ARE YOU BUSY?' she asked when he opened his front door to her much later that same night.

'No,' he said, looking down the corridor as he tucked her under his arm and ushered her into his flat. 'I was hoping you would come over tonight… I mean I didn't think you would, but I thought—'

'Can I talk?' she asked, clutching the strap of her handbag, which she let hang down in front of her.

'Aye,' he said. 'Can I take your coat?'

'Sure.' Somehow, the formality eased her into the discussion, not that she really knew what to say. Letting her bag sag in one hand she undid the buttons of her ankle length coat and pushed it back from her shoulders. When he didn't immediately take it, she peeked over her shoulder. 'Everything okay?'

'I just didn't… I thought there was…'

'More to it?' she asked and slid her coat down into her hands.

It was nearly one a.m. but this was her first chance to get to him. Press had been crazy tonight. The party afterward had left her mentally exhausted, but she wanted to be here, she had to talk to him while she had the gumption.

Being that it was so late she hadn't gone back to the hotel to change, so she was still in the halter neck waistcoat that left most of her back bare.

'I need to apologise,' she said as he took her coat and hung it by the door.

'Apologise?' he said, turning back to her and slipping his hands in his pockets. Again, she was left with her handbag hanging loose in front of her. 'I should be apologising for not coming tonight.'

'This is what I'm like,' she said, pacing away from him into the living room. 'I get so caught up in my own little world that I don't think about anyone else. I gave you no notice about tonight, and I expected you to be there. I didn't think to ask you about your personal life or what you do for a living, and that was entirely selfish of me. You could easily have had other plans tonight and I have no reason to assume that you would just drop everything for me.'

She paced back toward the entranceway blocking him from entering the living room until she paced away again. He stayed put. She focused straight ahead and paced to him and away, to him and away.

'My presumption must have sickened you; I'm disgusted with myself. I really didn't mean you any disrespect. I wouldn't, I mean I would disrespect you, but I don't mean to. My ex told me about this, about how I do this, about how I get so caught up in one thing, that I get this tunnel vision and I lose sight of everyone else's priorities, I am so—'

Her thoughts froze in her head when he snatched her arms and halted her. Bringing her eyes up to his, her lips parted but didn't manage to utter a word before his mouth covered hers. His serious look hadn't betrayed his intention but the gentle caress of his lips sampling hers didn't hide his objective now. Then his tongue touched her lip, and the tentative action showed her how she hung motionless, she knew his goal, but she hadn't shown hers. Throwing her bag to the floor, she seized his face in her hands and slanted her head, devouring him as thoroughly as she physically could.

'Tell me to stop,' he panted against her. 'I'll stop, if you tell me to stop.'

Already the heat on her skin was bringing her into a pinching sweat. The dizziness she experienced was nothing to do with heat, or with exhaustion, but everything to do with the man her nails were digging into right now.

Savouring him, she sang with her eyes still closed. Her head swam, floating into the mist of the moment she had never dreamt she would experience.

'Darcy,' he murmured, pressing his forehead down to hers, her hands locked at the back of his neck. 'Look at me, Darc.'

'I'm legal, Sloan, I swear it,' she teased him into a smile and found herself again tracing that dimple.

'No more singing?' he asked.

'I'm not nervous, not with you,' she said in truth and brought his mouth to hers again.

***

HER SINGING HADN'T LEFT for the night, she was singing again as he handed her the bottle of water and flopped onto his side on the bed next to her.

'What are you nervous about now?' he teased.

She poked his ribs while she gulped from the bottle and lowered it in a satisfied groan. 'Sometimes the moment just requires a musical interlude… There is nothing like a long drink of ice-cold water after incredible sex, don't you think?'

'Sure, Tyke,' he said, taking the bottle away from her, he capped it and got up from the bed again, taking a sidestep toward the window.

'Are you expecting someone?' she asked.

There she was in the darkness, those big, round, eyes gazing up at him with that innocent adoration. Innocent, he thought to himself, boy was he wrong. The woman was daring, or rather ferocious. He had never been with a woman who was so exuberant, uninhibited didn't cover it. She was wild, so full of energy and exhilaration that if he hadn't been involved in the process, he was sure the sight would have exhausted him. As it was with every moment of her ecstasy, she increased his. Seeing her unbridled pleasure only made him want to increase it and see more, and more. There were no facades with this girl, what you saw was what you got.

'Have I told you today how beautiful you are?' he asked, putting the water on the windowsill and edging back to the bed.

'You've never told me I'm beautiful,' she said, frowning at the bed a moment. 'I don't think anyone has ever called me beautiful.'

'You have to be kidding,' he said, dropping onto the bed with her again. 'You're the most beautiful woman I have ever known.'

Bringing her index finger toward his face, she narrowed her eyes. 'I'm not into heavy bondage, or threesomes.'

'Okay,' he said on a laugh. 'That's… good to know. What's the difference between heavy and light bondage?'

'Is that the start of a joke?' she asked, flattening his duvet over her body when she lay back.

'No,' he said, vaulting to the top of the bed to join her. 'You made the distinction, I was just curious.'

She looked so at home, so right, against his sheets. All of the pillows had disappeared from the bed and were currently scattered across the floor, so she was flat on her back. Keeping one hand on the duvet, which she held at her chest she flattened her palm on his cheek as he loomed over her, propped on his elbow. She caressed him for a moment, giving him the chance to memorise her face.

'Will you kiss me if I show you my breasts again?'

Her playful nature had him smiling more in bed than he ever had with any other woman. In all his life, he had never laughed with another woman, another human, as much as he did with her.

'Try it,' he said.

She pulled the duvet down and he took his chance to examine her chest. As she moved to pull it back up, his hand stopped her and pinned her down. He breathed her nipple into his mouth and swirled it with his tongue. She recoiled in laughter and grabbed his hair with her free hand.

'That's cheating!' she screeched, pulling his head away from her flesh.

'You didn't specify where I should kiss you,' he said.

She kicked the duvet away from their bodies completely. 'Well, if that's the case!'

He let her take control, but his arms held her tight against him. She rolled on top of him and kissed his jaw before sucking the flesh of his neck into her mouth. He was about to protest when she kissed her way up to his mouth and her tongue delved into his mouth. All control switched to him when her action brought him to full attention. He had her on her back with her fingers locked between his when she arched against him, prompting his mouth lower.

Then came the dreaded sound, the sound he had hoped not to hear – the source of the sound that he had been looking for at the window. The front door opened and closed with an unceremonious slam. Footsteps followed, and then stopped.

Sloan lifted his mouth from her cleavage and saw her looking down at him. The trust she gave him in that stare didn't hide her wariness.

'Tell me you don't have a girlfriend,' she whispered, and his lips turned upward again.

'It's Doug,' he replied. 'I should go and talk to him.'

He tried to roll away from her, but she locked her fingers between his, digging those talons into the back of his hands. 'I don't want him to see me naked,' she hissed.

Of all the things he might have expected her to say that wasn't one of them. 'Neither do I.'

Whether or not she heard his attempt at humour, he didn't know. She was too busy worrying that bottom lip of hers with her teeth and staring at the door as if waiting for it to open at any second. That was his concern too in fairness, which was why he wanted to go out and see Doug. If he went now, he could prevent the snooping photographer from walking in on them.

Sloan vowed that tomorrow he would fix a lock to that door. He jumped out of bed and grabbed his jeans from the floor, pulling them up he glanced back at the woman once again swathed in his duvet. Her lips were moving but he couldn't hear what she was singing. She did manage to throw a smile in his direction though, so whatever it was, it was working to calm her. He winked at her and ventured into the light of the living room.

'I'm not going to ask,' Doug said from his position on the couch.

'Ask what?' Sloan said, heading into the kitchen.

'Don't bullshit a bullshitter,' he said, popping off the sofa to join Sloan in the kitchen. 'It's three in the morning and you're still wide awake… Your neck looks ripe and unless we got a cat in the last twelve hours, you didn't do that clawing on your own.'

Sloan hadn't thought to put on a tee shirt though acknowledging the mistake was a bit late now. Doug still peered at Sloan's back with a tad of horror but more admiration. Sloan turned away from the man to take his attention from Darcy's handiwork.

'Are you going to deny it now?' Doug asked. 'She's a wildcat I'll give you that. I get why you don't want to give her up yet.'

'Yet?' Sloan parroted. 'I'm not giving her up at all.'

'So she took the news well then?'

'News?'

'Your job,' Doug said, reaching into the fridge for a beer.

'What I do has nothing to do with what she does.'

'Right,' Doug said, opening the beer. 'Except it does because all of your friends, colleagues, and superiors are desperately trying to get any tiny titbit and you've got her locked up naked in your bedroom.'

'That's not my problem.'

'Except it will be,' Doug said. 'When Toby finds out.'

'And how is that going to happen?'

Doug shrugged and he swallowed down the pale amber liquid. 'I can't keep quiet forever. She might be worth giving up your career for but she's not worth me giving up mine. I keep quiet for much longer and Toby will have my balls as much as yours… and I don't have the pretty damsel kissing mine all better.'

Sloan took a step toward Doug but clenching his fists at his sides he willed himself to calm down. 'If this is a problem for you, you know where the door is.'

'You'd kick me out? For a girl?'

'Not like we were best mates in the first place,' Sloan said, backing off. 'I was doing Nick a favour.'

'Oh cheers.'

'Now I know why he wouldn't take you in,' Sloan said folding his arms.

'Fiona is over there,' Doug grumbled under his breath.

'Right,' Sloan said. 'Nick's married sister.'

'Not for much longer.'

'But she was married when you shagged her.'

'Stand there as righteous as you want Sloan,' Doug said marching for the front door. 'But you've got your priorities all fucked up, why top rank a girl who'll dump you at the first sign of the green. Trust me man, she'll leave you in the dust.'

Doug slammed the door on his exit and the relief Sloan felt was short lived. If Doug was mad, there was every chance that he would get straight on the phone to Toby and have the full pack of hounds at Sloan's door by morning.

He couldn't think about that now. Now, he had business to finish. Filling two sports bottles with water he put them into the fridge, if cold water was what she needed, then that's what he would provide.

'He's gone,' Sloan said when he pushed open the bedroom door.

But when he rounded it, he saw her sitting on the end of the bed zipping up her boot.

'I heard,' she said, crossing to the mirror.

'How much?'

'I heard the door slam,' she said, pulling her hair away from her face and wiping the remnants of lip stain from her chin. She gave up, probably realising most of it was stubble burn. He ran his palm over his jaw. 'He's angry.'

'I kicked him out,' Sloan said.

She popped upright. 'He doesn't live here?'

'I was helping out a friend, giving him somewhere to kip down,' Sloan said, slipping his hands in his pockets and resting his shoulder on the door.

'But you kicked him out because of me?'

'It was never meant to be a permanent arrangement.'

'Angry will be an understatement then,' she said, tying her hair back with a band from her wrist. She always seemed to have one of these and she tied her hair high at the back of her head, leaving a mass of chestnut curls haloing her. Five long strides in those killer boots and she was in front of him. 'Excuse me.'

'You're excused,' he said without moving.

'Johnny, I have to go,' she said. Though she clutched at his biceps and tried to move him, he stayed put. 'Please, I don't want to be famous.'

Trouble was, she already was, whether she wanted it or not. Without taking his hands from his pockets he leaned forward and touched his mouth to hers. She accepted the kiss but only for a second before stepping back.

'Stay,' he said.

'I can't,' she said, and he tried to kiss her again. 'Please, I have to go… I'm already the talk of the village.'

Again, he tried to kiss her, with every step forward he took she had to take one back. One more and he would have her back in his bed. He kissed her and this time her hands slid from his arms to his shoulders. Yes, he almost had her.

'I promised my father,' she murmured against his mouth as he again stole it from her words. 'I wouldn't embarrass my family… the village… What will they say if I'm caught having an affair…' Her mutterings seemed to be more for her benefit than his, so he let her carry on as he kissed down the column of her throat. 'Me in bed… with Johnny Sloan of all people.'

This he did hear, and he took his mouth from her body. 'Meaning?'

'What?' she asked, running her hands into his hair.

'You, in bed, with Johnny Sloan of all people… What does that mean?'

'It means… I don't know,' she said her hands stilling at the back of his neck. 'It means you and I are… well we're hardly the most likely couple are we.'

Releasing her from his embrace he took a few paces away, one hand found its way to his hair. 'You can run as fast and as far as you like,' he growled.

'I didn't mean any disrespect,' she said.

'Sure,' he said. 'No one ever does, do they?' When he turned to look at her, he could read her clueless eyes, but it didn't quell his anger. 'Your family were pretty well to do, right? Strong, lucrative family business, popular with the locals… and then there's you, trotting along right into place; another Inverquay princess, falling into line… What the hell did I expect?'

'Wait a minute!' she snapped. 'Don't speak to me like that! I didn't say anything bad about you, I never did. You have no right to stand there and insult me! So what if I took on the family business? It's my duty, I love my work! I won't apologise for that!'

'You could have done it anywhere,' he said. 'Anywhere in the world! You stayed there because it won you points! No one ever whispers about you do they Darcy? No! Darcy Holmes is a perfect example of everything a good Quay girl should be!'

'There is nothing wrong with being proud of where you come from! Most of your friends still stay in town! We all look out for each other! You! You were the one who thought you were too good for us! Riding out of town on that big stupid bike of yours like you were some kind of hard man! But you're not! You are a coward! You ran because you couldn't face who you are! That's not our fault!' Her finger came up as she highlighted each point. Her brows came down and despite the floating lilt of her voice she was angry, there was no mistaking it.

But so was he. No baby steps for him. He took one stride and brought himself directly to her. 'You know nothing about me, or about my life. You don't know what's my fault. You don't know what I live with.'

She snorted and her hands found her hips. 'Do you think? That's the thing with small towns, everyone knows everyone's business! I could stand here and rhyme off a dozen things I've heard you accused of!'

'And you believe it?'

'I believe you didn't stick around long enough to correct them! I believe you didn't stand up to your accusers and prove your innocence!'

'I don't need to prove anything to you or to anyone!'

'Not until you've proved it to yourself,' she growled.

His hands came up to link at the back of his head, but she flinched, he saw it, and he took a staggering step back. 'You think I'm a piece of shit, a piece of shit that would hurt you? Is that what you're expecting? Is that what you think of me?'

She sucked her lower lip into her mouth and slowly drew it out against her teeth. 'I wouldn't be here if I believed those stories,' she muttered.

'Stories,' he said, again crowding closer before reminding himself of her reaction and backing off a little. 'What stories?'

'About you and Josie, about the baby she lost.'

'What?' he barked. A frenetic laugh seeped from his throat, he turned his back on her and walked to the window again. 'Jose certainly had fun with the truth after I left, didn't she?'

'You left,' Darcy said. 'There was no other version of events. Everyone knew how your father treated you. Josie was hurt when you left; she said a lot of things… a lot of horrible things… Mostly she won't even have your name spoken around her, even now.'

'Close, are you?' he asked glaring over his shoulder.

'Josie Richmond and me?' she asked, and she shook her head. 'Josie doesn't… mix with the lower classes anymore.'

'Sorry?'

'Ritchie…' she started. Her mouth moved but he could see from the way her eyes searched for words that she couldn't find any.

'What?' he asked.

'He made a lot of money,' she said. 'An awful lot.'

'So? I thought you said she didn't marry him.'

'She didn't,' Darcy said. 'But she took a big chunk of that cash with her.'

'How did that happen?' he asked but she just shrugged. 'How much are we talking?'

She shrugged again. 'No one knows exactly, except Ritchie I would guess, enough that he barely got away with the shirt on his back… He stays in a cabin by the Loch now; he doesn't come into town much.'

'She hasn't lost her touch then,' Sloan said more to himself than her.

'She's a very beautiful woman, and so classy. She could have any man in town.'

Sloan frowned at her unable to tell how serious she was being. 'Beauty's not worth much when it's only skin deep.'

'Maybe,' Darcy said and stepped around him.

He wanted to stop her when she opened his bedroom door. He wanted to stop her when she walked out of the room. Listening to her footfalls move through his living room, they paused, and he supposed she was retrieving her bag and coat.

An incredible night marred by something that neither of them could change. She was the Quay through and through. Yet, he had tried from the moment he clicked his bike into gear to put that place as far behind him as he could.

What he was, or rather wasn't, wasn't her fault. She couldn't help being from the Quay any more than he could. Trying to breathe out the anger he strolled to his still open bedroom door then leaned on the doorframe to watch the diagonal corner. The front door opened and flooded the room with light from the close. She paused and looked back, he wanted to tell her something; he wanted to ask her to stay. But those lips of hers were moving again, and the whisper of the Stones on her lips was enough to silence him. Their eyes locked, but neither flinched, and then she was gone, as quickly and as quietly as she had appeared.

FIVE

'WHERE'S THE…? Oh shit,' Sloan stopped as soon as he walked into Nick's office at the Daily National the following day. 'What is this? An intervention?'

'He can't stay with me,' Nick said despite Doug sitting on the opposite side of his desk, arms folded, staring out the window like a petulant child.

'Or me,' Sloan said, remaining by the door.

'You agreed to take him, what changed?'

'I don't need either of you taking pity on—'

'Sit down,' Nick said when Doug got out his seat; he obeyed and flopped back down. 'We're going to get this straightened out… I haven't got the room, Sloan.'

'Thought your girl had a place,' Sloan said.

'She gave that up when I promised her my sister was going to be out of my place by the end of the month.'

'There you go,' Sloan said. 'The end of the month is next weekend, you'll have room. He can stay in a hotel till then.'

'That was three months ago,' Nick said. 'Bella's ready for moving out. She doesn't see why it's a problem for us. Damn independent woman.'

'So let her go,' Sloan said.

Doug snorted out a laugh. 'This guy's more in love than you are,' he grumbled over his shoulder. 'He's crushed on this girl for nearly a decade and still lost her over a stupid bet.'

'Thank you, Doug.'

'How do you lose a girl over a bet?' Sloan asked.

Doug drew in a long breath and turned in his chair, but Nick got to his feet. 'We're not here to talk about B and I.'

'She's hot,' Doug said. 'Not as stacked as your girl. Bella's like… fearless, like really, nothing fazes this woman, and she does what she wants when she wants, whenever.'

'Would you shut up about, Bella,' Nick said.

'Singing her praises, man,' Doug said. 'You know I'm in love with her.'

'As in love with any woman as you could ever be,' Nick said, moving around the desk to sit on the corner of it.

'Is that what this is about?' Sloan asked. 'Is he putting moves on your girl?'

Nick and Doug looked at each other and smiled. 'He tries,' Nick said. 'B takes care of herself.'

'I might need to meet this girl,' Sloan said, widening his stance.

'Done,' Nick said. 'You can meet her anytime you want, providing you take this prick back.'

'No can do, Nick.'

Doug held up his hands, palms to the ceiling indicating he had already explained this to Nick. 'Do you want to tell me what happened?' Nick asked.

This time it was Sloan's turn to meet Doug's eyes. 'Not especially,' Sloan said.

'Where Doug's concerned, it's always a woman,'

Nick said. 'Right?'

'Now, wait a minute,' Doug protested. 'This is nothing to do with a woman.'

'Except it is,' Nick said. 'Because you told me it was last night.'

'Right,' Doug said. 'But not in the usual way. I didn't touch her… I wish.'

Sloan took a step forward, but Nick pounced up from the desk. 'He caused havoc in my sister's marriage and made me lie to my girlfriend,' Nick said. 'I know how tempting it can be to put him through a wall.'

'I never made you lie to Bella and the havoc was consensual.' Nick caught his buddy's eye and he sighed. 'Fine whatever; I never did a thing like that to Sloan… He doesn't even have a sister… Do you?'

'No,' Sloan said.

'See.'

'So what's the problem?' Nick asked. 'Is he not clearing his mess? Leaving the toilet seat up, what?'

'Your friend has a problem keeping his mouth shut,' Sloan growled.

'What? You've got a few on the go?' Nick asked, turning his attention to Doug. 'That's not usually a problem for you… In fact, that's right up your alley.'

'Oh, he's only got one,' Doug said slinking out of his chair. 'One very special one.'

'Laidlaw,' Sloan growled through grit teeth.

'She's very special,' Doug said as he ambled closer. 'You're not ashamed of her, are you?'

'Leave it.'

'Nick can be trusted,' Doug said, dropping his arm around Nick and giving him a pat on the back. 'He'll be very impressed. He's had his own choice of women in his time… but even he would have to bow to your skills.'

'What is going on here?' Nick asked.

'He's fucking Darcy Holmes,' Doug said.

Sloan lunged forward but Nick got between them and as Doug stepped back Nick grabbed Sloan. 'Hey! Not here! It's not worth it!'

'You're a fuck, you know that?' Sloan barked at Doug but shoved Nick back. 'The both of you can go fuck yourselves.'

Nick slammed the door away from Sloan's grip before he could get through it. 'It's none of my business, mate, none of my business.'

Sloan frowned. 'What?'

'I had to write a story on my girl once, it was totally consensual, but she would have had my balls if I got so much as a comma out of place. Whatever you've got going on, it's your business.'

'Did you hear me?' Doug asked, appearing again in the periphery. 'He's fucking the woman Toby would sell his mother for a sentence about.'

'It's none of your business either,' Nick said, shoving Doug. 'What are you doing getting mixed up in his shit? You keep your nose clean.'

'What are you, my mother?' Doug snarled.

'You want to do this?' Nick asked. 'Now? You want to have it out, like this?'

'This isn't my shit,' Doug said, pointing at Sloan. 'This is his shit.'

'So keep your snout out,' Nick said. 'You want to get involved in his life, you better be prepared for the consequences.'

Doug pointed to Sloan again. 'He's got her number! He knows everything about her! The whole world wants her and he has her!'

'Is that your problem?' Nick asked. 'Did you ever think that this girl doesn't want to be found?'

'Man, you're soft,' Doug said, dropping his hand. 'The pair of you!'

Doug moved for the door. 'Where are you going now?' Nick asked.

'Someone has to look out for the paper,' Doug said grabbing the door handle. 'I'm going to talk to Toby.'

'What will that achieve?' Nick asked.

'The National deserves a go at this. We can't miss our chance at the story. What do we do if someone else picks up her trail? What happens if she leads the competition straight to Sloan? One of our own! Can you imagine the embarrassment for the paper?'

'And I'm sure Toby will take appropriate action,' Nick said. 'It's not going to embarrass you.'

'Aye, but—'

'But nothing,' Nick said. 'If Sloan hasn't taken this to Toby himself, I'm guessing he's prepared for the consequences, should there be any.'

Sloan hadn't really thought about it and developments last night made it unlikely that their names would be linked now but appreciating Nick's help, he nodded.

'There you go,' Nick said. 'Toby can't do much if Sloan here denies all knowledge. Which I guess he would do if cornered on it… If he were going to give up the girl, he'd have done it by now.'

'You're crazy! We could make a fortune!' Doug declared.

'Off a woman who doesn't want it? Unlikely,' Nick said.

'What is wrong with you? You used to be the best! You were a pit bull!'

'What is the most important thing in this world to me?' he asked.

Doug sighed. 'Bella.'

'Right, and who did I promise to never hurt again?'

'Bella,' Doug said again.

'What did you swear to me you would never interfere in again?'

'You and Bella,' Doug said.

'Do you think Bella would be happy to hear about us being the cause of a woman's downfall?'

Sloan was surprised how Doug sloped back to the desk and down into the seat. Nick spoke to him like a disapproving parent but he took it. Doug accepted the chiding, which told Sloan two things. Firstly, whatever Doug did cost Nick dearly, and secondly, there was nothing in the world that would cause Nick to risk his relationship with Bella.

'This girl must really be something,' Sloan muttered.

'So must yours,' Nick said. 'You better know what you're doing. I'll keep Doug quiet but if the shit hits the fan…'

'Your names won't be mentioned,' Sloan said. 'It's appreciated.'

'It's only worth it if she feels the same way, mate,' Nick said. 'Find it out quick before you lose more than you stand to gain.'

Somehow Sloan registered the wisdom in Nick's words and realised he must have been there before. Sloan left the office wondering at what had happened with him and Darcy. They had spent only one night together and yet it was already serious, if not between them then for his career and his friendships.

Sloan knew he would never spill her secrets, what he knew of them, which he realised wasn't very much. He knew who she was through reputation, just as she did about him. The things he had learned in the last week had endeared him. He could never have imagined that Hayley's granddaughter, the girl he had a momentary encounter with on his last night in the village would mean so much to him that he would think about risking his livelihood, his reputation, and friendships.

What's more, he thought as he made his way to his desk. Little Darcy Holmes hadn't been a blip on his screen in all the years he grew up in the Quay. If it could hold one such delectable secret, how many more did he miss? Was Darcy right, did he take the coward's way out? Did he run away before he could be driven out? Where would he be now if it wasn't for his dramatic exit? Was that it? Drama? Whether or not he left to be dramatic was immaterial now because every year he didn't return it became harder to go back. He had become an enigma; Darcy had first viewed him with wonder, like she was faced with a real-life mythical marvel. Now, she laughed with him, she opened up to him and she trusted him.

Sloan froze, that was it, for whatever reason, she trusted him – completely. Could it be simply because of their shared turf that he had the gift of her trust without having to earn it? If that was the case, he should be thankful to Inverquay. She wouldn't have appeared in a stranger's flat in the way she did his, he was certain of it. Yet, all she knew of him was negative, the rumours and gossip from a place he had long left behind – but she came to him. Could it be that she didn't give much credence to the stories? If the sample Darcy had given him of Josie's stories were anything to go by then he had been painted as a monster back home. But she trusted him… why?

***

DARCY WAS STARING at the ceiling for the third night in a row when her mobile vibrating on the bedside table broke her reverie. Unlinking her fingers from beneath her chest, she picked up the phone and answered it with her eyes closed.

'I'm not drunk, or high, or sleeping with careless, disease-ridden celebrities,' she sighed into the receiver.

'That's good to know, especially that last part.'

Darcy sat upright in an instant. 'I thought you were my dad,' she said on one exhaled breath. 'I don't want to talk to you.'

'Don't hang up. You've been ignoring my calls for three days. I know, I was bastard. I deserve to be bound, and lashed, and publicly humiliated. I'm sorry.'

Darcy blinked into the darkness that surrounded her. 'You didn't apologise in your message.'

'It's not the kind of thing that should be done on a voicemail, and I'd have told you that if you returned my calls.'

'Sloan—'

He inhaled a long hissing breath through his teeth. 'She's gone for the surname. What happened to Johnny? You're the only person that's used my first name since I was a kid. I was getting used to hearing it again. I like the sound of my name on your lips.'

'I appreciate your apology, honestly, I do, and I apologise too. You weren't the only one out of line. I shouldn't have said what I did.'

'Okay then,' he said. 'So when are you coming to visit?'

'We had fun,' she said. 'I've not had a night like that in… Well… it was fun.'

'Don't go with, it's not you it's me, too cliché,' he said.

'It's not you,' she said. 'It is me.'

'Right,' he said. 'Except you've got you and you're not sharing with me. Sounds like I'm the one you have a problem with.'

She had to smile, he was being sweet, but she also had to be strong. 'I have no idea what is around the corner,' Darcy said. 'Things have been a whirlwind of mayhem since I left the Quay. I just want to do what I came here to do and go home, that's it.'

'And you don't want your buddy to be a part of that?'

'You're not my buddy,' she said.

'That's not what you said last week.'

'I can't get caught up in sex,' she said. 'It was amazing. But things could go either way for me, and I don't want to drag you into that.'

'So, you used me for my body and now you're casting me aside?'

Her jaw fell. 'No!' she protested. 'This is nothing to do with your body.'

'But it was the other night… You were happy to get me naked and have your wicked way, but now I'm not good enough to pick the phone up to.'

Exhaling a laugh, she lay back on her bed. 'Johnny,' she breathed.

'Progress,' he said. 'I'll try again… When are you coming to visit? Don't make me beg, I'm a proud man, or so I've been told.'

'I don't want to cause you any issues. For the sake of great sex—'

'In this thirty second conversation you've referred to our night as fun, amazing and great, a night that deserves those adjectives, deserves to be repeated.'

'Johnny, sex is so—'

'Not what this is about,' he said. His playful tone was gone, and his new deep intonation made her shiver. 'I want to see you. I want to talk to you, to know you're okay. If you happen to stay over then great, I know I'll enjoy every second of it. But I won't rush you and I won't let you back out because you're scared.'

'I'm not scared,' she said.

'Sure you are,' he said. 'So am I. It's what happens. When you can make love for the first time on the same night you have your first fight and still miss each other from the second that door closes between you, separating you… It's not something to walk away from… Or have I got it wrong? Did you miss me?' Everything he said was so completely true that it made her heart pound as though it were trying to escape her chest. 'I suppose if you could go three days without returning my calls, I—'

'I missed you,' she murmured. 'You were supposed to stop me.'

'I was going to,' he said. 'Until your Mick told me I couldn't get what I wanted.'

Now she had to laugh. 'Don't listen to my stupid singing… And I was talking to me, you idiot.'

'So you want me?'

'Don't get cocky,' she said, her smile glowing in her cheeks. 'I thought maybe I was too much for you.'

'Too much?' he asked.

'I've been asked in the past to… you know… tone it down.'

'Babe, don't ever change a thing, promise me.'

'Johnny—'

'Tyke, you're the most incredible woman I know, in any sense and I wouldn't change a thing, not for all the money in the world.'

'Did you fix things with your friend?' she asked, rolling off the bed.

'It's all taken care of,' he said.

'Did I cause any trouble?' she asked, pulling on her jeans as she tucked her phone against her shoulder and grabbed her tee shirt from the drawer.

Tucking it under her arm, she sat on the end of the bed to put her feet in her mules.

'No,' Sloan said. 'It wasn't about you, not really. You're safe here, this is your refuge, remember?'

'I don't want to cause you any trouble.'

'Then come and visit me,' he said. 'I want to say sorry properly.'

'What does that involve?' she asked, scooping her hair into a beanie hat and pulling her tee shirt on over the phone before covering herself with his hoodie again.

'I'm not telling,' he said. 'I'm an action kind of guy.'

At that she left her hotel room, sliding her card key into her back pocket. 'You better get the lights and the camera ready then,' she said. 'I'll be over in fifteen minutes.'

SIX

'ISN'T LIFE BEAUTIFUL?' Darcy declared as she stood on the bed, one foot on either side of Sloan as he lay with his hands locked behind his head.

'It is from this angle,' he said.

She laughed and dropped to her knees straddling his hips. 'I don't think I've been this excited since… since… I don't know if I've ever been this excited!'

Sloan slid his hands under the pleated plaid mini skirt she was wearing and admired the pale pink satin bra she shimmied in his direction as she dropped her lips to his chest. 'Let's have sex again!' she proclaimed, the hum of her lips tickling on his skin.

He lifted his hands to grip her schoolgirl bunches and pull her head up. 'I don't know if I like this side of you.'

'You always see my outfits before the world,' she pouted. 'I'm Britney.'

'I get it,' he said, flashing his dimple. 'And I didn't mean the outfit. The outfit…' He nodded in approval. 'It works… although the fact that you probably had this outfit when we first met should probably unsettle me.'

'I did not,' she said. 'Quayside High would never let a girl wear a skirt this short, at least in my day. Now I think they wear what they want… If the outfit isn't the problem, what is? We've almost made it to week seven and no one has figured us out yet.'

The seventh show was tomorrow night, and she was still in the competition. Interest in her had waned when it was revealed one of the other contestants was transsexual with a Z-list celebrity ex. Remaining tight lipped had meant when the more interesting story came along Darcy was old news. There were still reporters that followed her occasionally but for the most part she got the publicity on show night and hid from it the rest of the week. She did what she had to with sets and coaches, costumes and routines but the rest of the time she spent here with Sloan.

'You're excited because you're leaving me,' he said. 'We've only been together six weeks but—'

'Are we counting the first week?' she asked, and he nodded. 'So our first date was in the doorway?'

'Hey, it was the only one that's taken place outside,' he said.

Repeatedly he asked her to dinner, or out for drinks, or movies but she shunned going out in public for the privacy of home. Though he teased her that she was embarrassed to be with him, he was very supportive. She cooked dinner and he showed off his rusty barman skills that he had learned in his first jobs after leaving the Quay. Movie nights were common, but the film tended to be suspended in favour of making out on the couch, which always ended up in the bedroom.

They had broached most subjects; she had brought Sloan up to date on most of the Quay gossip. Sloan had educated her as much as possible on the finer points of football and other sports. When she got bored, she had a habit of removing her clothes and his until he stopped talking and got on with the action he always raved about.

The only thing she still wasn't sure about was exactly what he did for a living, she knew his hours were somewhat flexible, but he worked to tight deadlines. Other than that, he hadn't gone into specifics, but he had assured her it wasn't illegal.

One subject she stayed as far away from as possible was the future. Sloan spoke as though they would be together forever. Apparently, it hadn't occurred to him that her life was in the Quay while his was right here. Long distance relationships never worked but the odds were much worse when one side of the partnership refused to visit the other. Sloan was still cagey about his past and she didn't push. When he wanted to talk, she had told him she would be there for him, and they would get there eventually… if they could get over his aversion to visiting the Quay.

'I'm not excited to be leaving you,' she said, resting her cheek on his sternum and listening to his heartbeat while he finger combed her bunches. 'I'm excited that I get to go home.'

After tomorrow night's show, the remaining contestants were spending a week in their hometowns. Various nights through the week were planned in the Quay, ending with a final show the following Saturday, after that she would be back in the city.

'What happens if you get kicked off next Saturday?' Turning her head, she glared up at him. 'I'm just asking, I don't think it's going to happen, I—'

Snatching his pillow, she pushed it to his face and then hit his chest with hit. 'Damn right it won't happen. Don't jinx me. I haven't gone through this mayhem for the last month and a half for nothing!'

She shrieked when he grabbed her and pinned

her down on the bed beneath him. 'You got me out of it,' he said and tickled his tongue along her clavicle until she creased with laughter at a ticklish spot.

'And you've been so worth it, baby,' she said, stroking his hair from his face when he relaxed his head between her breasts.

They lay like that for what could have been a few seconds, or a few hours just cherishing each other until he lifted his head and looked at her. She smiled and waited for him to ask the question she could see on his lips.

'What are you doing this for?'

'What?' she asked.

'You didn't know we were going to meet. You've always said you don't want the fame or the career… What made you come here and do this?'

Shifting into a seated position, she faced him, and he sat up in front of her. 'It'll sound insane,' she said but he remained silent, which prompted her on. 'Do you remember old Mrs Rickett, the music teacher?'

'Old hag,' he muttered. 'I remember.'

'She had a heart attack, about five years ago.'

'Shit, sorry,' he said.

Sliding her hand into his she smiled. 'She was an old hag… But she clung on, we all took our turns keeping her alive, there were five of us. It took two hours for the air ambulance to arrive… Then we lost little Maisy after a car accident… We lost three youngsters on the Loch last year because we didn't have enough emergency equipment to run a proper rescue… We're too remote.'

'It's always been the way,' he said. 'It's sad, but with the weather and the terrain…'

'I know!' she said and released him to get off the bed. 'But why does everyone just accept that? It's not right!'

'No, it's not,' he said. 'But for every tragedy there

is a miracle… Like you and Hayes, that was amazing, Tyke.'

'Who thought saving a life would cause so much aggravation,' she sighed, wrapping her arms around herself as she reached the window.

Hayes hadn't been released from hospital, instead he had undergone a triple bypass and news was still bleak. But his people were still in touch with her, apparently, she hadn't been forgotten even if she wished she had been.

'I know these things, about CPR and such, because I have to… But we should have a proper facility.'

'Facility?'

'A community run venture,' she said, turning to him. 'We've been trying to raise money for two years and we're still more than a hundred grand short.'

'A hundred grand,' he said. 'Isn't that the prize money?' She nodded. 'So you plan to hand over your winnings as soon as you get them.'

'It's a community venture,' she said. 'If we can get enough money to have it up and running, we can put together an emergency team that can respond, with proper equipment and training and… What are you smiling at? '

'You're amazing.'

She shook her head. 'I didn't tell them I was doing this,' she said. 'Any of them, well other than Hayley and my father… They know I'm here now, the village, after all the press attention… But they don't know why.'

'Why wouldn't you tell them?' he asked.

'No expectation, no disappointment,' she said. 'I don't want to let them down if I don't win.'

She watched him get off the bed and come to her. 'You will win.' He gathered her into his arms. 'I've got money riding on it, you better win,' he teased, kissing her hair.

'If I do win, I can donate the money to the cause. If not, there are other things to try.'

'It explains why you went for the obscure show and none of the major ones that come with obligatory contracts.'

'You won't tell anyone, will you?' she said. 'Not even Gloria.'

'No,' he said, pressing his lips to her hair but she felt the way he tensed. The way he always tensed when she brought up talking to anyone in the village.

'You could always come with me,' she said, rubbing her cheek against his skin.

He pulled her back and gazed down at her. 'Are you serious?'

'I know we always joke that you don't come to the Saturday night shows—'

'To save your reputation in the village,' he said. 'Aye.'

'I don't care who knows about us, Johnny,' she said. 'You have to know that by now.'

Releasing her, he stepped away turning his back to her. That tension hadn't left his shoulders but when she let her fingertips reach him, he shrugged her off. 'You shouldn't have to say things like that,' he growled.

'I don't know what you want from me,' she said. 'Do you want me to go through the yellow pages and call everyone we know and tell them about us?'

'No,' he snapped and paced across the room to retrieve his jeans, which he then pulled over his boxers. 'This isn't about that… Do you think I really give a shit who knows about us? Do you think I give a flying fuck about anyone from that God forsaken town?'

The words hit her in the gut with an almighty thud, but she toughened herself and shook her head. 'No,' she said, reaching for the shirt they had discarded over the side lamp less than an hour before. 'I guess I don't… It's my mistake.'

'Darc,' he said, she pulled the shirt on and made for the front room. 'Darcy, come on, I didn't mean you, babe.'

'No?' she snarled, spinning on the spot with only two buttons done across her chest. 'I'm from that God forsaken town, you son of a bitch! You are from that town! You might not care about yourself, or about me, but I do! I care about you, and I care about me! But this… this will never be anything! Us? It's a joke, Sloan! Everything you loathe you see in me!'

Saying nothing more she grabbed her coat from a hook and slid her feet into the dolly shoes she had worn over here. The socks were lost somewhere in his room, but she didn't care.

'You are not walking out of here!'

'What are you going to do to stop me?' she snapped, throwing open the door. 'None of it is true! None of it! Maybe the man the town raves about would make me stay! Maybe he would have the balls to face the truth! To face his past! To man up for the sake of his woman! But you can't do it! You can't! You'll let me walk out of here! You'll let me go back to the town you despise, and you'll sit here, brooding, and cursing all alone! Is it worth it Sloan? Is it? Sitting here sad and alone while the rest of us fight for something? It's never easy! Not for anyone! But we face up to our responsibility… You're not a rebel! You're no renegade! People think you are this crazy, wild man! This fearless warrior! But it's not true… You're angry, you're sad, and you're alone… I hope that's enough to keep you warm at night.' Turning her back she took a step toward the hall and then paused before bringing her attention back to him.

'You know, for a man who claims to want to forget his past, you're doing a great job of wallowing in it, more than a decade after you left… Those of us in town have moved on from those days, but you… you relive every day you spent there here in this life, you let it dictate your life… and it's pathetic. Goodbye Sloan.'

***

BROODING, CURSING… sad, angry, pathetic! Darcy made herself lift her hand in a wave to Mrs Wellholm who was closing her curtains when Darcy hiked up her skirt and vaulted the wall at the back of her garden. She kicked the dirt beneath her feet and replayed the argument again; she had gone off the deep end as usual. Though she hadn't been back in town a full day she already wanted to get back to the city. After the show last night, she spent the remainder of the night in the hotel. Her morning had consisted of a round of press interviews and after that, she was bussed back to Inverquay arriving just after dinner. Terry, her agent, had hurried her into the hotel – the only hotel in town. The hotel, which was now fully booked with camera crew, lighting folk, the stage crew and a bunch of hair, make-up, and wardrobe people.

Terry insisted she stay at the hotel that they had taken over as it was more secure. But Darcy couldn't think of a threat in this village she had grown up in that she hadn't faced before. Leaving Terry to a meeting with his staff she had snuck out a rear window that the kids used to escape family events that were held in the hotel. This was the only place for ten miles that you could get a meal that you didn't make yourself. As such every reception, party, and wake took place here in this hotel. Terry might know show business, but she knew her town and right now, she was going home.

Keeping off the main road she cut across the gardens of the neighbouring houses and into the fields heading straight for the glitter of stars on the Loch. She didn't have to reach its shores but if she kept it in sight through the surrounding trees, she would come to a clearing. Inverquay had no streetlights, zip, but the moonlight offered enough of a compass. When she hit the clearing, she would see the stars, those beautiful, infinite stars that would put everything in perspective for her.

When she found it, she barely had a chance to look up before she heard the music, pumping through the trees. Narrowing her eyes, she crept forward and realised that there was something on at the community centre. It was only ten metres away and the usual crowd hung outside respecting the smoking ban, as they only did on warmer nights.

She could try to creep through the trees, but she would eventually have to cut across the road that ran to the community centre to get to her home. Setting her shoulders back, she reminded herself that this was her town. She had no reason to hide, even if Terry had confused her with all his talk of security. In all her time in the city she was used to hiding herself, playing down her presence to prevent being noticed. But this was home, she didn't need to do that here.

If she was lucky, she might actually find some friends to talk to, something she had sorely missed while keeping her head down in the city. She had stopped herself from talking to anyone other than her father and grandmother. The questions of her motives would be plentiful, and she hated to lie; she was awful at it.

Reaching the edge of the trees, she strode through and paused, noting each figure she saw. She hadn't clocked everyone when she heard a loud screech and the crowd parted.

'Ah! Darcy!'

Lottie came running toward her and Darcy's grin

about burst from her face as she was pulled into her friend's arms. Expecting her exuberance, Darcy hadn't expected everyone else's. Before she knew it, she was pulled into the arms of a dozen other people.

'You'll crease my dress,' she laughed.

'What of it there is.'

Much to her surprise when Darcy took her eyes to the voice of disdain she saw Josie Richmond, someone she would never have expected to see at a community event.

'Josie,' she said. 'You look good.'

'Wish I could say the same for you,' the tall blonde skulked closer, looking Darcy up and down while she took a long draw from a cigarette.

Darcy usually complained about wearing heels higher than an inch or two but tonight she was thankful for the spikes Terry's stylist had insisted on for her. Darcy hit barely five seven with the heels, but Josie was five eleven easily. Still the woman managed her perfected nose snub.

'You really have lowered yourself,' Josie said. 'I'm surprised at you.'

'I'm sorry you feel that way,' Darcy said and lifted the corner of her dress. 'It's a costume, nothing more.'

'You look great,' Lottie said and the others around her nodded in agreement.

Darcy recognised the faces of Julia, the girl they went to school with that now ran the post office; Grant, the local butcher; Colin, who ran the hotel with his wife Beatrice, who was as usual right at his side. Then there was Ricky, Stephen, Drew, and their usual mob.

The total number of people loitering around hit about twelve, but no one spoke a word as Josie came closer. 'The ugly duckling becomes the swan,' Josie said. 'You always were such a meek little thing. Still, I don't suppose we need ask how you've kept yourself in the limelight this long.'

Was that what the town thought? That she was sleeping her way to the top? Trying not the show her discomfort at the accusation Darcy swallowed the bitter sickness from her throat.

'I'm sorry you feel that way,' she said but her hands had already slid across her stomach and she knew her shoulders no longer held her posture.

'She always was one to go after what she wanted.'

Everyone turned to the new voice to see Donnie at the top of the ramp leading to the front entrance.

'At least you were dumped for a good cause,' Josie mocked.

'Dumped,' Donnie said, stomping down the ramp. 'I got rid of her… Look at the state of her.'

'She's standing right there,' Lottie said. 'Don't be a pig.'

'Never wanted to cause a whisper.' Donnie leaned in close to her. 'Never wanted a drama, never a scandal… What do you think this shit is?' he growled almost spitting at her with disgust.

To her horror she realised almost everyone had subtly stepped back as if physical distance would ensure no one mistook them for her allies. 'It's nothing to do with that, Donnie,' Darcy said. 'I'm not causing drama.'

'Showing up here like that?'

Darcy looked down at her dress. Yes, the corset bodice clung but the skirt flared at her hips in a fit of tousled monochromatic layers of silk and lace, even if it did stop just under her derriere. 'I was put in this.'

'Aye, right,' Donnie said. 'Convenient.'

Darcy saw the way he stepped back and called the insult over his shoulder looking for support.

'They say the quiet ones are the ones to watch,' Josie said. 'I'm personally outraged that they would bring this sleaze to our town… Of course, if Darcy here brought them—'

'Sleaze?' Darcy said. 'It's a singing competition!'

'Oh aye? How come the whole village knows you're ready to carry my coat,' Donnie said, grabbing for her chest, which caused her to leap back.

'Don't touch me,' Darcy growled.

'Come on,' Donnie said, sidling closer. 'You're begging for it in that get up, Sweetheart.' His arms came toward her, and others joined Josie's laugh, he pulled her against him. 'You like causing a show now,' Donnie said, squeezing her closer though she tried to wriggle away. 'That's it, Sweetheart, move for me.'

'Hey!' Lottie shouted. 'Leave her alone.'

'You're worse than her,' Donnie said over his shoulder. 'Is there a man in town you haven't had at some point Lots?'

That was the point that Darcy knew she was on her own. Lottie blushed and shuffled away with her head hung low. Darcy couldn't blame her, the fellas around all let out their own catcalls, and she folded her arms as she backed further into the shadows.

The attention off her for a moment Darcy tried to wriggle away but Donnie kept her locked in his arms. 'Let me go,' she growled.

'Not in this lifetime,' he snarled. 'I told you there would be consequences for leaving me.'

It happened in that moment, the moment she never in her life believed to be real even after experiencing it. A rumbling roar in the distance barely registered as the jeering continued. The more she struggled to get out of Donnie's arms the louder his taunts and laughs.

The thunder got louder, until it deafened the crowd to silence and thumped from inside her chest. Donnie frowned past her, and she got her chance to look over her shoulder. Her jaw fell when she saw it, that damn monster of a bike hidden behind the glare of the single headlamp. It couldn't be. Skidding to a halt in a spray of gravel, the crowd shrieked and scattered through the makeshift parking area, which was really just a glorified layby.

The pulsing grumble of the engine vibrated beneath her feet; he had scraped to a halt that close to her. Was he mad? Was she? Did she care when she watched him take his gloved hands from the handlebars and reach up to pull off the helmet concealing his identity from the gaping onlookers.

Her smile crept up when Sloan pulled it off and held it toward her. 'Need a ride?'

The gasp from the spectators was audible above the sound of the engine. The whispers started straight away but she didn't hear them. With one last shove, she rid herself of Donnie's unwelcome embrace and snatched the helmet from him.

'I thought you'd never get here,' she muttered.

She held onto him and slung her leg over the back of the bike.

The sight of his dimple told her that he didn't care who was mad either, not right now. 'Traffic was a bitch, Tyke,' he said over his shoulder as she pulled on the helmet.

Giving the engine a long rev followed by another, everyone around them jumped to attention assuring to get as far from the spurt of gravel and out of the path of the town's original cool rider.

With the rumble of thunder from the engine, she wrapped her arms around his waist and threw her head back with laughter as he roared away from the incredulous witnesses.

***

'THAT WAS LIKE SOMETHING out a movie!' Darcy exclaimed as she flipped her head back and put his helmet on her kitchen table. 'Bam! There you were; that was incredible! You're my hero! There I am thinking, damn, I'm screwed and then bam! There you are!'

She threw her arms around him, and he barely had time to catch her before she was almost crawling up him trying to find his lips, but only reaching his jaw. 'I'm so sorry, baby,' she murmured, her hands searching for the zip of his jacket. 'I was so horrible, so horrible to you… I'll make it up to you, I promise, Johnny, I'm so sorry.'

'Hey,' he said, snatching her wrists and holding them together and away from him to stop her ardent onslaught. 'I came here to talk to you.'

'You came all this way to talk to me?' she asked, blinking at him with those big doe eyes. 'You came to break up with me.' She shrugged herself from his grip.

'It's a hell of a long way to come to end things, don't you think?'

'You tell me,' she said, leaning on one of the wooden kitchen chairs. Her defences were up; he could see it in her straight away from the way those brows of hers came together.

'You were right,' he said, taking off his leathers. 'I came here to tell you that you were right.'

'About what?' she asked, appearing genuinely taken aback.

'You won't hear it from me often I'll tell you that now. I have been a coward and I was stupid to blame you for things that were nothing to do with you. But I've been struggling with these demons a long time – we're used to each other now.'

'I never meant to hurt you,' she whispered. Her eyes fell to the empty fruit bowl in the centre of the table. 'I did, I know I did. I lashed out at you because you lashed out at me. It wasn't right.'

'You were within your rights,' he said, rounding the table. 'No one's ever spoken to me like that, at least no one I wouldn't as soon put through a wall as see again.'

'I'd understand if you didn't want to see me again,' she said. 'I don't like looking at myself much these days.'

'I'll look enough for both of us,' he said, venturing to take her grip from the back of the chair.

'You came all this way to tell me I was right?' she asked.

'That I could have done on the phone... I came here to do this,' he said, leaning down to take her mouth with his.

He felt the way her mouth clung to his as though she would never have the chance to sample him again. As much as she tried to build the fervour, he kept his caresses slow, measured, gentle... they had more ground to cover before he took her up to bed.

'My bedroom's upstairs,' she said, clenching his tee shirt in her fists. 'I only have one.'

'Do you want me to take the couch?' he murmured against her to which she shoved his chest.

'Don't even think about it,' she said, snatching his mouth again.

'The villagers will talk,' he said while she nudged him backward to what he assumed was the stairway.

'They already are.'

'Johnny Sloan walks out of here in the morning and the townies will know just what went on in here last night,' he teased.

She shook her head while nipping at his neck. 'They'll guess, but they could never imagine what wonders of pleasure you are capable of.'

'We are capable of,' he said, gripping her hair to

tip her mouth up to his but she held back, her mouth twisted in an evil leer.

'Anyway,' she purred. 'Who said you'd be released in the morning.'

His own smile joined the intrigued rise of his eyebrow. Talking could wait; he linked their hands and let her lead him up the stairs.

SEVEN

DARCY GROANED AND ROLLED onto her front, further coiling herself in the bed sheet. 'Baby,' she whimpered. 'Answer the phone.'

Sloan smiled and hung his towel over the fireguard. He had forgotten how the quirks of country living could be so charming. Growing up he was used to an open fire in every room. In the city, he had never come across a real one yet.

'I would, Tyke,' he said. 'But it's not my house. Remember?'

This reminder had her rolling to her back and forcing open one eye. 'We're in the Quay,' she grumbled at him as she observed him standing, cleaned, and fully clothed by her bed. He nodded and she groaned again. 'I forgot.'

'No kidding,' he said. 'Do you want me to get it?'

Sitting up in a half-hearted attempt to appear awake she caught herself in a yawn. 'Why are you so awake?' she griped while moving to the side of the bed he had occupied to reach for the phone. 'More's the point, why are you dressed? Who said that was allowed?'

She didn't give him the chance to respond because she answered the phone, flopping back down in bed the moment she said hello. There she was, he thought as he watched her arm fall over her eyes, the only person in the world capable of bringing him back. Why he had got on that bike and made the journey he didn't know. What he did know was as soon as the thought entered his mind there was no talking him out of it. He was going to get to her, one way or another, he couldn't leave things the way they had been.

Her house was modest, the kitchen was the largest room, and it met the living room through a wide archway and the front door led into the functional room. Downstairs there was a WC under the stairs and upstairs consisted of her bedroom and an en suite with a shower over the bath. The house was more homely than anywhere he had lived, filled with soft furnishings and pictures transforming an otherwise humble house to a home.

Looking out of the long window that stretched further than the width of the bed, he saw the slope of the hills behind them and the glimpses of the viewpoint path they had discussed.

'Give me an hour,' she yawned again. 'Okay half an hour, Terry, I'm so sorry.'

Her apology was entirely sarcastic. If he hadn't known from her tone, he would have from the way she threw the phone down onto its cradle.

'I hate men,' she sighed. 'Except you, you don't count.'

'Uh, thanks,' he hazarded. 'I'm sure I was a guy last night.'

A sly smile crept to her lips and her arm flopped from her eyes to the top of her head. 'I'm sure you were too,' she said. 'I'm not sure you are this morning though.

I'm still naked.' She kicked the sheet from her body giving him a blissful full-frontal view. 'What kind of man is up and dressed, ready to leave a woman all cold and alone when she was hoping for a little heated honey for breakfast?'

'Heated honey,' he said, joining her on the bed. She rolled toward him with that predatory purr in her throat. 'I like that.'

'You're up,' she said, pushing him down in the bed to lie on top of him like he was a topper for her mattress. She buried her nose in his neck and groaned. 'And you're clean.' She brought her eyes up to his. 'You're leaving me, aren't you?'

Slithering one hand around her waist, he splayed his hand on her lower back while the other tangled its way into her hair. She offered no hesitation when he guided her mouth to his. 'I'll be back.'

'Maybe I don't want you later,' she said, catching his lip between her teeth. 'Maybe I want you now.'

'Okay,' he said. 'I won't come back.'

He moved as if to roll her away, but she threw her arms around his neck and clung to him with her lusciously naked body. 'If I don't let go then you have to take me with you.'

'Oh, that would go down really well with the old man.'

Relaxing, her eyes snapped to his. 'You're going to see your dad?'

'Thought about it,' he said. 'But I was heading over to Gloria's.'

She sat up, straddling him, resting her hands on his thighs behind her. 'You want me to come with you?'

'I'm a big boy,' Sloan said enjoying the way her position pushed her chest toward him.

'I remember,' she purred, wriggling in his lap.

'Don't,' he said snatching her hips to still her.

'I'm trying to contain myself as it is… If you're quick, I'll give you a ride to wherever you promised to be in half an hour.'

She slumped as though she didn't want the reminder but the illusion that they were going to spend any quality time with each other right now was well and truly shattered.

'You can wipe that smug smile off your face,' she said, throwing her leg off him and clambering to her feet. 'I have a date.'

His hands stopped on his jeans where he had straightened them as he sat on the side of the bed. 'Excuse me?'

She opened the wardrobe and frowned before closing it again and going to a set of high drawers next to it. 'I have a lunch date,' she said, retrieving underwear from a drawer and then crouched to pull out a pair of jeans. She turned them on him. 'If I showed up on a date wearing jeans, would you think I hadn't made the effort?'

'Who the hell are you dating? I wouldn't have come all this way if I knew you were skipping around town hooking up with other guys. What the hell was last night? You wish I'd left you with that loser?'

Scowling at him, she threw the jeans at his chest. 'I was heartbroken yesterday. I was ready to jack in the whole lot just to get back to you and apologise! This date is, well it's—'

'What? What is it?'

'Terry was putting pressure on me in the city. He said it would raise my profile if I was seen around town… I didn't want to be seen around town, so I told him…'

'You told him?' Sloan asked stepping toward her causing her to shrink in front of him.

'I told him to tell the press I was seeing someone from the Quay. It got everyone off my back. But now have to… find a boyfriend.'

'You have a boyfriend,' he said, getting closer still. 'And he's from the Quay.'

'What?'

'What the hell am I? Chopped liver?' he asked on a pronounced shrug.

'Oh, baby,' she muttered and hung her hands at the back of his neck.

'Are we fuck buddies now? Is that it? Johnny Sloan hits town with a hell of a bang… Did I spend all of yesterday afternoon more than twenty miles over the speed limit risking life and limb for a woman who—'

Her mouth silenced him with a long, smacking kiss. 'Adores you,' she said and kissed him again. 'I do… But I didn't know you were coming.'

'So you were happy for me to read in the paper you were screwing around up here?'

'I never thought I would be called on it,' she said. 'Terry brought it up yesterday and—'

'Who are you going out with?' he asked. 'Who's the boyfriend?'

'You won't remember him,' she said.

'Try me.'

'Simon Morris, he used to—'

'Run boat trips on the Loch,' Sloan said on a scowl. 'He's at least ten years older than you… and gay, from what I remember.'

'See nothing to worry about,' she said pressing her mouth to the underside of his jaw. 'Although he only came out about five years ago, so how you know he's—'

'Watch it,' he said, giving her behind a slap as she scampered away.

'It's lunch with a friend,' she called from the bathroom, and he heard the shower turn on. She then appeared around the doorframe, leaning her head on her hands where she grasped the wood. 'I haven't told him he's meant to be my boyfriend yet. But he loves a good tease.'

'He touches you and I'll kill him – gay or not.'

'You sound so serious when you say that.' She laughed while going into the bathroom and reappeared wrapped in a towel. When she looked at him again, he didn't let his expression convey anything but the utmost sincerity. 'Fascinating,' she breathed.

'What?'

'I would never in a million years have pegged you as the jealous type.'

'I'm not,' he protested and busied himself with stripping down the bed.

'In the city I prance about on stage wearing next to nothing, men get to see what you enjoy every night of the week but… you've never been angry about it.'

'This is different. I'm proud of you up there,' he said. 'You're vulnerable one-on-one.'

'I'm not vulnerable here,' she said. 'Everyone knows me here. Nothing bad could happen—'

'It could have last night,' he said.

Recalling how she felt last night, she realised he could be right. She was scared last night; even with a dozen people around them she was vulnerable.

'Donnie's an idiot,' she said. 'He was showing off for the crowd.'

'And that's the ex you listened to when he told you that you were selfish? Tell me you see now that he's a dick.'

She shrugged. 'I am selfish. If it wasn't for me, you wouldn't be here now.'

'Exactly,' he said, closing the gap between them and pulling her close. 'You don't let anyone walk over you. I was a pussy and you called me on it. It's about time I man up for the sake of my woman.'

Her words on his lips had her burying her head against his chest. 'Don't quote me. I hate myself.'

Cupping her face, he drew her eyes up to his. 'I don't hate you. In fact, I'm thinking it's quite the opposite.'

Something in her shifted and her look of wretchedness turned to terror before his very eyes. 'Johnny,' she stuttered. The clatter of her front door letterbox had her leaping to attention. 'The door! I'm naked!'

'I'd noticed,' he said.

She ran into the bathroom. 'The window above the stairs,' she said. 'Have a look and tell me who it is.'

Sloan didn't want to point out that he probably wouldn't recognise any vehicles. Instead, he did as told and poked his head around the bedroom door to look out the narrow window above the stairs that gave him a view out the front. 'No car, or any vehicle,' he called to her.

'It could be Simon,' she said through the splashes of the shower. 'God that would be amazing. If he came here, I wouldn't have to worry about everyone talking about last night.'

'You're worried about people knowing about us?'

The shower went off and he heard her moving around in the bathroom. His question sounded like an accusation, and he knew he was a hypocrite. Leaning back against the door his hand went to his forehead trying to erase his own guilt with his palm. His life was the one that would fall apart if their relationship hit the wires.

'I'm not worried,' she said. 'But I don't want anyone prying into our private life.'

'You don't?'

She appeared back in the room wearing

underwear and jeans and she snatched a shirt from the wardrobe, her hair was wet but in a flick of a motion he barely registered she had it piled on her head with a few loose ringlets escaping from the binds. It made her look natural but feral. Without a scrap of make-up, she was still the most beautiful woman he'd ever seen.

The doorbell went and she hurried toward him. 'Do you want to go out the back?'

'Are you sneaking one boyfriend out in favour of another?'

The corner of her mouth tipped up, but she kissed his cheek and rushed past. 'You're welcome to stay if you want. But it might be painful for you to see us together, after the profound experience you had with him in your youth, you know the one you won't tell me about.'

'Get!' he said, lunging at her again but she shrieked and ran down the stairs.

'I'll fight him for you if I have to,' she called back up the stairs.

He shook his head, grabbed his things, and followed her. As she answered the front, he let himself out the back to where they had parked his bike the previous night.

***

'THE RUMOURS… tell me they are true.'

'Rumours?' Darcy asked, sitting on the floor at her coffee table to pour the tea.

It had been Simon at the door and much as she would have rather rolled around with Johnny a little more it was nice to have time with a friend – quiet time without worrying about prying eyes and camera flashes.

'That Johnny Sloan is back in town and getting his male juices all over you… so to speak.'

'His male juices,' she smiled, handing Simon his tea. 'He'll like that.'

'So it is true,' Simon gasped. 'I knew it. I knew it had to be when I saw Josie Richmond's face at the shop this morning. It was quite a picture. How on earth did that happen? Please, you must tell me everything.'

'There's nothing really to tell,' she said, sliding up onto the couch after pouring her own tea.

'Nothing to tell, please,' Simon shook his head. 'I don't believe it for a second, this is Johnny Sloan! The career Don Juan, the rebel without a cause! Live fast, die young! Johnny Sloan!'

'I know his name,' Darcy said and for the first time she understood Johnny's frustration at his so-called reputation.

'You must tell me how it happened.' He put his tea on the table and moved closer. 'Let me guess,' he said with a grandiose arm gesture. 'Your eyes met over a crowded press conference. There he was a symbol of your past, of your misspent youth!'

Darcy laughed. 'We didn't know each other back then,' she said. 'Not really.'

'Oh,' Simon said now somewhat deflated. Lifting his teacup again, he took a long sip. 'Was I at least right about the press conference? I've never seen your name in his column.'

'Sorry?'

'I suppose there would be no reason to, your event might be sporting but it's not exactly a sport.'

'What?'

'It does make sense to ally yourself with someone in the industry,' he said. 'I'm sure he's been able to give you valuable advice.'

'Advice?' she repeated.

'Well, yes,' Simon said. 'He's been with that newspaper for so long now, he's reported for almost every section over the years. I'm sure he knows just how to make sure the undesirables don't corner you. There was a time we thought he was shaping up to be a real voice. Gloria thought he had finally found his passion with journalism. But over the past couple of years, he's been flat. Gloria's been so worried about him, she'll be so happy he's home.'

Darcy fumbled for the chain around her neck and tried to fathom the words being said. Simon was twittering on, but she only caught the odd word. "…National… press… tabloid… journalism…." could it be? No. He knew she didn't want publicity; he knew she avoided the press at all lengths.

But he had never come right out and told her what he did for a living. Whenever it came up, he distracted her. He encouraged her not to read the papers, telling her they would only upset her with their misconceptions. True, they had printed mostly lies about her, but she knew from Terry that some of the facts that came out turned out to be true. She didn't think much of it; the law of averages would suggest they would get it right eventually. She would have to talk to Terry, find out if the paper continually getting it right was Sloan's. But no, she should speak to Sloan, find out first if it was true.

Hearing the words now though, the pieces fell into place. It had to be right. It explained how he knew the best way to sneak her in. How he knew she would require a password for him at the box office. How he knew where she would be, what the procedures were, and it explained why he avoided her shows, and why he didn't volunteer to be her Quay boyfriend. Her head fell into her hands, in the blink of an eye Simon was at her side.

'Are you okay? Have I said something wrong?'

'No,' she said, squeezing his hand and finding his concerned gaze. 'I'm just tired and I have rehearsals for tonight.'

'You're singing at the bar?'

She nodded. 'Just a couple of numbers, no cameras but I don't imagine I'll get much of a reception.'

'Nonsense,' Simon said. 'I'll be there, front row, the dutiful boyfriend.'

She managed to smile at his kindness. He had accepted the deception as soon as she brought it up, he laughed along just as she knew he would and now she knew why. The rumours about her and Johnny might be true but a press abstainer like herself couldn't consort with one of the instigators. Or rather he couldn't be seen with her, not unless he wanted his own career to be questioned. She knew it. He had to give them all of her or nothing. But was that it? Was he protecting her and keeping their romance a secret, or was it sinister? Did he intend to reveal everything just as soon as he had the full scoop from beginning to end? That would mean as soon as she was kicked off the show, he would leave her and yet he spoke as if they were going to be together forever. Of course, if he knew that wasn't going to be the case it was definitely the easiest way to charm her. She worried that he hadn't faced the reality of their diverging lives. Maybe he did but the outcome was written for him already. He had his exit strategy planned.

'Thank you,' she said. 'I should get ready.'

Seeing Simon out was easy enough, he seemed oblivious to her shock. Closing the door, she took a long breath and closed her eyes. She wanted to hit him, she wanted him here right this moment so that she could shout and scream and have him beg her forgiveness.

Then there was the other part of her. The part of her that felt for him what he almost said that very morning. The part of her that wanted to believe he was protecting her, that he hadn't revealed their relationship to anyone. The part of her that wanted to believe the man jealous at the thought of her with another man really was who she thought he was. It would take one hell of an actor to pretend to the degree he had. Then again, Johnny Sloan was known for his loose morals and there could be some cash in the truth of what had happened between them. The closer she got to the final the higher the stakes. The fewer people on the show the more those remaining were coveted and there were only six of them left. Could that be why he had asked about her plans if she was kicked off this week? If she was then she could stay here, and he wouldn't have to face her wrath. That could also explain why he was here.

She had been cruel to him in their argument and yet he came here, he followed her. Why would he do that? Why would he come to her, here of all places, he could have waited until she was back in the city. Maybe didn't he expect her to be back there. Rumours that the competition was fixed were rife and the way Jet, the transsexual with the celebrity ex, had shot up through the ranks was anything to go by then there could be truth in that.

Sloan had lied to her, she thought as she sloped up the stairs. Whichever way she looked at it, he had lied, it may have been through omission, but she had trusted him. Trusted him with her secrets, she had told him the truth of why she was taking part. Her hands covered her face again when she lay back on the bed. Still covered in the crumpled sheets Sloan had left there that morning.

She had trusted him with her heart. Could it be that she was that naive? Did she give Sloan credit where it wasn't due? But how could he possibly have told her the truth after she forced her way into his life, which was exactly what she had done.

That left her with two choices. She either gave up on them, kicked him out without ceremony believing that he was the rat he'd been accused of being all these years. Or she thought staring up at the ceiling she trusted that he was protecting her, and she did the same in return by ensuring that no one in the press got even a whiff of their connection. Unless the whole thing was a stitch up, he stood to lose a lot more than she did if the truth of their relationship came out to his superiors.

***

'PEOPLE ARE FICKLE,' Simon leaned in to shout at Darcy who nodded while accepting another glass of champagne from a passer-by.

Right now, she was being rewarded for raising the profile of the town. The place was packed, and she knew every face, except for some of the cronies around Terry but none of them had moved from his booth all night.

She had dutifully sung her three numbers and her worries about being ill received were unfounded. Until this point, she had been backstage and so had been saved any ambush of questions. Now she was being plied with drink and the word "encore" was being hollered in her direction. The whole place had a party atmosphere, and she was so happy that her community enjoyed the attention. Luckily, the opinions of last night were in the minority and sure enough Josie and Donnie had scowled at her for most of the night.

"Encore" was turning into more of a chant, and she laughed as she sipped her champagne and Simon shrugged.

'I think you'll have to give them what they want,' he shouted in her ear.

Glancing over at Terry she saw that he was on his phone, looking rather annoyed that the commotion was interrupting him. Sticking his free finger in his ear he shuffled out the booth and headed for the door. She figured if the boss wasn't in the room, then she had to be off the clock.

'I suppose I will,' she called back to Simon and sipped the champagne again.

As she put the glass down and prepared to get back on stage the chanting died from a room of voices to half the room, to half a dozen, and to nothing until there was deathly silence, even the background tunes stopped. Looking around she saw everyone was fixed on the same position, following their gaze she saw him. Standing just inside the swinging doors of the bar he looked like the outlaw stepping into a western saloon. It was all in the eyes she decided because he was wearing the same jeans and tee shirt as he had that morning, with his heavy boots and leather jacket that she was sure he would have left her house wearing too, even if she didn't see them. When she spoke to him this morning, she didn't think cowboy, but she did now, in the way he met everyone's stare while looking at no one. Intimidating the room without an action or word and yet appearing indifferent to them all.

She saw the moment he clocked his prey. Stalking toward the table he sought, Sloan bypassed her, and his own cousins. The attendees fell over themselves to get out of his way and he didn't have to divert his path once. He only came to a halt when he reached the booth furthest from the stage.

'We have to talk,' he growled. Those piercing eyes of his locked onto Josie Richmond.

Josie drew in a long breath while rolling her eyes and lifting her shrug from her elbows to her shoulders. 'Why on earth would I—'

'Now.'

The word seemed to be enough. Her bored eyes became alert, but she was quick to try and hide them behind her remote veneer. Taking another bored breath,

Josie stood from the booth and took her time about getting out of it. Sloan didn't give an inch; he took her arm and began to guide her to the door. No one got in the way. Josie kept her nose in the air as though this was nothing more than a minor inconvenience.

Darcy was as drawn in as everyone else and scrutinised Josie's superior attitude for so long that she almost missed Sloan's eyes on her. Glancing at him, she did a double take when she realised he was checking her out. Only when he got right up close by did he meet her eyes, Darcy knew her cheeks flushed when he winked but he didn't miss a step in marching Josie from the bar. The door swung shut behind them and the room remained in silence.

'Any requests?' Darcy hollered and bounced toward the stage, trying to draw the curious eyes from each other and quell the wagging tongues before they started.

***

'YOU ARE A WOMAN in demand,' Sloan said from his place at her kitchen table when Darcy entered the house several hours later.

'You idiot,' she gasped, her hand finding her chest and her bag hit the floor. 'You scared me. Why are you sitting here in the dark?'

'I told you I'd be back,' he said. 'Weren't you expecting me?'

'I don't know,' she said, slipping out of her coat. 'You said that before you marched Josie out of the bar, neither of you was seen for the rest of the night.'

'Aye, we were at it in Winchers Hollow,' he said, pouncing out of his chair referencing the cave up from the Witches Lock.

'Gloria told you then,' Darcy said, sitting at the

table to unbuckle her sandals.

'About the kid I beat out of Josie… And the drugs I forced her to take, and the places I pressured her into sex, aye, Glo told me.'

'I told you the stories were crazy.'

'I'm surprised you looked at me twice, if half those stories were true, about the assaults, and the crime… You're a brave woman.'

'I'm a glutton for punishment… I knew what I was letting myself in for,' she said, kicking off the sandals and bringing herself to her feet just a couple of inches from him.

'What?' he asked when she stayed static in front of him just gazing up at him.

'Nothing,' she said with a shake of her head but the way her smile grew increased how self-conscious he felt.

'Do I have a bug on me or something?' he asked.

'No,' she laughed. 'I just… I never tell you just hot you are, do I?'

'Thanks,' he said without believing a word of it. 'How much champagne did you drink?'

'It's not real champagne,' she said. 'No one around here drinks real champagne. Do you want to tell me how things went with your dad?'

'I only spoke to Gloria,' he said. 'I'm pacing myself.'

'Was she happy to see you?'

'Aye,' he said, remembering the tears in his aunt's eyes when he strolled through her front door. 'I think she was.'

'See,' Darcy said. 'You're not as loathed around here as you think.'

'I think Josie would tell you different,' he said.

'Ach well, she as good as called me a slapper last night. What does she know?'

'You didn't tell me that,' he said, sliding his arms around her until she leant against his chest. 'What else did she say?'

'She said that under absolutely no circumstances should I trust Johnny Sloan to come within twenty feet of me.'

'She did?'

'No,' Darcy laughed and took his hand. 'I just thought it might prompt you into wanting to come to bed with me. I know how you love to rebel.' Her attempt to move to the stairs had him remaining motionless and she bounced back. 'Something wrong?'

'You,' he said, taking his turn to stare at her with the same awe she bestowed on him. 'How did I get so lucky?'

'The lucky bit happens up the stairs,' she said, nodding and darting her eyes to the stairway.

Her effortless nature filled him with such satisfaction. He hadn't believed it was possible to be content standing in the dark in a room with a woman who could fire his imagination and his loins with just one graze of her thumb. She was doing it right now as she moved it back and forth on his hand.

'Can I tell you a secret?' she asked, creeping closer to him, her eyes flitting around as though watching out for being overheard. When her body touched his she pulled him down to whisper in his ear. 'I've never done it on the kitchen table.'

As she drew back, he let himself glance at the table. 'This one?' he asked, releasing her hand to push on the tabletop. 'Sturdy enough… That's just a crime Miss. Holmes.'

'I should probably find someone to rectify that with me, shouldn't I? Can you think of anyone who might be willing to be naughty with me?'

'I have it on good authority that the bad boy is

back in town.'

'No,' she gasped and let herself be gathered into his arms where he unceremoniously lifted her and dropped her down on the tabletop.

'Spread 'em,' he growled.

She complied, snatching his neck, her legs wound their way around his hips, and she pulled him close. Never had he felt so valued. He truly believed that there was no one she would rather share this moment with than himself.

EIGHT

'WHO WOULD HAVE THOUGHT he was such a wanker.'

'Me Lottie,' Darcy said as she turned the pastry dough and rolled it thinner. 'Why do you think I dumped him?'

'I know you said he had attitude,' Lottie said, stocking the scones in the front display of the bakery counter as Darcy began cutting the pastry and lining the pie tins. They were talking through the long, industrial hatch between kitchen and front shop. 'But that was ridiculous.'

'He was drunk,' Darcy said.

'I can believe it,' Lottie said. 'But he's always drunk.'

'He wasn't drunk last night.'

'You mean when Sloan came in and huckled Josie out?' Lottie asked, pausing with her hand on her hip to look back at her friend. 'What is the story there?'

'Story?' Darcy asked, taking her attention to her Danishes.

'Aye, the way he swooped in the other night to rescue you like some phantom biker. I didn't even know you two knew each other, what is he doing helping you? And how come he appeared back in town the very day you come back?'

'I wasn't away in Never, Never Land,' Darcy said, opening the oven for her pies. 'I was in the city.'

'So you didn't see him in the city?'

'He didn't come anywhere near me at the bar last night,' she said deliberately avoiding the question.

'And that's another thing,' Lottie said, shaking her tongs at the hatch. 'No one has seen him in daylight. He's appeared the last two nights and then just disappears.' Darcy approached the hatch to see her friend looking back still shaking her tongs. 'Grace says he's a vampire, or a ghost. You know the stories about those woods.'

'You think he's some kind of supernatural creature that only comes out at night?'

'Could be, these stories have to come from somewhere.'

'Aye, fair point,' Darcy said. 'Why don't you ask him yourself?'

Lottie frowned and Darcy nodded behind her.

Her friend spun around to see Sloan on the other side of the counter next to his aunt Gloria.

'Ask me what?' he asked.

'He looks pretty real to me. Hold on.' Ducking under the counter, she popped back up. 'Think fast,' Darcy said and tossed the bulb to Sloan who caught it and examined it with a frown.

'Garlic,' he said. 'Thanks.'

Confused as he was Darcy smiled at a blushing Lottie. 'I think you're safe.'

'Good afternoon, Darcy,' Gloria called to her. 'It's nice to see you in there again.'

'Five shows,' Darcy said, holding up her crossed fingers. 'Then I'll be back for good.'

'We're all rooting for you,' Gloria said.

Darcy didn't miss the way she stole a glance up at her nephew.

'I'm going on break,' Lottie said, having not yet made eye contact with Sloan she hurried off out the side door leaving the front counter unattended.

'Lottie doesn't seem herself,' Gloria said. 'Is she okay?'

'She thinks the town is being taken over by supernatural beings,' Darcy answered, taking off her gloves and binning them. 'What can I get you?'

'If you're busy, don't—'

'No,' Darcy said. 'I'm just waiting for my—' A loud buzzer sounded, and she held up her finger until it stopped. '…timer. Take your time and peruse the menu. I'll be one second.'

Darcy moved to the back of the kitchen and opened the second of the large ovens to pull out a tray of her cookies.

'Box it up, I'll take the lot.'

Darcy looked over her shoulder to see Sloan sloping into the kitchen as if he owned the place. 'Can I help you sir?' She smiled, balancing the tray of cookies, which was twice the length of her. 'This area is off limits to customers.'

'Is that so?' he asked as she slid the cookies onto the counter and shook off her gloves.

'And you can't have all my cookies they are for you know actual paying customers.'

He swung her into his arms and urged her back against the floured counter she had been rolling out her pastry on. 'Who wants the cookies,' he said, breathing the flesh of her neck into his mouth.

'Johnny,' she breathed. 'The hatch is open.'

'And?' he asked sampling her lips.

'People might see us.'

'Haven't you heard,' he said. 'I have a thing for breaking the rules.'

'And I don't,' she said, plastering her hands to his chest and pushing him back.

'You're very strict in the kitchen,' he said, mirroring her stern expression. 'You weren't so serious on your kitchen table last night.' She found herself blushing again while his hands squeezed her behind. 'Come on, Tyke; give me some bang for my buck.'

Shrieking out a laugh, she nudged his chest. 'That was a terrible line!' she laughed. 'Anyway, no bucks, and no bangs – you get whatever you want on the house.'

'Oh, do I?' he asked and tried to kiss her again.

'I am not on the menu.' She slid her hands to his waist where she tried to urge him back again, but he resisted. 'Not until we're alone in the dark later,' she muttered against him feeling her resolve wane when he nibbled at her ear.

'I hope you don't give all of your customer's this treatment,' he said.

His lips cruised to her shoulder making her knees wobble, he directed her arm upward to wrap it around him and he lifted her from the floor. 'Not here,' she exhaled.

'Where?'

'No,' she said, shaking her head and snatching his hands from around her. 'Your aunt is out there; the front is unattended.'

'Can we come back and christen this kitchen later?'

With a nod and a laugh, he finally relented and put her back on the floor. She turned her attention back to the cookies, but bounced upright when his hands were again on her backside. Frowning over her shoulder she slapped at his hand with the spatula.

'Flour,' he said, holding up his hands in innocence. 'You have flour on you.'

Just at that she noticed that he two had handprints on his chest and waist. There was a trail of flour up to his neck and she found herself giggling. 'This is a disaster,' she said as she pointed out her observation.

'Don't think I'll be doing any visiting in this state,' he said, trying to brush the flour away.

'I don't think you'd need to explain to your family what your girlfriend does for a living,' she said but gasped when he snatched flour from her worktable and threw it on her top.

'Not so funny now, is it?' he said, enjoying her horror.

'You bastard,' she gaped. 'That costs money you know. It's not just there for your amusement.' Turning away, she took a handful and threw it back at him this time it landed on his jeans. 'That ought to dowse your fire.' She squealed, her hand covering her mouth to stifle her laugh.

'Come here,' he grumbled.

She only managed to shake her head, but he stalked toward her, and she leapt back.

'No!' she screeched, waving her spatula at him. 'We're even now! I'm armed!' Holding the spatula out like a sword, her back hit the freestanding steel fridge. 'Baby…' She tried to calm him because there was no escape now that she pushed herself against the appliance. 'Think about this, before you do anything too… Ahh!' She let out a screech when he doubled and tossed her straight over his shoulder. 'Johnny!' She laughed. 'Please! Oh, God! Please, baby!'

The cold steel of the counter got her first as he flattened her on her back against the workspace covered in flour. 'Usually when you're screaming for me like that you don't find it nearly so funny,' he mumbled and grabbed the flour.

'I'll do what you want,' she said, trying to get up as he held her down with one hand and the flour up in the other. 'I swear I'll be your slave for life!'

Trying her best to show him those big doe eyes he had told her he was a sucker for she watched him relax and lower the flour. 'Just you don't be forgetting who the boss in this duo is.'

Her jaw dropped as he turned and in a moment of sheer insanity, she grabbed for the bag he still held. Catching him off guard she almost had it, but his grip met hers and before either of them could react the bag exploded between them. The flour billowed up, down, left, and right, despite standing in front of each other they lost sight of the other for a clear half minute while the flour settled around them.

Both were as dumbstruck as the other was. Blinking flour from their eyes and spitting it from their mouths, they both seemed to realise their own ridiculousness in the same moment. When their eyes met the horror ebbed to humour.

'What happened in here!' Lottie exclaimed.

Darcy turned to see her friend scurrying into the kitchen but all she could do was look at Sloan. 'Industrial accident,' he said, shaking flour from his hair.

Darcy slapped his stomach only to create another cloud of flour. 'It all happened so fast,' Darcy said.

'The place is a mess… you ruined the cookies!' Lottie said.

'I'll pay for that,' Sloan said, his fingers curling around Darcy's shoulders. 'I'll give you a ride home.'

'I'm not getting on that bike like this,' she said, letting herself be led. 'We'll create a hazard for other drivers!' Lottie gawked as the couple shuffled toward her. 'You might have been right about the ghost thing.'

'Ghost?' Sloan asked.

'Forget it. Will you lock up for me?' she asked Lottie who blindly nodded.

'Darc?' Lottie asked as the pair reached the kitchen door. Darcy turned back to her friend. 'You did meet him in the city.'

Darcy looked from Sloan to Lottie and let herself smile before bringing her finger to her lips in the universal silence gesture.

***

'I'M GOING TO BILL YOU,' Darcy said, elbowing Sloan in the ribs when they left the main street to head for her street.

Gloria had been very amused by the state of them. Darcy didn't need to ask; it was obvious Sloan had told Gloria all about their relationship. Oddly, the knowledge only reinforced her belief in him and in them. It fostered a desire in her to tell the world about their bond and only made her resent her time in the show more. Reminding herself that it was only temporary she resisted the urge to link her arm in his and appreciate this rare time they had together outdoors.

Turning onto her street she was about to cross the road when she saw it. The momentary pause shook her to her senses, and she grabbed Sloan's arm and dragged him back into the trees behind the houses.

'Tyke,' he said. 'Watch it, we're nearly home.'

He took her dramatic move as a seduction because he turned her into his arms and pinned her to a tree. 'No,' she said, shaking her head.

'If I kiss you anywhere right now, I'll get a mouthful of flour.' He smiled down at her. 'Tempting as you are—'

'News vans,' she muttered. 'They're outside the

house.'

'What?' he frowned and released her to peek through the trees.

'Shit,' she muttered and paced away.

'This is not a disaster,' he said.

'Look at me,' she said, holding her hands out to her sides. 'Look at us! They'll put us together in an instant.'

Darcy had to think fast. The press was there so they thought there was news, they hadn't been eager to chase her here two days ago. The journey wasn't worth it for a reality show contestant who didn't want to speak to them anyway. Someone had told them a story, something that made them think it was worth being here.

She paused a moment looking at Sloan who was still shaking flour from his clothes. The flour had to go, she thought. They couldn't explain that, and it put them together even if they were seen apart. They had a story, but she knew her town. Without word she turned for the loch and started to run. Sloan had to be not far behind her, he wouldn't let her go alone but it didn't matter at least one of them had to clean up. Pulling off her apron she let it fall as she unbuttoned her shirt.

Curling the bend of the Loch side she headed up the steep incline to the north, the water was always colder in the cove, but it was private.

'Darc!'

He was following she thought stopping long enough to kick off her skirt next to her shirt. When he saw she had stopped, he stopped too. But he was still forty feet away. Blue Oyster Cult was going round in her head as she looked at him. She knew he knew what she was planning; he had to. Or maybe the words of the song were seeping out of her as they had before.

She didn't respond when he called her again. Instead, she turned and started running again. This time taking the death-defying leap from the cliff above the Loch and straightening her body to dive the thirty feet into the Cove.

The water was ice cold, but it did its job, coating her from head to toe in her plunge. Her body froze and she fought to keep her limbs moving to get her back to the surface. Whether it took seconds or hours she didn't know, what she did know was when she broke the surface that long, intense breath that filled her aching lungs was the sweetest breath she had ever taken.

'You're crazy!'

Shaking the water from her face, she treaded water and looked up the cliff toward his figure, still at the top. 'Chicken!'

She laughed but she didn't grudge him his choice, the water was freezing cold here. The water got no sun in this corner because of the towering cliffs on each side. In truth it wasn't much more than a ravine, diving the Cove was somewhat of a rite of passage and she hadn't done it since she was teenager. Everyone had to do it at least once, but few she knew ever risked it twice.

As she regained feeling in her limbs, she held herself rigid when she saw he wasn't one to be beaten. In disappearing from the cliff edge, she assumed he was climbing down the wimp way. But no, he reappeared in a flash of movement above her. Scrambling to reach the edge she moved to give him the widest target to land in. Watching his body shift in the air she was taken by how toned he was. His gooseflesh was as naked as hers, but he held form and didn't show an ounce of fear as he broke through the water. Swimming back out to the centre of the Cove she whooshed around in the water trying to locate him. Her heart hammered against her chest. What if he was hurt, what if hit the rocks? What if…

She shrieked when her body was pulled back, and

she found herself dunked under the water. 'You prick!' she sputtered as she surfaced and found herself imprisoned in his arms.

'Me?' he asked. 'What is this a suicide pact?'

'You made it didn't you,' she said, looping her arms around his neck. 'We're safe down here.'

'Do you do this often?' he asked.

'I was fourteen when I did it for the first and last time, you?'

'Eleven,' he said. 'But boys are different.'

'How many times did you do it?' she asked.

'Whenever there was a girl to show off for,' he said. 'Course none of them jumped it first.'

'I'm unique,' she teased and pulled him closer. 'Someone tipped off the press about something.'

'I get that,' he said. 'But now you're in your underwear.'

'If I'm going to get caught for something it should be something good right?' she said, noting his teeth chattering as much as hers. 'Do you think if we had sex right now it would warm us up?'

'Tempting as that is,' he said. 'And as many times as I leapt into this water hoping for that reaction from a girl – I think we'd die of hypothermia before either of us came.' She laughed. 'And if I'm honest, and it takes a real man to admit this, I'm not sure I'd be capable under these circumstances.'

'What if we come back in the summer?' she asked, wrapping her legs around his waist.

'You got it, babe,' he said, clinging to her for what she was sure was dear life.

'The city's made you soft,' she said, finger combing his hair from his face.

'This Baltic water has made me soft,' he said. 'Please tell me you have a plan beyond this.'

She kissed him, intrigued by the sensation of

frigid lips against each other while tongues remained warm and slick. The juxtaposition was unusual but not unpleasant. 'Can you swim?' she asked to which he just scowled at her. She kissed him again and turned to swim.

Holding her breath to dunk under the water and through to the lagoon, where the water was somewhat warmer let them pick up pace. The rain must have been heavy and frequent recently she noted when she had to duck under a thick veil of water falling from the hills above, then, only thirty yards beyond the waterfall was her salvation.

Pulling herself ashore she turned to ensure that Sloan was still with her. The swim seemed to have toughened him up because when he joined her, he was far more alert.

'What is this place?' he asked her.

They rounded the boulder scattered loch edge, and he caught sight of the wooden shack, with lights on in its front window and a stream of smoke from the chimney.

'Don't worry, he's a friend,' she said and carried on to the house. She let out a whistle and a few seconds later the huge black Husky she was looking for bounded toward her. Sloan got in front of her when it approached but she smiled and linked their hands. 'It's okay, this is Rocky.'

Dropping to her knees she nuzzled the dog, running her hands through his warm fur while he licked at her face. 'What the hell have you got yourself into now, Holmes?'

Her face lit up at the sound of his voice, she hadn't heard it in so long, and she had missed his friendly manner. 'Ritchie,' she sighed pulling herself up to her feet. 'You wouldn't believe me if I told you.'

'Who you got there?' he called to her. She started for the house with Rocky trotting along at one side and

Sloan at the other. 'You know who he looks like?'

'You say anyone other than Johnny Sloan and you'll be way off the mark.'

'You're kidding me,' he hollered. 'It's a regular convention… Get yourselves in here.'

Ritchie disappeared into the house and Sloan took her arm. 'Josie's ex Ritchie,' Sloan asked. 'The one she left at the altar?'

'He's glad to be rid of her,' Darcy said patting his chest in reassurance. 'And I'm sure you can contain your jealousy while the man gives you a change of clothes.'

'Jealousy?'

'If you feel the need to fight about it, there is nowhere better,' Darcy said, holding her hands up to the wilderness around them. 'Ritchie was pretty much ousted by the town when Josie started telling her stories… Give him a break.'

'Have you slept with him?'

Darcy stopped and looked at him. 'Do you think it's my mission in life to run around after Josie Richmond's sloppy seconds?' she asked. 'I don't pay any heed to the rumour mill and the man needed a friend. He lets me swim in the loch here whenever I want.'

'It's not his Loch,' Sloan muttered.

'It's an hour back to town by road,' she said. 'If you're too proud to let a good person help you because he screwed your ex then you better start walking. I don't judge a person based on other people's opinions; I make up my own mind. He has always been very good to me.'

'I couldn't give a fuck about Josie,' he said.

'There you go then,' she said and turned for the house again, but he drew her back.

'You didn't answer my question,' he bellyached.

'How about that,' she said, still not answering it and instead going straight for the house with the dog loyally guarding her.

'I'm scared to ask,' Ritchie said when Darcy entered. He threw her a thick, soft towel and she dried herself off.

'It's a long story.' Darcy had always liked Ritchie's cabin. The room they stood in now took up half of the whole building. With a low ceiling they were cocooned in wood, in here there was no overhead light, although there was electricity to the place, she knew he never used it.

Johnny entered and another towel got tossed to him. Ritchie then disappeared into the bedroom. Darcy had always said his bedroom was tiny and Ritchie's explanation was that smaller rooms were easier to heat in the winter, both the bedroom and living space had an open fire, although the living room's was significantly larger.

'I was expecting you to be at mine when I got home on Sunday,' she called toward the bedroom while wrapping herself in the towel.

Paying Johnny no heed she moved around him as though he wasn't there to the single row of kitchen units made of the same wood as the walls. They blended in, so much so that in certain lights they were completely invisible. She took mugs and coffee from a cupboard and began to make the drinks while the water Ritchie already had hanging over the fire boiled.

'It's a circus,' Ritchie called but soon after appeared back in the room. Making his way to Johnny, he handed him a pile of clothes and nodded to the bedroom. 'You can change in there if you want.'

'It is not a circus,' Darcy said, taking the cups to the mantle.

'You've not been on this end of the coverage. You've been leading those city folk a merry dance down there.'

Ritchie dropped into the big wooden framed

chair she had upholstered for him. Rocky propped his head on his master's knee and welcomed the casual hand Ritchie relaxed on it.

'You're such an old man,' Darcy said with a shake of her head and went about taking the towel they used for the hot kettle.

'It's heavy,' Ritchie said. When he leaned forward Rocky was unceremonious pushed out of the way only to be put in the way between the pair. 'Do you want me to get it?'

'The city hasn't made me that weak,' she said, carrying on with her work.

'This from the woman who makes me chop wood for her house every other month.'

'You remember that splinter I got?' she teased, putting the kettle back on its hook. 'I have a phobia.'

'Phobia, my arse,' Ritchie said, taking his drink from her. 'Hurry up and get changed then come back out so I can make fun of you some more… I've missed you, Darc.'

Darcy smiled down at the man with the dog's head again in his lap. Ritchie lifted his hand toward her, and she took it, squeezing it tightly to remind herself that he was real. This taste of normality after the craziness of the past couple of months had tears moistening her eyes.

'I still can't believe you really went through with this.'

'I told you not to worry about me.'

'Yet, here you are,' he said. 'I've told you, no one would think any less of you—'

'Don't.'

'Come home, Darcy. We need you here.'

Johnny cleared his throat and Darcy turned to see him – now clothed in Ritchie's clothes – standing in the middle of the room. 'Am I interrupting?'

Heat of embarrassment flooded Darcy's cheeks.

Johnny had no right to look at Ritchie with that contempt painted on his face. 'I'll get changed.'

'You didn't tell me how you came to be in the loch with the town legend.'

'There are news vans outside my place,' she said. Re-adjusting her towel she sat on the rug in front of the fire. Her hand found Rocky's fur and she tucked her feet under herself. Staring up at Ritchie she saw the lines of concern etching deeper on his face.

'Trespass law 1865, section three—'

'Ritch,' she said her smile matching his concern as it so often did. 'I'm okay.'

'This is the Hamlin guy, isn't it?' Ritchie asked.

'Terry says the press are good for—'

'I told you I didn't like the guy,' Ritchie said, his brows going ever higher. 'Didn't I? Didn't I tell you that there was something about him?'

'The man had you kick Rocky out; of course you didn't like him.'

'The man is only interested in money.'

'As most people are in this industry,' she answered.

'Someone should be looking out for you down there,' Ritchie said.

This time when he leaned forward Rocky stayed put so his head was sandwiched between Ritchie's thigh and torso, but he didn't seem to mind.

'I'm fine,' Darcy said, taking his hand again. 'I don't need looking after.'

'I'm looking out for her.'

Darcy again found herself looking at Johnny as did Ritchie. 'Sure you are, mate,' Ritchie said. "Cause we all know how seriously you take your responsibilities.'

'Pardon me?' Sloan said.

'Don't talk to him like that,' Darcy said. 'He's been good to me. You know what it's like to be a victim of the Richmond rumour machine. Do you want us to cast aspersions on you too?'

'Right,' Ritchie said with his focus on the floor like a child chastised by a parent. He shook it off and brought his attention back to Johnny. 'She's right. I apologise.'

Darcy clambered to her feet and left the men alone to go and get changed, hoping – naively – that they would take the time to bond. Though when she came back out both were as silent as when she had entered.

'I suppose I've put it off long enough,' Darcy said and held her hand toward Ritchie. 'I need your keys.'

NINE

FIFTEEN MINUTES LATER and they were on the road back to town. The air in the truck was thick with unspoken words. Johnny was the first to break the silence.

'Are you going to deny it now?'

'Deny what?' she asked, keeping an eye on the sheep up ahead that looked poised to jump out on the road the minute she took her eye off them.

'That you've fucked him.'

'What is your problem?' she asked, shifting up a gear when they passed the sheep.

'You had clothes at his place. You were perfectly comfortable wandering around in your underwear.'

'I'm sorry, was I supposed to be faithful to you after that thirty second conversation we had the night you left town over ten years ago?'

'No, but you—'

'Or maybe you think I've been having clandestine meetings with him in the last seven weeks. Let me tell you… the journey between here and the city is at least five hours, and that's in perfect driving conditions. Unless you think he can fly.'

'Darc, you know fine well—'

'Or maybe you're telling me that you were a virgin when we first slept together, is that it? Were you saving yourself and expected me to as well?'

'No, Darc—'

'Then I don't see how that part of my past is any of your business.'

'I think denying it now would be redundant,' Johnny mumbled to himself.

Darcy stole a glance at him and saw his expression filled with anger and disappointment staring at the passing heathery hillsides. How could she tell him the truth of her relationship with Ritchie? No one would understand, she and Ritchie had long ago realised what the village had thought of them. She wouldn't apologise for doing a good deed, and since then Ritchie had felt the need to repay it a thousand times over. No, she couldn't jeopardise Ritchie's dignity, not to appease Johnny's ego.

'I'll drop you off at Glo's,' Darcy said. 'We'll reach her side of the village first, that way the press won't see us together.'

'What? You expect me to tuck tail and hide?'

'No,' she said. 'But there is no need to drag you into this circus.'

Darcy wanted to tell him that she knew the truth but that raised the question. Why didn't Sloan tell the truth? He sat there affronted, acting as though she should apologise for keeping his identity a secret, except she was the one looking out for him.

'We're not hiding from the village anymore,' he said. 'They have to know that I appeared here because of you.'

'Maybe,' she answered noting all accusation had gone from his tone.

'But you still accept that we won't be seen in public together; that I won't be seen with you.'

The road was straight enough, and his sombre tone had her eyes meeting his. 'Yes,' she said after a beat.

More unsaid words hung in the air, and she wondered if she was the only one aware of them. Whatever he thought about her reply he didn't say a word. The vehicle remained quiet for the next twenty minutes. Johnny was again the one to break the silence. This time he asked her about the shows she had that week, then about the big show that was due to be broadcast at the weekend. He asked about her outfits, about her confidence level, and basically made small talk all the way to Glo's.

Darcy drove up the long dirt drive and turned the car in the narrow paddock that doubled as a play space for Glo's grandchildren, Johnny's second cousins, of which there were many.

'Are you sure you don't want me to come back with you?' Johnny asked, staring out the windscreen.

'I can handle it,' she said careful to keep the smile he had cultivated in her voice.

'Right,' he said, releasing his seatbelt.

When his hand touched the door, she couldn't let him go, not like this but she wasn't sure what she wanted to say, she grabbed for his knee, and he paused.

'Baby,' she whispered, surprising herself with the quiver in her voice.

'I used to think it was this town,' he said. His body still twisted in the direction of the door; his chin tipped down to talk to her but the growl in his voice kept him from looking at her. 'I thought it was cursed. I couldn't believe that so much bad luck could befall one family. I looked around me and none of the other faces were particularly happy either, so it had to be the town — that's why I vowed never to come back here. But it's not the town is it, Tyke? The town doesn't make any of our choices for us. We put ourselves there. We only have ourselves to blame.'

Darcy didn't have the chance to ask any more questions. He pushed open the door and slammed it behind him. She watched as he stalked to the house and shoved through the door without ceremony. Something in him still hurt, that torture he endured growing up was still there and had only been made worse since he returned… at her urging.

This thought stayed with her all the way home. She wondered if she had made him worse, made it worse, whatever it was in him that still warred with his past, with his family. Except it wasn't his family either, it was his father, his mother, the past that she had still to pry from him. Yet, she didn't want to pry; she couldn't make his pain any worse. Some part of him had to blame her for the pain because she had dragged him back here under severe protest.

Pulling on the handbrake, Darcy surveyed the terrain around her. She parked at the rear of the house, but the street wasn't exactly huge, it wasn't even a street, not really, more of a dirt track. Without any choice, she got out and locked the truck. That in itself was foreign in those parts, she couldn't remember the last time she'd locked anything in this town. Times were changing; and it was her fault. The town was being dragged kicking and screaming into the twenty-first century because she had a crazy notion of making some money by being on the small screen. All these choices that she had made – with the best of intentions – affected all of these people, people she cared about, people she loved. Staying as low as she could she moved in a creeping run over the narrow embankment behind the house. No one had noticed her… yet – she was only yards away from the house.

Someone shouted, then someone else and before

she had time to process, she was in the middle of a swarm. Whether it was ten people, or a thousand Darcy couldn't tell, she couldn't hear either, every question became a shout drowned out by the scores of shouts filling the once tranquil town around her. Choosing not to curl into a ball and ignore it she set her gait, lifted her chin and with nothing but sheer determination she marched forward. The swarm moved with her, and each jostle moved her from her path but keeping the house in sight she realised the swarm had taken her around the edge of her property and she was closer to the front now. Picking up her pace she almost yelled with joy when she snatched the bannister on her front steps. Using it to leverage herself forward she propelled herself up the first three steps. Her front door wasn't locked, and she could only hope that the hordes hadn't breached her home.

To this day she didn't know what made her do it. Something caught the corner of her eye and whatever it was made her turn, just slightly, but the sight made her pause mid step. The roar of shouts around her faded to nothing and she just stared, tipping her head to the side she peered closer sure she was mistaken.

Only when his wave joined his smile did she realise that no, this was real. Tipping her head back in the universal "come here" gesture she saw him start to move and didn't wait anymore. She ran up the last of the stairs, aware now of the shouting focused on her soon-to-be visitor. The door closed behind her, and she crossed as far into the room as she could, before she could turn the door opened again letting the sound of the riot outside to flare and fade once again as the door clattered shut.

'I'm scared to ask,' she said with her hands on her hips. 'But what in the hell are you doing here?'

'Gorgeous,' he said with that sparkling smile she was sure was responsible for many a broken heart, or at least hymen. 'Glad to see me?'

'And you just happened to be here?' she asked, flicking on the kettle, and searching the fridge for something to eat; dinnertime had come and gone and now she was starved.

'I wouldn't say that.'

'Good,' she said, slamming the fridge and turning the frustration of the day on him. 'We might be a little out of the way here Doug but we're not stupid. What are you doing here?'

'Hey, hey,' he said hold his hands up. 'I'm here to help.'

'Help?' she asked. 'How exactly are you going to help?'

'Where's Sloan?'

'You're here for your buddy,' she asked running through as many scenarios in her mind as she could muster in the seconds she had to strategize.

'Is he here?'

'No.'

'All the better then,' Doug said with that smile again. 'I wouldn't leave you alone to deal with the horde.'

'Except how could you possibly know they were here?' she said, turning her sweetest, most innocent smile on him. The tactic worked because his bravado faltered. 'If you saw it on the news then you wouldn't possibly have had the time to get up here. And this is the first time they have got any footage of me because I've not been home all day. Johnny hasn't been anywhere near a camera at least to my knowledge and being that I just left him a few minutes ago I can guarantee he hasn't been in touch with you either.'

'Well, I… Sloan told me that he was—'

'Save it,' she said, gesturing for him to stop. 'I'm tired, I'm sick of playing games.'

'Okay.'

'I know who he is okay.'

'Who he—'

'Sloan,' she said. 'I know he's a journalist.'

'He told you,' Doug asked.

While he sounded as relieved as she felt she also noted his incredulity.

'He didn't tell me,' she said. 'He doesn't know I know.'

'Why not?'

'A friend told me,' she said.

'And you're not angry?'

On a sigh she shrugged. 'At first,' she said. 'Maybe I still am… Not about what he does but it would have been nice if he had been the one to tell me.'

'I'm lost,' Doug said. 'You know, but he doesn't know that you know?' She nodded. 'And you're angry but you're not angry, except you are… I….'

'It's confusing, isn't it?' she asked and delighted in his confusion for a moment. Serve him right to be the one in the dark; she had been for long enough. 'Are you hungry?'

'Aye.'

'Let's have dinner,' she said. 'I'll fill you in.'

***

'RIGHT,' Glo said, shutting the back door on her grandchildren. 'Now you can tell me why you're huffing and puffing.'

'I'm not,' Johnny said, snatching the remote from the back of the couch and flicked the TV away from Ben 10, he continued through the channels to give him a distraction from his aunt.

'You've been like a bear with a sore head since you thumped your way in here earlier.'

'You want me to leave, I'll leave,' he snapped, throwing the remote to the couch and spinning on the spot.

Glo appeared in front of him. 'Did I say that? Sit down, I want to help.'

'I don't need help.'

'Course you don't,' she said, taking his arm and leading him around the couch to sit him down then took a seat next to him. 'You and Darcy were in rare form when you left the bakery. What happened?'

'What do people say about her?' Sloan asked his aunt.

He should be ashamed that he was asking but the village had no shame in gossiping about him even years after he left.

'Darcy?'

'Aye, Darcy,' he said. 'What do you know about her past?'

'Johnny,' Glo said with a dose of warning. 'You of all people should know not to pay any heed to gossip.'

'Just because you tell me doesn't mean I'm going to believe it.'

'If you want to know anything about her, shouldn't you be asking her?'

'We've never really had a chance to… When I tried, she… she told me it wasn't my business.'

'This wouldn't have anything to do with Ritchie McHugh's Explorer, would it?' Sloan's head snapped up and he glared at his aunt. 'I saw it going down the drive after you came in. If you need to get clean in a hurry out here the loch is the best place.'

'Tell me what I have to know.'

'You don't have to know anything,' Glo said. 'Has there been talk about her and Ritchie? Maybe… But I don't pay much attention to it, there's been talk about everyone in this town. Darcy's a good girl and I shouldn't have to tell you that. If anything has happened between her and Ritchie, then it's their business. You should be encouraged that she's not the type to kiss and tell, it means when she's home she won't be giving up your intimate secrets.'

'When she's home…' he said and thought about that.

Darcy hadn't shared gossip with him, even gossip about him. Like she said, she didn't pay it any heed. She didn't spread stories, true or not and she was probably the only discreet person left in the village.

'It strikes me,' Glo said, taking him from his verve with her positive tone. 'You wouldn't care anything about her past if you didn't care about her.'

'You know I care about her,' he said. His aunt's smile only widened.

'Really cared about her,' Glo said. 'Perhaps a "till death do us part…" kind of care.'

'You think I'm going to marry her?'

Glo laughed. 'You don't have to sound quite so surprised. It's hardly unusual for men and women in love to make a commitment.'

'If she won't give me a simple answer on whether or not she's slept with someone, what would she say if I proposed?'

'You don't know until you ask her. And I don't blame her for not answering you if you asked her that way.'

'What way?'

'So accusatory as if she has done something wrong. The double standard never fails to amaze me, has she questioned you on past conquests? If she did, would you be anything but proud of them? No. But if you throw that accusation at her as though her own needs and desires are wrong then of course she's going to be defensive.'

Johnny had to admit that what his aunt said made sense. Darcy had been nothing but accepting of his every need, she'd accepted his stubborn arrogance, and welcomed his every embrace. Yet, she held back from him and maybe seeing how easy and relaxed she was around Ritchie set him on alert.

'I can't imagine my life without her now,' Johnny admitted. 'It's not like we're physically together twenty-four, seven but somehow, she's always there… Is that crazy?'

'No,' Glo said with a much more content smile on her face now.

'Anything good, bad, or… indifferent, anything that happens, I want to tell her. I want her reaction; I want her opinion… Sometimes in the middle of nowhere, for no reason she pops into my head, and I need to talk to her. I crave her, Glo and I… I'm not sure I know how to deal with that.'

'It's all positive,' Glo said, wrapping her hand around his. 'She's a good girl and she'd never break your heart. I know it. You have to tell her.'

'I do, I… in my own way, I… I talk about forever, I try to make plans but she… when I do, it's like… She's not there with me, Glo, I know it. I might feel this strongly about her, but it's not mutual. I don't know how I know that, but I do. '

Glo took a moment and the smile settled into something much more serious. 'I'm sure I'm stating the obvious here but…'

'What?' he asked, sensing his aunt's hesitation. 'Is it the gossip? Did Jose say something I should—'

'Are you staying?'

'What?'

'Geography, Johnny. Of course, she's scared, she's probably more scared than you are. Darcy is a girl who thrives on home; her life is here, her family, her friends, her business. Darcy has never made a secret of how happy she is here… And now she's fallen for a man who not only lives hundreds of miles away but who has made no secret of how much he hates the home she loves.'

Suddenly, so much made sense. Glo had cut through all the crap that he had failed to see. No, not failed, chosen, he had chosen not to see the obvious. If he wanted Darcy, then he had to want Inverquay too; he couldn't take her from her home. What would she do in the city? What could she do? She would be miserable. But he would be miserable here. He couldn't come back here. Moving back would be more than just a physical move it would mean changing the way he had thought about this place for as long as he could remember.

He had to admit that worrying about it was probably moot, when Darcy found out about his profession, when she found out that he had lied then she wouldn't be interested in what their future could hold. This thought stuck, stagnating in his brain until he reviled himself.

'Being in love in a good thing,' Glo said but her words seemed distant now, so distant they didn't sound real, and yet the heat of her hand still curled around his. 'You would be surprised at what love does to people, what it makes people overcome. Somehow in the shadow of love nothing is as important as the object of that love.'

'Darcy!'

The screeching sound of her name startled him from his thoughts. Snapping back into reality he turned to the sound of her name only to realise it had come from the TV. Dozens of people crowded her outside her own home. A dark flock of jabbering journalists moved in synchrony around her like a flock of starlings dipping and floating on each air current, while Darcy was pushed and jostled.

Red clouded his vision. Her chin may have been

up, but the set of her jaw told him she gritted her teeth. That the distant, hard expression in her eyes masked a gloom that he imagined he had only added to. Again, she was pushed and although her body stumbled her expression didn't falter. She shouldn't be alone, he should have been at her side, screw the press, screw Toby, and The National. His girl needed help, she needed protection, and support, and he was here cowering in fear for his job.

His own expression hardened. Darcy ascended her stairs on the screen, he was about to push up from the couch to say damn it all and get to her when she glanced to the left then paused. Her whole body remained frozen as the herd behind her brayed for attention, then slowly she turned and fixed on something the camera didn't see. Her head tipped to one side and then she nodded as though beckoning to someone. In a flash she was inside and gone from the snooping camera. Just as he thought the shot was over, the commentator of the programme said something about a curious stranger welcomed to her home. At that, the crowd was forced apart and someone bounced onto her stairs. He ran up them and turned, taking an imaginary hat from his head he bowed to the crowd in an overtly theatrical gesture. Only when the man straightened and winked at the crowd did Johnny's heart still. The door banged shut behind him and the camera cut back to the presenter.

'He's not from the village,' Glo said.

Johnny had forgotten that his aunt shared the couch with him. 'No, he's not.'

'I wonder how Darcy knows him,' she said.

Much as Sloan knew Glo wasn't expecting an answer he gave it to her when he left the couch. 'He's my flatmate… or he was.'

***

'YOU'RE AN AMAZING cook,' Doug said, slurping the spaghetti sauce into his mouth. 'I knew you could bake but—'

'Just answer the question,' she said, pushing her own plate away.

'How should I know?' Doug asked. 'All this lying can't be healthy though.'

'No,' she said, losing herself in the flame of the candle between them. 'But he hasn't told me, he must have his reasons for that. I know he's protecting me but—'

'How do you know that?' Doug asked, wiping up the sauce from his plate with a slice of garlic bread.

'Why else would he be doing it?'

'Maybe he's going to screw you over, sell secrets of your sexcapades when you're all washed out from the show.'

'He wouldn't do that,' she said with a laugh in her voice.

'How do you know that?'

'Because he's not like that,' she said, taking Doug's plate away before he licked the glaze from the crockery.

'You don't know that. You've only been seeing each other for a couple of months.'

'You don't believe it either,' she said, running water into the sink.

'How do you know that?'

'Would you stop asking me that,' she said, turning away from the sink. Swinging his chair back onto two legs his hands locked behind his head.

'You women,' he said with a shake of his head. 'You never can make up your mind, can you?'

'What?' she asked.

'You never make things simple, do you? You're

lying to him because he's lying to you. Sloan wants me to keep his secret from you, and you want me to keep your secret from him. No wonder these things turn into such dramas, why can't anyone be honest?'

'Oh, and I suppose you're so righteous.'

'Not righteous,' Doug said, unlinking his fingers and planting his palms on the table. 'But I'm honest. A woman knows what she's getting from me.'

'Lucky ladies,' Darcy said and turned back to her dishes.

'Why is that people only lie to the ones they love?'

'Love?' she said and found herself looking at him again.

'Sure,' Doug shrugged. 'Why else would we be going through this drama if you didn't love him?'

'Johnny and I have never—'

'Bella was just the same. It's weird that,' Doug said, taking himself from his chair to rake in the fridge. 'Nick knew he was in love, head over heels, never denied it… except to Bella. B just denied it entirely, even to herself, just like you.'

'I have no idea who you're talking about.'

'Look,' Doug said, slamming the fridge. 'You want to play your games then play them, both of you. But at least when Bella screwed Nick around the only thing that was hurt was him. You screw Sloan around and he'll be ruined; finished. Do you get that? His career would be over.'

'You're saying he's not protecting me; he's protecting himself – his career.'

'I'm saying that you hold all the cards. He's ready to give it up for you. Sloan doesn't give a shit about the paper. He could take Nick and I down with him – course Nick would probably let him because it would make Bella happy to hear he was virtuous – me, not so much. I like my job. I love it. I'm good at it.'

'Okay,' Darcy said. 'So let's do it, now, here, you and me.'

'Much as I appreciate the invitation, I like my face the way it is thanks.'

'An interview,' she said, rolling her eyes and ignoring his deliberate misinterpretation. 'I do an interview with you, it goes into your newspaper, and then Johnny has nothing to worry about.'

'If I'm honest,' Doug said, sitting back at the table and muttering to himself. 'I can't believe I am actually about to say this.'

'Say what?'

'It wouldn't be smart.'

'What wouldn't?'

'For you to do an interview. The baying mob out there…' He pointed as though to emphasise his argument. 'It'll only get worse. You give them what you want, and they'll only want more. Hmm,' he said to himself and drifting into his own world. 'Kind of like a woman I suppose.'

She clicked her fingers to bring him back. 'More?'

'Yeah.' He left his chair and began hunting in cupboards this time. 'You answer one question, and they'll ask another, it's inexhaustible. You're hot property right now, so if you give in that just opens the floodgates.'

'I could give you an exclusive,' she said, sitting at the table and propping her head on her palm. 'Tell them I'll only talk to you.'

'Flattering as that is, Gorgeous,' he said over his shoulder before opening another cupboard. 'I'm not a journalist.'

'I thought you said you worked at the newspaper with Johnny.'

'I do,' he said.

'What are you? A tea boy?'

This brought out a laugh from him. 'I'm a photographer… and I've been stung by interviewing a friend's girlfriend before. Like I said, I like my face. I learned my lesson.'

'You're making no sense.'

'I'll introduce you to Bella one day.'

'Who is this Bella? And what are you looking for?'

'Dessert,' Doug said and gave up his search.

Darcy opened a cupboard beneath where he had been and produced three tins of her baked treats. Doug took his place at the table and dug into all of the tins.

'Are you going to answer my other question now?'

'Bella is Nick's girlfriend, he's my best friend. They went through a… debacle before they got it together too.'

'And now it's all moonlight and roses for them?' she asked, propping her chin on her palm again.

'Hardly,' he half scoffed and choked. After swallowing down the lump of pastry in his throat he carried on. 'They are forever dealing with one drama or another. His sister is married to her brother, or was… I don't know, I think they're divorced now… maybe. Ach, who can keep track.'

'Sounds like its more trouble than it's worth.'

Doug surveyed her for a second then he put the lid back on the tin he had been delving in and pushed them all aside. 'I'm going to tell you something now. Something I've never told anyone. Something I'll deny if you tell anyone I said it.'

'Okay,' she said now intrigued having never seen Doug this serious. 'Go on.'

'I'm jealous as all hell of what they have.'

'You're what?'

'Don't get me wrong,' Doug said reverting to his old self. 'I don't want to be tied down. I like keeping my options open. Bella's a great girl but she's not one to be on a leash, Nick has his hands full with her, I don't envy him that…'

'But?'

'But he's different,' Doug said, picking at a piece of stray pastry that had escaped his chops. 'The sky could fall in – and in our job sometimes it feels like it has – Armageddon could be upon us but he… nothing gets to him, not like it used to. He was never a big stressor, he was always laid back but… now it's not frivolous, nothing is frivolous, he's happy, he has this… contentment that he carries around. Back before Bella people would think he was indifferent, that his casual attitude was apathy. Now he still has that nonchalance, but everything is important now, he listens, he reacts, he cares.'

'And you think it's because of Bella?'

'I know it is. I tease him that he reacts to every situation as WWBD.' Her frown made him explain. 'What would Bella do? Funny thing is it doesn't bother him that I tease him. He likes any reminder that he got the girl, the girl he loved for almost a decade without ever saying it to her. Can you imagine that? Loving someone that deeply, being so crazy in love that you can bypass the physical and just be with them, just be friends with them and have that as enough.'

'It obviously wasn't enough if they're physical now.'

'He tells me he ached for her,' Doug said. Darcy wondered if he realised he was talking aloud. The look in his eye was distant as though digging up thoughts from his deepest, darkest secrets trove and somehow uttering them aloud without conscious thought. 'I can't even imagine what that's like. I know what it's like to look at a woman and desire her but to treasure every glance, every whisper, every touch… I thought he was crazy, I think he thought he was too. But when he looked at Sloan in that office… I don't know what it was but in that one look Nick sympathised, he told Sloan without words that he understood and somehow Sloan got that. Like they're in some exclusive club with this secret handshake, only instead of a handshake they have this secret stare and—'

'Doug?' she said. Her words sounded like a shout although she had only whispered them. From the way he physically started and shook himself from that daze she wondered again if he had forgotten she was there. 'You've lost me, I don't know what office you're talking about or—'

Music pierced the air and after shaking himself again Doug took his mobile from his inside pocket, with one look at the name on the screen he took himself from the room to the hall with the stairway and answered.

'Usually it's only the ladies that miss me.'

'What are you doing in there?' Sloan snapped at his friend. 'What are you doing here?'

'I don't know if you've noticed but I'm not the only one with an interest.'

'But you're the only one that made the evening news.'

Doug heard the growl in Sloan's voice and turned his back to the kitchen. 'She invited me in.'

'I know,' Sloan said. 'I saw it.'

'She cooked for me,' Doug said, scuffing his foot on the bottom stair. 'The only woman who has ever done that for me is my mother.'

'That's because you think a meal means commitment.'

'Wow, do you think I should be worried that she asked me to spend the night then?'

'You so much as think about going up those stairs and I'll—'

'Hey, I turned her down, I was polite, but she's pretty forward huh?'

'Laidlaw, if you—'

'Shouldn't you have more faith in the girl...? Damn, why do all my friends think I'm scum?'

The last part had been rhetorical, but Sloan answered anyway. 'Because you've never met a woman you haven't taken the first opportunity to seduce.'

'Well if that's the way you feel, why don't you come over here and... Oh, wait, that's right because you're lying to the woman about who you are and if these cameras caught your mug, then your career would be over.'

'Don't think for one second that I wouldn't...'

'Wouldn't what? What will you do, Sloan? The woman has enough on her plate without you lumping on more. Just give her a break. You push too much now and you'll lose her altogether.' Her footsteps came up behind him. 'I've got to go,' Doug said and without waiting for a reply he hung up the phone.

TEN

FOR MOST OF THE NIGHT, she had tossed and turned trying to decide what was the best way forward. Doug's warning had plagued her thoughts, she could ruin Johnny, ruin his career, ruin what he had spent years building. If he lost everything because of her then they would have to stay together, she didn't want him to resent her for his sacrifice. Still, she was left with the original problem too: geography. Things had been complicated before she had learned about his career. Although he spoke as though they were going to be together forever, she had always been aware of home. Home was a place she loved, a place of normality that seemed so distant to her now even as she lay in her own bed. She wanted to be here, wanted to be home, and back to her life. Johnny did not. He left town when he was young because he hated it. The place she loved he hated, and how could they build any kind of relationship on that? In this town she was known, loved, and she had purpose. In the big, bad, city she would be lost, just like she was now.

Her alarm had gone off already; she'd turned it off but hadn't moved. Normally she bounced out of bed ready to face the day ahead. Since being with Johnny she leapt into each day with glee, waking up next to him gave her a security she had never known. He might have only spent a couple of nights in this bed with her but already it felt empty. Rolling her head on her pillow she stared at his vacant one. How had things got so complicated? Was Doug right that we only lie to those we love. Much as she hated to admit it this whole situation only had one end – no matter which way she twisted it, no matter how she tried to contort, and organize the facts, every scenario ended the same. Now all she had to do was the necessary and decent thing.

Doug had already laid out breakfast when she got down the stairs an hour later. Granted, it was almost lunchtime, but she had a show tonight and wasn't in any hurry to get ready for that, or face the crowds outside if they were still there.

Doug's version of breakfast was unlike any she had ever known. Every food group was represented… The more she examined the spread as she skirted the table, she realised every food she had in the house was there.

'I was going to make pancakes.'

Doug loitered in the doorway tucking his shirt into his still open jeans. The toilet flushed behind him, and he had no shame about arranging himself into his underwear.

'You better wash your hands then,' she said, examining the contents of the table again. 'Why do you have Marmite out for pancakes? And hot dogs? And rice pudding?'

'I don't know how to make pancakes,' he said with a grin plastered on his face. 'I thought I would help you get a jump on it.'

'By clearing out my cupboards?' she said. His grin reminded her of an exuberant child. Although she shook her head at him, she had to smile. The man hadn't an ounce of shame, but his honesty was refreshing. 'I'll make pancakes for you if you do something for me after.'

She began mixing the batter.

'What?'

'I'll give you directions, and you can go and get Johnny.'

'Gorgeous, there's still a crowd outside and—'

'Not to bring him here,' she said, whisking it harder. 'I want you to take him home.'

'What?'

Coming to this conclusion hadn't been easy and she was glad that Doug had given her a distraction so that she didn't have to face Sloan. 'You were right about what Sloan has at stake. I don't want to cost him his career. I also sort of... goaded him into coming up here and... well... It's not my place to rush him into dealing with any family stuff. There's enough going on and—'

'You want me to break up with him for you?'

'Now I didn't say that,' she said, pointing at Doug with the frying pan. 'I just think it would be best for everyone if—'

'If he wasn't here.'

With a deep breath she put the pan over the gas flame and brought her attention back to Doug. 'I woke up alone this morning,' she said. 'Not because I wanted to or because he didn't want to be here. When circumstances are so strong that they can't be overcome for something so simple, it's time to take stock.'

Doug had been seated at the table. In a flash, he was in front of her. 'If you're ending it you have to tell him to his face. Don't do it like this.'

'I'm not doing it, not like anything. Tell him... tell him it's okay. I'll be back in the city at the start of next week. No matter what happens this weekend I'll come back.'

'And then what?'

'Then we'll talk.'

'Talk?'

'Doug,' she beseeched. 'Take him home, please.'

His expression betrayed his reluctance. If she wasn't mistaken, he was angry too. Though Doug's anger would be nothing on Johnny's, she knew that. By doing this she was sending a clear signal – that she didn't want him around. But that wasn't the truth of it; not at all. If she had her way they would be together now, they would have spent the night together, the day together and he would kiss her each night before a show. But he couldn't, they couldn't. The more she thought about the situation the more she wondered if his career was an excuse – for her. Telling herself that she was doing this to protect him was easy on her conscience. To ensure his career was safe she could prove now that she would sacrifice anything in favour of giving him what he needed. He couldn't leave her because of his career but she would give him this out, she would take the pressure off. She could do this alone. She would do this alone.

***

THE CROWD WERE cheering, the music was live, and the atmosphere thick with joy. Yet, she couldn't bring herself to get into it. She couldn't relax. Every element of the evening was perfect for her to have the show of her life, but it wasn't there.

After the pancakes Doug had gathered what few of his things he had together and stood inside the back door. Having told Toby, his boss, that Darcy had kicked him straight out the back of the house last night soon after he entered through the front it was important that his exit was discreet. She hugged him and he kissed her cheek but neither had said a word. When she stepped away, out of view, he opened the door to creep out avoiding the flashes and shouts still at the front. But when the door closed behind him Darcy was alone. Despite the throngs of people outside screaming her name with adoration in her life, she had never felt so isolated. If she was honest, without the hope of being in Johnny's arms all she wanted to do was to go to Hayley's care home and crawl into bed with the woman who had taught her all the life lessons she could. Until now Darcy had never appreciated that this was one lesson that had to be learned alone. Heartbreak had no name until now, not for her. Now her world was consumed with the bleak, black loneliness of sacrifice.

The crowd had had their encore, but she remained here in the wings. The audience still shouted though most had gone back to their drinks now that the band was playing without her. Pushing past a column of boxes that held all of the hall's accumulated decorations from over the years; Darcy reached for the door that went to the only separate room backstage that was used for anyone and everyone to get changed usually before the annual Christmas pantomime.

Her hand didn't make contact with the door; another warm hand closed around hers seizing her reach. Opening her mouth, her eyes moved upward but she could never mistake his touch even in this dark gloom.

'You didn't think it would be that easy, did you?' The weight of his voice was as heavy as the dark air around him.

'It wasn't supposed to be easy,' she said, mimicking his tone.

'You thought you could send Doug over and I'd run away like the dutiful pup?'

'I was trying to do what is best,' she said. 'For

both of us.'

Again, when she went for the door handle his hand snatched hers away. 'Best? You don't get to decide anything for me.'

'Fine, I was doing what was best for me,' she said.

'So it's best for you to dump me through my mate? Cheers.'

'I wasn't dumping you.'

'Aye, right, I heard that one, try again,' he said.

'Where do you get off? Standing there indignantly when I'm doing what is absolutely the best thing for you!'

'What do you know about what's best for me? First, you bitch at me that it was best to come here. Now, I'm here you tell me to fuck off? Just who are you lady?'

'Right, I've been wrong all along. Hate me if that works, just get out of here.'

Again, she went for the handle, this time he took her hand and dragged her to the opposite wall of the narrow space. 'What are you playing at, Darc? What is all of this about? I'm not a toy you get to pick and put down when it suits you.'

'I don't care what you think at this point, Sloan,' she snarled, whipping her hand out of his. 'You really have some nerve.'

'I have nerve?'

'Yeah, you,' she said. 'I'm trying to do what is best for you. Get out of town! It's what you want, isn't it?'

'I came here for you,' he said.

'If you did then your reasons were wrong,' she said. 'You can't do anything for me here. Here I'm fine, I'm happy, I'm home. I don't hate this place the way you do.'

'I'm doing this for you. I'm here for you. I'm here because you wanted me to—'

'No,' she said. 'I don't want you to be here for me. I wanted you to fix what's wrong for you.'

'What's wrong?'

Her hand covered his chest over his heart. 'In here. Something was taken from you. Or, you didn't get something you should have, and—'

Batting her hand from his body, he paced away. 'Spare me the psychobabble.'

'Excuse me for caring.'

'Caring,' he said. 'You've got a funny way of showing it. I came here to prove to you how much I cared.'

'I had that information in the city.'

'So why did you—'

'Your anger isn't healthy. People shouldn't speak about you the way they do. It's hurtful.'

'So it was about saving face?' he asked. 'You could admit you screwed Johnny Sloan after all the rumours had been corrected?'

'Forget it,' she said. 'Forget it. Forget it.'

'I thought we had something special. I wanted this to be special—'

'No, you didn't,' she said, admitting that his righteous anger was getting to her. 'If you did, you'd have told me the truth.'

The flicker of surprise was just like that silence that had hung between them in the Explorer yesterday.

'The truth… this is about… what truth?'

'You can't admit it, can you?' She folded her arms. 'Okay, Sloan, stand there and tell me that you told me everything, tell me what you do for a living.'

'You know,' he murmured.

'Yes, Johnny I know—'

'Doug's a little—'

'I knew before he arrived,' she said.

'You're angry because—'

'No! I'm not angry about your job, but don't you see? Getting away from here, getting away from me is the only thing you can do.'

'I don't accept that.'

'You should never have come here,' she said. 'It's made things worse… But maybe it's better we face facts now.'

'Face facts?'

'You can't be seen with me, unless you're willing to sell our story – will you do that?'

'Of course not.'

'Then you have to go,' she said. 'If they find out what we've done, what we've been doing it could end your career.'

'No, I—'

He approached, so she backed away. 'I understand. I know you wanted to protect me, to protect us.'

'I don't care what my boss—'

'I do,' she said, licking her lips. Reality was so much easier to face when it was in your head and not staring you in the face. 'It might mean nothing right now, but what would you be ruining your career for?'

'I'm not—'

'How will you feel in five weeks when this is all over? When the show is done, and I'm standing in your flat telling you goodbye? Because I will. I can't leave the Quay. I know you hate it, and everything about it. But don't you understand that every ounce of your hate is worth half the weight of my love for the place? You had it bad, you haven't told me about your family, about your troubles, but no one feels as strongly as you do without good reason. I'm sorry Johnny,' she said and took his hand. 'I wish it could be better. I wish you could find something to love as much as I love this town.'

'You are breaking up with me.'

'I thought we could sit down and talk about it when I got back to the city, but maybe it's better that it happens here. Now you have another reason to hate the place, another bad memory to add to all the others. You can lock them tight here and forget any of us ever existed. Pretend that Inverquay doesn't exist. We'll leave you alone, all of us. You can forget your father, and Josie, and Donnie, and Lottie, forget Gracie, and Julia, Grant, and Colin, forget all your cousins, your old crew, Ricky, and Stephen, and Drew, forget Ritchie McHugh… Forget Glo… forget me.'

'Dar—'

Covering his mouth with her fingertips, she moved against him, pushing her lips up to his. After the kiss, she sang in a breath against him.

Knowing she would never again in her life see him brought too much emotion to process in the narrow window they had, so with a smile she turned her back, and marched out on stage for one last encore.

ELEVEN

'DIVA,' Jet said, standing a good foot higher her in the mirror. 'Stick out your chest. You've got 'em so use 'em.'

'You've got 'em too,' Darcy said smiling at the woman who'd become the closest thing to a friend she'd had in the city these past four weeks.

Semi-final night loomed ahead of them, now only she, Jet, and an older woman Gwen remained. Gwen believed that the competition extended to every area of their lives and felt it necessary to gain an advantage over her and Jet whenever she could. Jet explained to Darcy that this was Gwen's last chance. If she didn't make it now, she never would. Jet didn't hold her breath for Gwen's chances. Darcy would never say it aloud, but she didn't either.

'I should hope so too for what they cost me,' Jet said. 'I'll be getting every penny out of them I can.'

Darcy laughed when Jet nudged her, but it was quickly back to her lessons. 'Doesn't diva come from within?' Darcy asked when Jet pulled her shoulders back again.

'Absolutely,' Jet said. 'You have to own the room, and everyone in it. Give everyone attitude.'

'In a song?' Darcy asked.

'Tina Turner is not a diva,' Gwen said from where she sat in the back of a room smoking by a narrow window – the only one in the room.

'I didn't hear anyone asking you a question,' Jet said.

'She's a gay icon,' Gwen said with another draw. 'It's not the same thing.'

'You better hope it is,' Jet replied. "Cause with your forty a day habit she'll be all you're good for in those karaoke bars you'll be singing in after tonight.'

'At least I have an excuse,' Gwen said, stubbing the cigarette out on the window ledge. 'What's yours?'

'Eh, I was born in the wrong body, have you been paying attention? I use what I got to the max; I don't poison myself like you do.' Jet brought her attention back to Darcy. 'Now, we gotta teach you how to do it.'

'I wasn't given much,' Darcy said. 'A short body, and a big chest, that's it.'

Slumping down into the director's chair with her name on it, Darcy propped her hand under her chin.

'Your fella's still not been in touch, huh?' Jet asked, pulling her chair up alongside.

'I didn't really expect him to be,' she said.

Darcy hadn't told the full story because she couldn't. But Jet had noticed how she moped around, and after a couple of weeks of watching she'd intervened saying her "man troubles" were obvious.

'Expect has nothing to do with it,' Jet said, reaching for the hairbrush on their make-up bench.

Darcy's hair had been "relaxed" whatever that meant, but the curls were gone – she missed them, she missed everything, she wasn't the same girl who'd left home with good intentions, and a dream. Now she was a woman with a broken heart, failing dreams, a new hairdo, and a spray tan. Jet began to brush her hair, in long, languorous strokes.

Jet sang to her, having discovered Darcy's nervous habit quickly.

Darcy smiled and picked at the blush brush rolling around without the hairbrush to keep it in place. She obliged by taking the next line and they sang up to the chorus together.

'How cliché,' Gwen muttered.

'Ignore her honey,' Jet said. 'You do what it takes to put a smile on that pretty little face of yours. Just you wait and see, next week we'll blaze a trail, and that man of yours will be tripping over himself to make up with you – mark my words.'

The door thumped off the wall behind it, which blew a brusque wind into the room. All three women were startled by the action, but when they turned and saw Terry, none of them were surprised.

'I should've known,' Jet said, pushing up to full height – which had to be six four in those heels. 'We've told you to knock, you don't stumble in here like a drunken perv, what if we'd all been naked in here – you can't assault a woman—'

'These girls get their tits out for you, what's the difference?' Terry declared. Gwen snorted, but there wasn't time for further comment. 'Out.'

Terry's gaze was on her. For a moment, Darcy wanted to look past her usually invisible self to see who he was talking to. She got to her feet, but he pushed past Jet and shoved Darcy back into the seat.

'You stay,' he said to her. 'It's the other pair I want to scram.'

'Well, now—'

'You wait a minute,' Jet said. 'You can't order a

lady around like that.'

'I was talking to you, wasn't I?' he said, looking Jet up and down with disgust.

'I'll be okay,' Darcy said to her friend, Gwen had already left but she no doubt had head to pleasure before her time on stage, if what Jet had seen was anything to go by.

Jet didn't look happy, but she glared at the agent then left the room, closing the door behind her. The sound of the handle coincided with Terry dropping a stack of freshly printed sheets on Darcy's dressing table, and a biro appeared in her periphery.

'What's this?' she asked.

'Sign it.'

'What is it?'

'It's what you're here for. Now sign it, I've got things to do.'

'Terry, I'm sorry I don't—'

'What the fuck does it look like? It's a contract.'

'A contract for what? I already signed one at the start of the show. I promised not to divulge—'

'Not that bullshit,' he said. 'This'll see you through three albums.'

'It's a recording contract?'

'Maybe it does have a brain,' he muttered. 'Yes, Doll-face it's a recording contract.'

'You want me to sign my life away, just like that?'

'This is your life,' he said. 'I saw what you've got to go back to, and wow Doll-face, you're welcome.'

'I like my home,' she said, pushing out of her chair. 'I don't want a contract. If I wanted a contract, I'd have tried out for one of the bigger shows where I wouldn't have had to put up with the likes of you.'

'You better get used to it,' he said, shoving the pen at her.

'I won't sign it.'

'Aye, you will.'

'I won't,' she said. 'I don't want a contract. I'm only interested in the money.'

This had him coming up short, and then his anger dissolved into a slow, smug smile. 'Is that right,' he said. His eyes wandered all over her body, but it might as well have been his hands because the violation felt as thorough.

'My boyfriend won't appreciate you looking at me like that,' Darcy said without thinking she might have to back up her claims.

'Boyfriend,' Terry chuckled. 'Yeah right, if he even exists, he doesn't give a shit, letting you go out on stage every week shaking that tight little arse of yours, no one shows up for you. Do you think I didn't notice the empty seats? I've been selling your comp tickets for weeks. You've never used one, not once. You don't know a soul who cares enough to show up, not even the scent of money will bring them out the woodwork for you Doll-face.'

Though she wanted to argue he'd taken the wind from her sails. Flopping back into her seat, he tossed the pen on top of the contract. 'Sign it.'

'I haven't won anything,' she said.

'Doesn't matter, you want me to list the runners up of these bullshit shows? The runners up go further than most of the winners. Win, or lose, it doesn't matter,' he said, heading for the door again. 'We'll go a long way you and me Darcy, trust me I'll make it the ride of your life.'

Shivering at his innuendo she listened to him leave, and eyed the contract, her arms came around her in a solitary hug.

Another lyric crossed her lips, more forlorn than the others. Taking her eyes from the contract, she looked at the reflection of the woman she no longer recognised.

The one that sang a lot like she had once upon a time when she was safe and happy. The woman in the mirror lacked the same intensity, the same emotion.

A hand touched her shoulder, warm and heavy it drew Darcy's watery eyes upward. 'Are you okay?' Jet asked.

Her answer was to sing another couple of lines.

Jet crouched beside her, and Darcy welcomed the embrace, it had been four weeks, and she was still crying. At the time she'd known what they had was special, but she loved what he loathed they were destined to fail from that first case of mistaken identity in the woods behind the community centre.

***

'YOU'VE HAD A LONG day,' Glo said, handing a plated sandwich to Sloan then seating herself in the armchair in her living room.

'It's been a long month,' he said, taking out a huge chunk out the sandwich. 'Did I wake the kids?'

Glo shook her head. 'They're only here on a Saturday night. So you'll have your own room tomorrow.'

He shook his head. 'Won't be necessary,' he said, chomping on the sandwich again.

'I recorded the show for you,' Glo said, and he nodded again.

'How'd she do?'

'She's in the final,' Glo nodded.

'Obviously,' he said, gulping from the tall glass of juice she'd handed him before the sandwich. 'Is this awkward?'

'No,' Glo insisted. 'You're my nephew.'

'You look awkward,' he said.

Her hands slid up and down her thighs, and she

was very interested in her own nick-knacks. Slapping her hands onto her leggings covered knees she gave in and looked at him. 'I just don't understand what's really going on here. I love that you're here, that you came back. I want you to stay here.'

'I appreciate the offer, I do. I know having me here will raise questions, and your brother—'

'Your father,' she said. 'But I don't understand where you'll—'

'I'm staying at Darcy's,' he said, finishing his sandwich, and brushing his hands together over the plate.

'You're moving into her house? What did she say?'

'I'm hoping she'll say, "hi honey, the place looks great. I've missed you desperately." But more likely it'll be, "who do you think you are, get out of here now," or a variation on that theme.'

'You haven't told her?' Glo asked.

'Our last conversation was…' Bobbing his hand side to side, he then took another drink.

'What did she say?'

'It's tough to remember, it was four weeks ago.'

Glo sat back in her seat. 'You haven't spoken to her since she left here?' He shook his head. 'You sold your flat.' He nodded, still drinking. 'You quit your job.'

He finished with a satisfied, 'ah… that's right, I worked notice and everything. I'm doing this right.'

Moving from her seat to his couch, she took his hand in both of hers. 'Now, sweetheart you know I love you, and Darcy, and I'm rooting for you all the way…'

'But?'

Glo wasn't laughing, but she had to think she was talking to a crazy person, the look in her eyes said it all. 'You haven't actually told her any of this, have you?'

'It's a process,' he said. 'I have a plan.'

'You have a plan,' Glo said, patting his hand between hers. 'Do you have a back-up plan?'

'I'm confident.'

'Is that a no?' she squinted.

'I don't need a backup plan. She'll forgive me.'

'Forgive you what?' Glo asked then pointed at the TV. 'What if she wins next week? She'll be off to fame, and fortune, and—'

'She'll need someone to look after the house then won't she. Do you know she doesn't lock her doors?'

'No one locks their doors,' Glo said, and he glanced at the back door he'd used. 'If someone wanted to steal something, they'd need to do it in daylight, or get lost on the roads out of town.'

'Still, it's not very safe with the kids here and everything. What if someone wants to murder you in your bed?'

'You've been in the city too long,' Glo said. 'It's also one of the perks of being so far on this side of the village… Murders have to go past every other door in town before they get anywhere near here, so the chances are they'd stop somewhere there.'

'Good point,' he said with a worrying thought. 'I should get a chain for Darcy's door.'

'Do you think you're going to be raped and murdered in Darcy's bed?' she asked.

'No, but a lot of people know who Darcy is now.'

'That is a good point,' she said. 'It's a good idea.'

'I'll do it tomorrow,' he said.

'Have you really thought this through? Do you have a job?'

Sloan tapped his temple with his index finger. 'I'm working on it.'

Glo could only smile at her steadfast nephew. 'I'd forgotten how…'

'Crazy I am?' he asked.

'Sure,' she said. 'And how optimistic you are, how did you hold onto that through… everything?'

'I'm not sure I did,' he said, taking his dishes to the kitchen with Glo following on.

'You were so angry when you left, I thought…'

'That I would end up dead… or in jail?' he offered. 'Darcy told me that I went down in the annals of town history.'

'You've done all of this, I only hope…'

'It could all go wrong,' he conceded. 'But you take stock when you meet someone like Darcy. She has a reason, a purpose, she's determined, and dedicated, and—'

'Are you going to burst into song?' Glo asked.

'I'll leave that to Darc,' he said matching his smile to hers. 'I didn't have much to leave behind, and this place is… it's it to her. My life was better, happier, with her in it. I want a chance – that's all I want from her. The city will still be there, the National will still be there, the only thing I can't replace is Darcy.'

Clasping her hands together at her chest Glo squealed. 'You're really coming home for good?'

'If she'll have me,' he said and had been about to refill his glass when Glo snatched him into a hug.

'Darcy looked really good on the show tonight,' Glo mumbled against him.

'Not as good as she does when her eyes open first thing in the morning,' he said, sure Glo sighed. They held a few more seconds then she backed off swiping at her eyes though she tried to be discreet.

Sloan filled his glass and gave his aunt a moment, though what could have her teary he had no idea. He'd voided his life – the whole thing. Now he had to start again, in the place he'd chosen not to start in thirteen years ago. But this couldn't be further from a do over.

'I'll leave you in private to watch your lady in a

minute, but…'

Her words stalled, but they didn't need to because he'd sensed her hesitation. 'What?'

'There are just two things…'

'What?' he asked.

'Her father… and yours.'

'What about them?'

'Hayley's in the home so she's not around. Lottie won't mind catching you in your civvies, although she might climb into bed with you,' Glo said, eeking her face as though she shouldn't have. 'But if her father walks in to check on things, and you're wandering around without your clothes on, even with your clothes on, you're a strange man in his daughter's unattended house.'

'He'll tell on me, I get it.' He took one finger from the glass to point at his aunt, while touching his nose with the other index finger. 'I'm with you. We're on the same page. I'll talk to him. Tell him to keep it quiet.'

'How well do you know Ewan Holmes?' Glo asked propping herself against the sink.

'Darcy's dad?' he said trying to recall. 'I think we had a run in with him when the window at the bakery got broken.'

'That was you lot?' Glo asked straightening up. 'Hayley was heartbroken.'

'It was an accident,' he said. 'We were only fifteen. He didn't call the police about it; they never questioned us anyway… what should I know about him? We never saw him around much.'

'No one did,' Glo said. 'Darcy was raised by Hayley. Ewan loved his wife very, very much. When she died…'

'He wasn't around?'

'He did what he had to,' Glo said. 'Darcy was always cared for.'

'She speaks very highly of her childhood, she was

happy.'

'Ewan does better now; he comes into the village more. But he loves his daughter…'

'Why did you start that sentence with a but?' he asked. 'That's good, that's how it should be.' Glo just kept looking at him. 'I'm a bad apple… God, I've got my work cut out.'

'You were a bit of a tearaway.'

'Everyone hates me.'

'Darcy doesn't hate you.'

'She does,' Sloan said. 'Her reasons are different to everybody else's, but it's there.'

'Why are you living in her house then?'

'She'll be home in a week,' he said. 'I might need somewhere to stay when she's back, probably for a few days… maybe a week.'

Glo wrapped her arm around his waist and guided him back to the living room. 'What will you do if she doesn't come back?'

'She'll come back,' he said.

'How do you know?' Glo asked.

'I know.' He took a seat on the couch. Glo turned on the TV and handed him the remote control. 'Who is selling land around here?' he asked, bringing up the television planner.

'Land?' Glo asked. 'What are you going to build? A house?'

'We might need more room,' he said, blanking his expression while examining hers.

'I'd have to think about that. It depends how much you need.'

For now, he'd hold onto that, the house Darcy owned would be fine for them, he liked it. Plus, she had enough land that they could extend if it came to that. But the centre Darcy wanted to build would need land, close to the loch without disturbing the view, and with enough room for the air ambulance to land if it needed it. His plan didn't just involve moving into Darcy's house, and into heart. He meant to prove to her that he could embrace the town she loved.

'Just throwing it out there,' he said, scrolling down.

'Are you going to talk to your dad?'

Dropping the remote to the couch, he faced her. 'I'll have to,' he said. 'But I don't know where to begin.'

'You could start by talking to him.'

'What wife is he on now?'

'He loved your mother too,' she said.

'Don't I know it,' he said, picking up the remote control again, and mindlessly flicking. Glo snatched it from him and turned off the TV again.

'You loved your mother, he loved her. You loved the same woman, and you were both equally devastated when she died.'

'It was never as easy as that,' he said, finding himself feeling as well as acting like a petulant teenager – maybe Darcy had been right all along.

'You blame him,' she said, pushing one knee to the arm of the couch.

'He blames me,' Sloan said. 'Maybe he was right to.'

For a moment there was silence. 'It might be better to wait.'

'For what?' Sloan asked. 'I've barely had a conversation with the man in twenty years. What is it we're waiting for?'

'If Darcy was with you—'

'I'm not taking her anywhere near him,' Sloan said, leaping from the couch. 'I'll tell him I'm back in town as a courtesy. If he's got anything to say to me—'

'You're as bad as each other!' Glo shouted to cut him off but then lowered her volume so as not to wake the grandchildren. 'Where do you think your bullheadedness comes from? Your mother was calm as a lily-pond, and it's a wonder living with the two of you.'

'I'm not like him,' Sloan growled.

'You're more like him than you'd admit. He's exactly the same. I grew up in the same house as him, remember? I know what your father is like.'

'I don't see you inviting him round here for dinner,' Sloan said. 'I haven't seen him here once.'

'That's his choice,' Glo said. 'Just as it was yours to stay away from the Quay all those years.'

'I was a kid, what was I supposed to do?'

'Ask him,' Glo said. 'You won't be happy until you hear the words from the horse's mouth.'

'He never told you,' Sloan muttered. 'Did he? How many times did you ask him about it? Is that why he doesn't come here? Did he get tired of ignoring your questions? He ignored mine.' Somewhere he'd detached himself from the memories of his childhood, now as he thought about it for the first time in more years than he could count he still found it difficult to consolidate them with now. 'I found her. Did he tell you that?' he asked the rug under his feet. 'He made me stay in there with her, told me I should face what I'd done… did he tell you that?'

'No,' she said. 'He didn't.'

'No, he didn't,' Sloan said, slumping onto the couch. 'I want to watch my girl now.'

Glo came around the back of the couch, and kissed the top of his head, resting her hand on his shoulder. 'You're back where you belong. You're a good boy.'

Sloan squeezed her hand but didn't look back. All of the places and faces around here would bring back all of the things he'd pushed away. But for Darcy it was worth it… Long after Glo had gone to bed, he rewound, and watched her segments for the fourth time – he didn't need to watch the others. 'Come home soon, Tyke,' he said to the TV. 'I need you.'

***

'WHAT CAN I GET YOU?' Lottie asked, closing the bakery till, when she brought her eyes up a shadow loomed over her, and his black eyes landed on her. 'Oh, it's… God.'

'Sloan will suffice,' he said. 'Why do you look terrified?'

'Because you're… you're…'

'I'm what?' he asked, shifting his change from one hand to the other. 'This works out great.'

Dropping the coins back into his pocket, he reached over and took her hand, she squealed but he ignored it, and rounded the counter to pull her into the back kitchen.

'What are you going to do to me?' she panted.

'What do you think I'm going to do to you?' he asked.

Lottie was small, but bleach blonde hair, and too much eye make-up covered any beauty that might be beneath, of course the short skirt and bare legs would probably distract any man. At the moment she hunched in front of him, shoulders forward, and hands shaking, her eyes wide with what he assumed was terror.

'If you want to have sex with me you have to take me to dinner,' she said her shoulders losing some of their tension.

'Dinner,' he said.

'Or at least a drink,' she relaxed. 'I know what you've heard about me.'

'Funny, I haven't heard much of anything. I've been in town less than twelve hours, so I'm not on the phone tree yet.'

'We can't have sex while there are customers out front,' she said. 'Darcy doesn't like the place to be unattended.'

The corner of his mouth slid up. 'How many times did she catch you at it before she brought in that rule?'

'Three or four,' Lottie said. 'Just because she's not in town doesn't mean—'

'I don't want to have sex with you,' he said instantly offending her.

'Why not?'

'We probably did it when we were kids anyway,' he said but this only angered her more.

'You would've remembered having sex with me,' Lottie said. 'Believe me.' Shaking her hair back, she pushed a frizzing fringe past her forehead. 'If you come back in an hour—'

'I'm not coming back to have sex with you,' he said, squeezing her hand in a move meant to comfort.

'If you want to come to my house, I'll have to ask my mum.'

Now the other corner tipped up. 'You live with your mum?'

Lottie shrugged. 'I'm out most nights anyway, so it's cheaper. My mum says I'll have to move out when I get married.'

'You're getting married?'

She beamed. 'Are you asking me?'

'No,' he said, taking a reflexive step away and dropping her hand.

'Why not?' she asked with a faltering smile. 'Why do men always get that scared look in their eye when I say that?'

'I'm sure you'll make someone a wonderful wife,' Sloan said. 'It just won't be me.'

'I bring home baked goods,' she said.

Poor little Lottie had never quite left her teen years, and he smiled again, strange that there should be something comforting in that, but there was. 'I appreciate that. My girl brings home baked goods, and she can sing.'

'You mean Darcy,' Lottie huffed, and looked past him. 'She makes the best hot chocolate. No one's quite sure how she does it.'

'She spits in it,' he said.

'Really?' Lottie gasped.

'Makes it sweeter,' he said, noting never to drink hot chocolate served by Lottie.

'I had no idea,' Lottie said, sliding up onto the kitchen counter, her legs swinging.

'I need a favour,' he said, and her attention went to his belt. 'Not that kind of favour.'

'I'm not sure I'd be very good at—'

'When is the next community meeting?'

'There's one tomorrow night,' Lottie said.

'How do I get something on the agenda?' he asked.

'You'd have to talk to the Chair, but—'

'Who's the Chair?'

'They rotate on a—'

'Lottie?' he prompted.

'Nancy Pearce, it was supposed to be her husband Roger. But he's got haemorrhoids,' she said, catching a yawn with the back of her hand.

'Lovely, where do they stay?'

'She's the schoolteacher,' Lottie said, his expression asked his next question. 'At the schoolhouse.'

'Thanks,' he said, snagging a cookie from the tray behind her.

'Wait,' she said, grabbing his arm in both hands. 'You can't go over there.'

'Why not?'

'She won't talk to you. I mean you're not a community member.'

'I'm not?' he asked, taking off his anger hat, and replacing it with his dispirited one.

'You're a third, right?' she asked, considering it for a moment. 'You're the third—'

'Yes,' he sighed.

'I suppose with that, and if you're marrying Darcy—'

'Married,' he said. 'Who said married?'

'You're not?' she asked with a flare of hope in her eyes.

'Will it get me in the committee?' he asked, holding himself rigid.

'If you can prove it,' Lottie said.

Sloan released a long breath and smacked his lips to her foundation-clad forehead. 'You and I are going to be fast friends… What do they need to know?'

TWELVE

'I WILL NOT,' Darcy said again.

Her whole body was on fire, her heart hammered for freedom, and every muscle ached from the tension it had held all month. Tonight was different, now she was alone in a hotel room in the middle of a sinister, hard city. No one knew where she was, not a person on the planet knew how tough this week had been on her. Initially she got through by telling herself they were counting down the days – it hadn't helped. Every day it got worse, every day he got closer, more hateful, more out of control. Terry wanted her signature, and he'd made it clear he'd go to any lengths for it. She didn't have a safety net, and he knew it. No one could help her, she was all alone, and that only made him push harder. Other contestants in the competition had pushy parents, gaggles of giggling friends, an entourage, but she moved solo, no one held her hand, or gave her a pep-talk. Terry could do whatever he wanted to her, with her, in spite of her, and she couldn't fight back.

'Tomorrow,' he growled at her. 'I'll be back for

it tomorrow.'

Slamming the door behind himself, she choked on her own breath and collapsed to her knees. This couldn't go on. But she'd come this far, for a good cause, how could she let the town down now. Except he'd told her she couldn't win if she didn't sign. All of these weeks away from home, that sweet, optimistic woman who'd believed in the journey, the adventure, now wanted to choke on her own vomit – at least there was some hope in that.

Hayley was too ill to hear how she struggled, and her father didn't have the strength to help, and she couldn't put this on him anyway, he'd hated the idea of her leaving town from the beginning, even if it was only for a few weeks. Darcy hadn't considered how much a person could change in just a few weeks, most of her life coasted by on the same constant path. Life like this wasn't for someone like her, she was a small-town girl used to having a community looking out for her. Much as she hated to admit it the only thing left was to ask for help, and she could only think of one person in her life who could intimidate Terry – the man who intimidated every person who breathed the same air as him.

***

HIS PHONE RANG OUT. No one answered his door at home. Doug hadn't answered her voicemail, and so she bit the bullet, nothing could be worse than fearing Terry every minute of the day. Donning a headscarf, and oversized sunglasses she became the cliché.

Constant noise rattled her, and she stepped off the Daily National elevator to be faced with a room full of busy people leaving her lost. Venturing forward she stopped a woman just leaving her desk.

'I'm looking for Doug Laidlaw,' she muttered.

'Try in there,' the red head said, pointing to an office in the corner. 'Just go on in.'

Darcy nodded and made her way to the corner; with a light tap on the door, she took off her glasses, and opened it. Doug wasn't here, and she'd be impressed by the office if she wasn't stuck on the sight of a caramel haired, beautiful man, with a tiny brunette in his lap, sitting astride his lap… with his hand very obviously up her cotton tee shirt.

She'd been spotted, and the man took his lips away from the woman in his lap long enough to study her. The brunette noticed his attention shift and turned in his lap to look at her too. Neither appeared perturbed, or in much of a rush to disengage.

'I was told Doug would be in here… you're not Doug,' Darcy said.

'No, I'm not,' Caramel man said.

'Thank God,' the brunette straddling him muttered.

At that inspiration struck. 'You're Bella,' Darcy said, a broad grin already on her face, and her task momentarily forgotten.

'You're famous – why are you famous?' the man said. 'I know who she is, and I know who you are obviously.' He kissed Bella's lips briefly. 'How does she know who you are?'

'You're Darcy… I can't remember your last name,' Bella said.

'Holmes,' Darcy answered.

'Okay. What do you want with my Nick?'

'Nothing,' Darcy said quickly closing her hands in front of her. 'Nothing that your veiled anger implies anyway.'

'You're looking for Doug,' Nick said. 'Which means you're really looking for Sloan – see how I did that?'

'Who's the clever investigative journalist,' Bella said, pinching his cheek.

'Former,' he said, giving her derriere a slap as she climbed off him. 'Sloan's not here.'

'He's not at home either,' Darcy said. 'Should I be worried?'

'Doug told me what happened,' Nick said going to a mini fridge in the corner. 'Up in, Innerquay is it?'

'Inverquay,' she corrected.

Nick took a bottle of water from the fridge, and a coke, both of which he held toward her. She pointed at the water; he put the coke back and took a second bottle of water out. Giving her one bottle he took the other to Bella, then he took his seat at the desk, and gestured to the one opposite. Darcy took his offer because she had nowhere else to look at this point. Nick rolled forward, grabbing Bella's wrist in the process, and bringing her into his lap again.

'I think he got the message,' Nick said.

'What message?' Darcy asked.

'You served him his balls on a plate,' Nick said, but Bella gasped at him. 'Miss. Holmes,' he added respectfully, and kissed Bella's shoulder for good measure.

'Doug's a big fan,' Darcy said to Bella.

'Oh, I'm sure he is,' Bella said. 'Just which version of events did he give you?'

Darcy had been trying to gain points; instead, she was on the receiving end of some harsh curiosity. 'He didn't give me any version of... should I go out, and come back in again?'

Bella laughed which served to relax Nick. 'Don't be fooled. Doug's not harmless,' Bella said.

'I...'

'She's not interested in Doug,' Nick said into Bella's hair when she leant back against him like she would any other chair.

'What's she interested in then?'

'What do you want with Sloan now?' Nick asked Darcy.

Part of her wanted to pour out the whole story, but she was talking to a journalist and one she didn't know at that. So, she closed her mouth. 'It's not important,' Darcy muttered.

Leaving her chair she considered her options, but she hadn't got two steps when she realised, she had none. Sloan had been her last hope, and he wasn't around when she needed him; though he couldn't be blamed for that, she'd been the one to end the relationship.

Darcy sang to what she thought was herself.

'Hey.' Darcy looked over her shoulder to see Bella leaning over the desk, still sitting on Nick who was drinking from the water bottle. 'Give us a minute.'

'I—' Darcy started.

Nick lifted Bella's hips, and slid out from under her, leaving her in the seat. 'She means me,' Nick said. 'Be good.' He ran a finger across Bella's cheek.

'Back at you, Bracken,' Bella said in a way that made her think Nick was rarely good. He chuckled to himself but left the room without further complaint. 'Sit down.'

Darcy took the seat she'd vacated. 'Doug says he loves you very much.'

'Doug's a chancer,' Bella said.

'Oh no, I meant Doug says Nick loves you very much.'

'What's not to love,' Bella said. 'It wasn't exactly plain sailing for us.'

'I'm sorry to—'

'You come from a small town,' Bella said.

'Yes.'

'Nick is… he's everything I could want in a

man… but he is… a man.'

'I don't—'

'He was harsh,' Bella said, pulling Nick's chair into the desk. 'He might be great at his job, he's great at everything. But he didn't ask, why are you looking for Sloan?'

'Do you know where he is?'

Bella shook her head. 'I've never met him. I wouldn't know him if I fell over him. Whatever message Nick was talking about wasn't what brought you here was it?'

Darcy shook her head because she was sure if she opened her mouth her tears would start.

'Do you know anyone in town?' Bella asked peering closer, clearly knowing the answer to her own question. Darcy shook her head.

'Nick and I nearly didn't make it,' Bella said. 'Our story's long, and almost as tragic as it is comedic. A big part of our problem was me, I'm stubborn, and you wouldn't catch me showing any man I needed him… Nick knows without me asking.'

Darcy licked her lips. 'I don't—'

'You're a woman who needs help,' Bella said. 'Is that why you're looking for Sloan?'

'He's the only person in town I know… knew.'

'You have a long story too, don't you?' Bella asked. Darcy nodded. 'Do you want to talk about it?'

'You're all journalists,' Darcy howled, and the tears betrayed her.

'No,' Bella said, rushing around the desk to pull Darcy from her chair, and into a hug. 'Bite your lip, and take a deep breath… I'm not a journalist—I can't stand most of them, except the one I have sex with, I give him special dispensation.' Darcy sobbed out a laugh. 'Sloan's not here, whatever your story is… we're good people—'

'But Nick—'

'Wouldn't do a thing to upset me,' Bella said, leaning back and pushing Darcy's hair from her face.

'You're very lucky to have a man who cares for you so much.'

'Why don't you tell me about yours,' Bella said. 'We can decide if he has any redeeming qualities.'

'I'm not upset about him, I… I want to go home.'

And, just like that the story came out, all of it. Why she was here, what had happened on night one, how she had found herself in Johnny's bed… all the way through to her last conversation with him, and her most recent one with Terry.

'What a slime ball,' Bella said, handing Darcy a second bottle of water.

Though her tears had stopped she still held the balled-up tissue in her fist, but she took the bottle, and opened it. 'I don't want all my time here to have been for nothing. I love my home, and if I'd been told I could spend three months here and have nothing at the end of it – I'd have stayed home.'

'Yeah, except you could've been kicked out in week three.'

'I could've,' Darcy said. 'Then it would have been a holiday, and no one would have been any the wiser. If I gave it my best shot, and lost out legitimately—'

'It's a lot different from being blackmailed by a—'

The door opened. 'Just let me phone Be—' Nick turned and saw the women on the floor under his window. 'You're still here?'

'Who?' Bella asked.

'You, either of you.'

'Where did you think we would be?' Bella asked him.

'I don't know, out getting drunk.'

'Oh,' Bella said, pushing off the floor to slink toward him. 'You think that the only way to get through the devastating desertion of—'

Nick held up his hands. 'You hate everything with a penis right now, don't you?'

'Maybe,' Bella said, stopping her incursion mid-trek.

'Are you going to punish me later?' he asked, anticipating the spirited woman's actions.

Darcy laughed, but the couple remained focused on each other. 'I might do,' Bella said, moving toward him again, but this time was slower, more seductive. Nick groaned and snatched her toward him. 'I didn't say you could touch me.'

'Oh, punish me now,' he said, burying his face in her neck.

Darcy laughed again and clambered to her feet. 'I should leave you two alone, I interrupted earlier—'

'No,' Bella said. 'He's leaving. We have sex all the time. He's getting tired of it.'

'Am I?' he asked her throat.

'Stop pawing,' Bella said, shoving at his shoulders. 'If you're a good boy we can do it in the kitchen when Fiona's asleep.'

'Really?' Nick asked and released Bella immediately; he flicked on the light as he left the room, closing the door.

Darcy squinted up into the harsh light; she hadn't noticed how dark it was until he illuminated them. 'The kitchen?' Darcy asked, seeking out her handbag.

'His sister stays with us,' Bella said. 'Or with him… we don't get out of the bedroom much, and we have to be very quiet. She's my best friend, and sister in-law, or she was, or will be… it's complicated.'

'This is why I like home,' Darcy said, wiping the smudges from under her eyes, and blinking quickly to clear the redness from her eyes. 'Things are simple.'

'Things are never simple,' Bella said. 'I used to think my life was simple. I found out that was code for safe.'

'I don't see anything wrong with safe.'

'I wouldn't either if I was in your position,' Bella said, sitting on the desk when Darcy sat in the visitors chair again. 'Terry doesn't have to be in control. You have other options. What's going on with Hayes?'

'His people told me he was recovering, but that was two weeks ago. I haven't heard anything since.'

'Get in touch,' Bella said. 'Be proactive.'

'What for? I don't want to be famous.'

'He can work out a deal with you,' Bella said. 'At least you can tell him you're having trouble with Terry, he might arrange security.'

'I didn't do what I did for payment.'

'No,' Bella said. 'But one good turn deserves another... Terry can't do what he's doing.'

'What am I supposed to do about it?' Darcy asked. 'I'm a nothing from a tiny town. I have no contacts, no—'

'Phone the police,' Bella said. 'He's trying to intimidate you.'

'It's working,' Darcy said. 'But he knows I have no one.'

'You don't have no one,' Bella said. 'You have me, and Nick, my brother Alfie's a soft touch too... and he's single.'

'I appreciate that,' Darcy said. 'But there's a reason I came here in disguise. The press wants a story— I couldn't ask Nick to—'

'To what?' Bella said. 'No one has to ask him anything.'

'Have you met his boss?' Darcy asked.

'Toby,' Bella nodded.

'If you're pictured with me, or in the audience for me then Toby will know who you are, and who you're with. Even if you came to protect me in my hotel room, do you really think two women will really scare Terry? And, how will Nick react if he finds out you were endangered by me—'

'You wouldn't be responsible for a thing, but I'll admit I have a history with… unsavoury characters. Nick can be overprotective.'

'Johnny's very lucky,' Darcy said, fixing the strap of her shoe, then taking her headscarf from the back of her chair.

'Who?' Bella asked.

'Sloan,' Darcy said with a smile. 'I suppose I should've known better than to come here. First, I get Sloan involved, then Doug, now I'm involving you and your Nick too.'

'It's a shame what they all… do.'

'Typical, isn't it,' Darcy said, adjusting the scarf. 'I always took community for granted, until I found myself without it.'

'Leave me your number,' Bella said. 'I'll think of something. There are other men in the city.'

'Other men for what?' Nick asked from behind them.

'Shut the door,' Bella demanded. When Darcy turned, Doug was closing the door. Bella approached Nick in the middle of the room. 'I need my phone.'

'I don't have it,' he said.

'That was code for give me your phone, mine's at home,' Bella said, presenting her palm to him, he handed his over without another question.

'You and that phone are ridiculous,' he said. 'You're the most organised woman I know, why can't you organise to remember your phone?'

Bella was already walking away from him, and

was typing into the phone, when she held it to Darcy the contact had already been created, so she punched in her number. 'Phone it so you have our number,' Bella said to Darcy.

'Our number,' Nick muttered. 'I want to point out for the record that my girlfriend is putting women's numbers in my phone – nothing to do with me.'

'Does he step-out on you a lot?' Darcy asked.

'What?' Nick puffed, and Doug was guffawing.

Bella only smiled. 'He knows better than that.'

'I know it doesn't get any better,' Nick said, taking the phone when Bella offered it back.

'That's brilliant,' Doug wheezed. 'You should've seen your face.'

Darcy knew the three were close, maybe her statement had been out of line, but she hadn't meant offence. 'I'm sorry,' she said to Bella, then looked to Nick who just threw up his hands.

'I've heard it all before,' Nick said. 'Don't worry about it.'

'Pleasure seeing my two favourite girls together,' Doug said. 'Invite Darcy back to your place,' he said, slumping an arm around Nick. 'She's a great cook; the best. Bella can't cook.' He looked to Bella. 'Can you?'

Bella leaned in close. 'You'll never know,' she murmured.

'Oh, Beautiful, don't leave me hanging,' Doug said taking his arm from Nick to pull Bella into his embrace. 'I'll do tricks – whatever it takes. Leave lover-boy and ride off into the sunset with me, Beautiful, I've been patient.'

'Do you need somewhere to stay?' Nick asked, ignoring Doug slobbering over an amused Bella.

'No,' Darcy said, pointing over her shoulder. 'I have rehearsals anyway. I'll be late.'

Nick nodded. 'Should I phone you a taxi?'

'No,' Darcy said. 'Just tell Bella thank you for me.'

Nick looked over his shoulder at the same time Doug licked the side of Bella's neck more like an amorous pup than an ardent lover. 'Eurgh!' Bella screeched and curled away.

'Put her down,' Nick said, tugging at his friend, who held on tight.

Bella buckled in laughter. The sight of three friends enjoying each other without a care in the world made Darcy smile. Sliding on her glasses she glanced back once more then slipped out. Little Darcy Holmes didn't make waves, she'd do what she had to, keep her mouth shut, and her nose clean, and in less than a week she could go home. Until then, no matter what she wouldn't sign anything.

***

NOTHING COULD'VE PREPARED him. When you've lived your life with anger, with a hate for something so deeply embedded, you miss the moment the fury becomes fear. Because it does. Sometimes we feel aggrieved, and there's a sense of injustice that someone has to stand up for but the odd thing about Sloan's anger, and his fear was when he saw the man he'd lived with as a child get out of the typically flash Mercedes he froze. Often parental relationships are fraught especially through the teen years, but those emotions are replaced when we grow into adulthood, and our parents support us through thick and thin, and with maturity comes understanding, the teen angst was caused because the people who raised us cared, and wanted what was best for us.

However, when a parent betrays a child at any age, that's something that can't be rectified; maybe that was what Sloan wanted Darcy, and his aunt Glo to understand. The relationship couldn't be fixed. The men could talk for days, for weeks, pour over every detail of anything, and everything. The trouble was that betrayal festers – not anger, or hate, or fear, it breeds indifference. The betrayer valued something more than they valued the betrayee, and when the wronged party comes out of the other end stronger, and they did it without the person who betrayed them – what use are they?

Sloan understood that Darcy couldn't understand, no one can understand. When a parent chooses not to love a child, that child is left affected, deeply, it shapes everything about you. How can a person unloved by the one who is supposed to love you the most not develop a hardness? You're on your own in the world, now and forever. Your parents didn't love you; they didn't want to see you helped, they would rather hurt you, and that's what happed to Sloan, at perhaps the most impressionable age. His parents chose something else; they chose themselves, and he was superfluous. Intellectual arguments could only frustrate because something deep within you is planted there by the love of your parents, nothing else can replace that, and it can't be explained away. All the psychobabble in the world couldn't cure a terminal psychological disease – emotional abandonment.

'I was wondering how long it would take you,' John Sloan Senior said slamming the sleek silver door behind him.

Sloan kicked the heels of his heavy boots back against the wall that lined the perimeter of the drive and shoved off it much as he had when he was a teenager. Odd thing about parent/child relationships that go sour at a young age, often neither party know how to move the relationship forward, and so it remains locked, played out perpetually by repeat actions, and mistakes round, and round.

'Didn't hear you kicking in my door either,' Sloan said, his arms folded over his chest. He got his height, and his width from his dad, but the man was older now, and so had lost some of his physical stature. Thing about JS – as he was known to his friends – was that he could intimidate with a look, just as Sloan could. Except Sloan hadn't quite mastered the action of looking so equally indifferent and disgusted at the sight of another human – no, his dad was the master of superiority.

'What reason would I have for doing that?' JS asked.

'The same reason I'm here.'

'I hear you've taken up with Darcy Holmes,' JS said. 'It's a shame. I thought she had her head screwed on.'

'I do have a habit of corrupting people.'

'True.'

'I don't know why I bothered,' Sloan said, and turned to go.

'Are you staying long in the village?'

'What's it to you?'

'I assume with you in town that the gossips will have a field day.'

'Ah,' Sloan said, swaggering toward his father. 'So, I should leave the way I came in, is that it?'

'That might be best idea,' JS said.

'You're unbelievable,' Sloan said. 'Your only child comes home, and you can't muster a hello.'

'I'm your only parent, and I haven't heard from you for more than a decade. What do you expect?'

'She'd roll in her grave,' Sloan snarled. 'At the sight of you now.'

'She did all that with your growing up. She wouldn't recognise you, and neither do I.'

'You don't know me,' Sloan said.

'No, I don't,' JS said. 'I haven't known you since I walked in on you both. I told you then I could never forgive you.'

'It's about time we got one thing straight. I didn't cause her death. You managed that all by yourself. She loved me, which was something you could never forgive either of us for.'

'How can you remember anything?' JS barked. Sloan had squeezed a raw nerve in his father making that slick exterior falter. 'You were too young to remember.'

'Discovering your mother's dead body is not something you forget in a hurry,' Sloan said. 'I was twelve; it was three months to my birthday. I remember everything about that day, everything. I sat with her for hours, and when you came home you locked me in there with her.'

'You were happy to brood with her; the two of you deserved each other, always sulking over something.'

'We could've helped each other, you and I. She wanted to bring us together.'

'That would never have happened. You were no son of mine then, running around town like a common criminal. I wouldn't have you in my house. You should have left the Quay then.'

'At thirteen?' Sloan asked. Although after his father kicked him out, he hadn't slept another night under the old man's roof. Even at thirteen, he had his pride. 'Maybe I knew that's what you wanted. I had responsibilities here, to my family, my friends. I finished school. I'm not sure you knew that then, or now.'

'Is that what this is?' JS snorted. 'You're looking for some sort of recognition? Or is it money you need? How much trouble are you in? Always was your specialty.'

'The only trouble I've got is my girl, and that's trouble I welcome every day.'

'Got her pregnant, have you? How many other women have you gotten in "trouble" through the years? Darcy Holmes was a responsible woman, beautiful, and innocent. You should be ashamed of yourself, everyone in this town is ashamed of you, and no one wants you here. You should leave now, or you'll be driven out.'

'Not everyone is ashamed,' Sloan said. 'I was a kid when I left; I'm not a kid anymore. I can change opinions, I'll make it better.'

Leaping the wall, he paced to the paved corner he'd left his bike on. Parking out of sight gave him the element of surprise, and keeping it off the drive would cause aggravation, here was the evidence their relationship was stuck on stall.

Throwing a leg over the bike, he walked it into view, and revved the engine on, JS went straight back to superior. 'I can admit I did wrong,' Sloan shouted over the engine. 'That's the first step to fixing it… what's your excuse?'

***

TAKING THE LONG ROUTE back to Glo's was supposed to depressurise his frustrations, but high speeds, and narrow paths got his adrenaline pumping, which did nothing for his infuriation. Slamming into the house, he dropped his helmet to the floor, and marched into the lounge.

'It went well then?' Glo asked.

'He's not interested,' Sloan said, unzipping his jacket. 'He told me to leave town.'

Glo paused with the polish aimed at the windowsill. 'Are you going to listen to him?'

'Darc will be home in a couple of days,' Sloan said, rounding the couch to flop down, and cover his face with both hands. 'He thinks Darcy's pregnant.'

'Is she?' Glo asked.

'What?' he asked, dropping his hands. 'No… I don't think so.'

'John—'

'I can't categorically say for definite when I haven't spoken to her, or seen her, can I? But we were always careful.'

'Darcy's a good girl,' Glo said going back to her polishing. 'She would have been in touch with you.'

'I turned my phone off,' he admitted.

She stopped again. 'Why did you do that? What if she needs you?'

'She won't need me until she's home, and I'm already here,' Sloan said. 'All the kids at work kept calling…'

'What else did your dad say?'

'The same thing he's been saying for as long as I can remember. Mum's death was entirely my fault. I'm nothing but a disappointment, I should be ashamed of myself, everyone hates me, blah, blah, blah.'

'I don't hate you,' Glo said, sitting beside him, and taking his hand. 'And I don't care what you say Darcy Holmes is too sweet to hate anyone.'

'What's going on?' he asked. 'You hold my hand when you're giving me bad news.'

'I don't think with your father—okay…' She gave in to the curiosity he landed on her. 'I don't think this will make you feel better.'

Reaching under the couch, she pulled out today's copy of the National, and handed it to him. 'What's this?' he asked, scanning the article.

'It says she's the favourite, but it also says she's dating her manager, and that she's signed a recording contract for after the show.'

'I don't care,' he said, tossing the paper aside.

'How can you not care?' Glo asked. 'If she's

signed a contract she might never come back here. And, if she's seeing other men—'

'She's not dating him,' Sloan said glad of the distraction. Consoling Glo over an erroneous print piece was easier than admitting his relationship with his father was dead. The distraction also gave him an excuse for avoiding how he could explain that to Darcy.

'How do you know that, if—'

'I know what my girl likes,' Sloan said, retrieving the paper and pointing to the picture. 'It doesn't look like that.'

'But she could be so heartbroken, and—'

'Do you think he would make her feel better about losing me?'

'The pull of a contract—'

'She doesn't want a contract,' Sloan said.

'But—'

'She doesn't want it,' Sloan said. 'She'll be home on Sunday.'

'If she wins there'll be interviews, and—'

'She's coming home Glo,' he said, patting her hand in consolation. 'Trust me. If I wasn't enough to make her stay in the city nothing will be.'

Glo wasn't as convinced but she took his teasing with a nod and pulled him into a hug. 'I'm sorry JS is so—'

'Let's not talk about that anymore,' Sloan said. 'Everything will be better when Darcy's home. She'll make it all better.'

THIRTEEN

THE FOLLOWING NIGHT Sloan had just locked the door of the free-standing garage at the back of Darcy's property when he saw the car pull up. No one came to the back of the property, the road was barely a road, and the garage ran parallel to the house with a small, paved area of a dozen haphazard slabs. Obviously, the area had never been meant for this use, or any use, other than clandestine activities, because he'd bet the Mercedes driver wanted the element of surprise, and it was just through pure luck that Sloan had been here, in the right place, at the right time.

The Mercedes stopped, and Sloan folded his arms leaning back against the concrete waiting for JS to get out the car. He took his time about it but eventually the men faced each other.

'I didn't realise you were this serious,' JS said, glancing to the house. 'With Darcy.'

'Neither does she,' Sloan muttered.

'What?'

'Nothing. What are you doing here JS?'

'You're staying.'

'Yes. Did you think telling me off would scare me away? It didn't work then, and it won't work now.'

'I hadn't expected to see you.'

'You knew I was in town,' Sloan said.

JS faltered. 'I did… but I didn't expect to see you.'

'You thought I would scurry around the underground avoiding you,' he said, glancing back at the flash car. 'You weren't trying to surprise me, you're hiding. You don't want the town to know you're here.'

'Who knows you're staying here?' JS said, inspecting the view of the house again.

'What does it matter?' Sloan shouted holding his palms open. 'The rumour mill will make it up anyway. I'm Johnny Sloan the biggest rebel this town has ever known. I'm the bad boy, breaking all the rules, breaking hearts, breaking windows. If I gave a shit about what this town thought of me, I'd have left when you told me to at thirteen. I won't let them win. I won't let you win. What's right is right, and it's as simple as that… Darcy's about as wholesome as this town has ever known. I offered to sleep elsewhere when she was here, she couldn't care less. She was proud of me! For the first time in my life someone looked out for me, over and above themselves. You couldn't begin to understand what that's like. If you're here to tell me off, to buy me off, to scare me, I don't care what it is – this is where I'm meant to be. It took me thirteen years to realise it, maybe if I'd had a few more minutes in those woods with her – if I hadn't been a punk kid, I… This is my home, it always has been. What happened to you, to me, to mum, how I grew up, all the shit we went through it wasn't the town's fault, it was ours. You can run as fast, and as far as you like, but you can't run away from yourself.'

Sloan had left his leaning post and was only a

foot away from his father who must have heard every word, because he said, 'I know.'

Ready to argue, Sloan inhaled then processed JS' words. 'What?'

'I didn't expect to see you yesterday. I didn't expect to see you at all, and we've been on default defensive for years. I reacted to you because you reacted to me.'

Backing away Sloan found himself unable to formulate a response. They stood outside in the late dusk light. The house to one side, a stretch of grass then the garage behind Sloan. The gravel, stone path that doubled as a makeshift road was the only thing separating them from the instant, steep incline of the hills beyond.

'Should I invite you in?' Sloan asked him.

Without the bluster he didn't know how to relate to the man in front of him. Darcy's house couldn't be the site of a battle; he had more respect for her than that. But his father had come here under the flag of truce, hadn't he?

'We could start with that,' JS said.

The men had no sooner turned in the direction of the house than Sloan's pocket buzzed and blared out the low ringtone. 'Sorry,' Sloan said, retrieving the phone from inside his jacket. 'I just turned the thing on this afternoon it was lit up constantly with calls from the city but—' Reading the name on the screen, he stopped mid-sentence, mid-stride. Instead of diverting the call, he answered. 'Nick?'

'Where the hell have you been?' Nick screamed down the line so loud Sloan took the phone from his ear, and JS' eyebrows went up.

'What do you mean?'

'Your girl has been in the shit all week, what's the matter with you?'

'Darcy?' Sloan said, taking a back step toward the

garage. 'What's wrong?'

'What's right,' Nick sighed. 'She's in my flat crying to Bella about some guy I—'

'It'll take me a while, but I'll get there,' Sloan said. 'Leave the front door open, and don't let her leave.'

Hanging up he went straight to the garage. 'What's going on?' JS asked.

'We'll have to save the reunion,' Sloan said unlocking the garage door. 'I have to go.'

'Go where? You haven't packed, or—'

'She needs me,' Sloan said, throwing up the garage door. 'Nothing comes before that.'

***

DARCY HAD FOUND NICK'S address with startling ease. Calling Doug would have been her next port of call, but she wasn't in the mood for his easy humour. So she called the National. Maybe it had been her tears, or the desperation in her voice, but when she'd asked for the information, she had received it.

Now, she was in front of the door, knocking, extraordinarily self-conscious but she had no other choice.

'Don't even think about it!' Nick called over his shoulder on opening the door. When he saw her, he went instantly silent, and sombre. 'What happened?'

'I—'

'Come in,' he said, stepping out the way, and gesturing into the flat. The room was inviting, with warm woods, and browns, and reds, modern but very homely.

Bella had been on the couch, but she was off it when she saw Darcy. 'Oh, what happened?'

'I… I…' Darcy noticed another woman with rosy, red hair sat on a chair in front of another door. Bella welcomed Darcy into her arms while the other woman covered the top of her wine glass with her palm, and simply watched.

'Tell me what happened?' Bella asked, ushering Darcy onto the couch. She couldn't help but notice there was another glass of wine on the table next to what she assumed was Bella's. Again, she'd interrupted.

'I'm so sorry, I didn't know what… what to do and…'

'Did he touch you? Are you hurt?' Bella asked. 'Should we take you to the police? The hospital? Darc, if he tried anything on—'

'No, I—' Aware of Nick somewhere, she tried to seek him out.

Bella took the third glass and put it in Darcy's hand. 'Ignore him, he's not listening.'

'I don't want to—'

'If he reported everything he heard in this room, we would have our own newspaper,' Bella said. 'Tell me.'

'I quit,' Darcy said with the quiver returning to her voice.

'You quit?'

'Can you do that?' Nick asked, appearing at the back of the couch.

'I don't know,' Darcy answered but kept her attention on Bella. 'I don't, but I…'

'He was in your room again?' Bella asked, and Darcy nodded. 'He was pressuring you?'

Darcy nodded, and the redhead spoke. 'For what?' she asked, sliding her glass onto the table. 'It seems to me if all a man wants is a bit of slap and tickle, well… path of least resistance and all.'

'Thank you for your input, Fiona,' Bella said over her shoulder.

'You had sex with Doug,' Darcy said, and everyone in the room looked at her.

'Do you just say the first thing that comes into

your head?' Bella asked.

'Sometimes,' Darcy said, squirming a little.

'That's alright,' Nick said. 'Maybe she'll learn to keep her snout out.'

Clearly brother wasn't happy with sister, and clearly sister couldn't care less. 'It's not like I have a room to go to,' Fiona said to her brother managing to look down her nose at him although he stood, and she sat. Nick was tall so Darcy imagined Fiona had perfected this from being at a lower perch for most – or all – of her life.

'You know what you can do about that,' Nick said.

'Would you two stop it,' Bella said. 'I'm sorry about them.'

'We're never having kids,' he muttered to Bella who smiled up at him.

'What's all the practising for then?'

Darcy didn't know how long the couple had been together, but she imagined it was nice to still flirt with the person you loved even after the honeymoon period and because they lived together Darcy had to assume they'd been with each other a while.

'How long have you been together?' Darcy asked Bella, who was about to answer when Fiona did it for her.

'Since before or after the bet that broke them up?'

'Here,' Nick said, taking his wallet from the narrow table that ran the length of the back of the couch. 'Please take it and get out of here.'

Pulling a card from the wallet Nick tossed it at his sister.

'What's the limit?'

'None of your business,' Nick said. 'If there's anything more than a hotel room, and a meal on it I'll add it to your bill. How many months have you lived here rent-free now?'

'I wouldn't be getting a divorce if it wasn't for your friend,' Fiona said.

'Keep telling yourself that,' Nick shouted to his sister who entered the door behind the chair she'd been on, Darcy saw a flash of a broad bed before the door closed.

'I thought she didn't have a room,' Darcy said.

Nick's hands landed on the back of the couch, and he leaned down to the women. 'She doesn't, that's our room. She's everywhere.'

'You're a man at the end of his rope, aren't you?' Darcy asked, appreciating the chance to smile.

'Oh,' he growled. 'So close… I don't understand why we don't turf her out.'

'She's your sister, and my friend, we—'

'She's a nuisance, a parasite. If we had another room, it wouldn't be so bad, but—'

'Why don't you move,' Darcy said.

'What?' Nick asked, pushing his weight to his hands.

'Yeah,' Bella said. 'That's a brilliant idea.'

'What?' Nick said again.

'Why don't we move?' Bella asked Nick.

'Sell the flat from under her?' Nick asked and thought about it for a minute. 'I love it. Why hadn't we come to that conclusion ourselves?'

The couple shared a moment, and though Darcy wanted to be happy for them a stab of isolation reminded her what had brought her to their door.

'Do you think they can sue me for breaking the contract?' Darcy asked, taking a gulp of wine to whet her throat.

'The show's not until tomorrow night,' Nick said. 'You can still compete—'

'Uh,' Bella interrupted. 'The man keeps touching

her up, threatening her; would you send me back to that?'

'I'm not sending her back to anything,' Nick said. 'I made an observation.'

'Do you have any more money in that?' Bella asked Nick's wallet.

'I don't—'

'We need wine,' Bella said. 'More wine.'

Something went unsaid between the couple, and then Nick lowered his mouth to Bella's. 'I'll be ten minutes,' he said pocketing the wallet.

'Thirty,' Bella said, snatching his face, and kissing the bejeezus out of him. 'Love you.'

'Woman,' Nick muttered. 'Sends me out after that, women…' He grabbed his jacket and slammed out the flat.

'I didn't mean to cause such disruption in your night. I am sorry.'

'Don't apologise,' Bella said. 'I'm glad you came here. We have to figure out what you're going to do. Are your things still at the hotel?'

'I grabbed my jacket, and—'

'Which hotel were you staying at?'

'Nothing fancy it was the West Inn.'

'Great,' Bella said reaching past Darcy for the phone. 'I used to work there. I'll make sure they look after everything. Should I ask them to pack it up?'

'I… I… I don't know.'

'That's okay. I'll tell them to make sure no one goes into the room.'

Bella left her alone while making the call, and Darcy's thoughts went to home, to all the people she knew, the streets that held all her memories. To get the business more lucrative she had done a lot of work, Hayley's was the only place to go in town, but Darcy had expanded the business by creating a website, she fulfilled orders for all the towns around about Inverquay, in the summer months at least – winter would always be a problem because of the weather. She'd thought of herself as quite a savvy woman, but her trip to the big, bad city had erased all those delusions. The more she thought about it the more she realised that tying herself to the town, singing its praises, and keeping herself there had been safe, just like Bella had said.

Staying in Inverquay was easy. Growing the business was a natural progression for her. Sloan had been right after all; she was a Quay princess doing exactly what they expected of her. Much as she loved the bakery, she'd never done anything else. Maybe she did have other talents, other areas of expertise that would be more lucrative. The town would always be there, and she could help it without actually living there. Darcy might know every face, and every corner but that hadn't stopped the inhabitants from judging her at the first opportunity. Josie Richmond didn't hide her distain for anyone from the villagers. Josie could stay on her high horse and look down at them all while she was there. But how long would Josie Richmond last in the big city where no one would listen to her, no one would care?

Darcy had found out the hard way just how alone you could be, and how quickly. The town didn't need her, she needed the town, the residents brushed her off as insignificant because she played safe, lived safe, did nothing that would cause waves, or gossip. Always everyone's best friend Darcy Holmes, she was still friends with anyone who had ever done her wrong, Lottie had jumped into bed with all of her exes, but still she employed her, and gave her a raise every year. Ritchie was the only one who'd never asked anything of her, but the town had cast their aspersions, and he was no longer welcome. Sort of like Sloan, the town made a decision to ostracize and it was done, much like the reality shows of the day. You have been evicted please leave the myopic, insular community, and please, do not swear.

'It's done,' Bella said, re-entering the living room. 'No one will be allowed in your room. They've changed the door code too.'

'I think I have to sign,' Darcy said.

Bella paused mid-sit, took a moment, and then sat. 'Sign what?'

'The contract,' Darcy said. 'Why not? Why shouldn't I?'

'I thought you wanted to go home,' Bella asked.

'For what? What do I have waiting for me there? I'm crying for people who aren't here, they don't care. What am I going back to?'

'Your grandmother and your father.'

'My grandmother doesn't know I'm there even when I am. My father will be happy pottering about in his shed for another twenty years. No one in that town needs me. It's safe, that's why I'm so out of my depth here I've never experienced anything. If I were worldlier, I wouldn't be a coward in the face of a man who is completely out of line. He acts that way because he can, because I can't stand up for myself.'

'Signing a contract with him is giving him exactly what he wants,' Bella said. 'That will only encourage him.'

'I don't have to sign with him,' Darcy said. 'Hayes might still be interested, and if I put it out there that I'm interested.'

'I could have Nick ask around,' Bella said. 'He knows a few people. But I'd worry about you making this decision too quickly, not after the time you've had recently.'

'The only way to experience life is to live it,' Darcy said.

'What about the community project?'

'If I'm successful I can fund it, I don't have to live there to make it happen, do I?'

'No, I—'

'All my life I've been scared, I've fallen in line, done exactly what was expected. What do I stand for?'

'I think you stand for quite a lot,' Bella said. 'You came here and did all this, outside you comfort zone, for something you believed in. That's very admirable Darcy.'

'Did I?' she asked finishing her wine and holding out her glass for more. 'I'm passionate about the centre because someone has to be. Every morning I woke up, went to the bakery, worked every hour I had, helped out friends, neighbours, sang in the bar to pay for Hayley's care, for the mortgage payments on dad's house, and on mine.'

'I thought he stayed at Hayley's?'

Darcy nodded. 'She re-mortgaged a few years before I took over the business. She had some crack-pot idea about a second shop, except the town isn't big enough for a second shop. She signed the papers, and got the money—'

'What happened to it?' Bella asked.

'Haven't a clue,' Darcy said. 'I didn't find out about it until I was taking over the reins. Her mind started going early, but she hid it well. She took the mortgage out on the house and not on the shop at least, we own that still – the house was worth more.'

'Does your dad work?'

'Hasn't in as long as I can remember,' Darcy said. 'He's happy, he keeps busy, but he doesn't always cope well with people. Most of the time he's okay, but it's the other times… It makes his behaviour volatile, which isn't the best mix for holding down steady employment.'

'Don't you think going on the road would just be running away from those problems? They will still be there.'

'I can pay the mortgages without being there. Lottie knows how to run the shop, although I'm sure she's turned it into a brothel by now.' Darcy smiled at the memory of her friend. 'They don't need me… I've been scared all my life, and this is me finally admitting it. I am a perfect Quay princess. Sloan had the right idea all along. It'll never be enough, the Quay will take, and take, and never be satisfied. Get out or you'll be swallowed up there. From birth to death with no life in-between, that's what a small town does to you. If you're not gossip fodder, you don't exist. You're a mug. I'm a mug… I need to start looking out for me.'

'And singing is that what makes you happy?' Bella asked.

'I did it for the money,' Darcy said. 'In the bar, the competition, all of it I was just whoring my voice, I don't suppose Lottie, and I are that different.

Bella topped up her glass with what was left in Fiona's glass, and then poured the last of the bottle into Darcy's glass. 'What makes you happy?'

'I have no idea,' Darcy said gulping the wine again.

'That's a cop out,' Bella said. 'There must have been a time in your life when you were happy, completely content.' Darcy examined the liquid in her glass again, smiling at the memory that jumped into her consciousness. 'I saw that smile, tell me.'

'I can't,' Darcy shook her head and hid her mouth with her glass. 'It's silly, you wouldn't understand.'

'Try me.'

'It involves my bakery,' Darcy said edging closer, pulling her knees onto the couch. 'An industrial sack of flour and…' the smile grew heavy.

'And?' Bella asked.

'Sloan,' Darcy said. 'We were messing around… it was Sloan.'

'So what's wrong with that picture?'

'He hates the town, and everything associated with it,' Darcy said. 'Which includes me.'

'Why would he take you to bed if he hated you? Aside from the fact that he's a man.'

'I don't want to deconstruct my relationship with Sloan,' Darcy said. 'We're opposites.'

'Okay, but you've just said you're not going back to the Quay. Why not call him up, and tell him you're not going back? You're welcome to stay here for as long as you want. But Nick's mine, and he's the only man here. So, he'll never make you smile like that.'

Darcy appreciated Bella's humour, but it couldn't warm her own. 'Sloan's… an enigma. I'm not woman enough to understand him, to handle him.'

'It sounds to me like you did fine.'

'Fine wasn't enough though, was it?' Darcy said. 'Do you see him fighting for me? He won't even pick up his phone.'

'Men are stupid when their egos are bashed. He'll get over it. Remember, from his point of view you're an attractive, talented woman on her way to fame, and stardom, he could be intimidated by that.'

'Johnny Sloan?' Darcy said and found herself laughing. 'Intimidated… Oh honey, I don't think so.'

***

NICK HAD RETURNED, Fiona had left, and the time had vanished. Darcy got what they called a brief version of the couple's history, but the story took more than an hour, though she had asked a lot of questions, and the couple had fought, flirted, kissed, made up, and disagreed again. Darcy couldn't remember falling asleep, but Nick had pulled out the sofa bed for her, Bella changed the sheets, and Darcy apologised for invading their space and time. Bella told her they would make decisions tomorrow and gave her a nightie to wear. After staring at the ceiling for what felt like hours, she must have fallen asleep, though after the wine they'd drunk she was surprised she hadn't puked or passed out.

Her eyes opened to shadows on the ceiling, and for a moment she couldn't remember where she was. The panic gripping her heart didn't come from that, no, a noise near the door had done that, squeezing her eyes closed she tried to convince herself she imagined the zipping sound, and the stumble of heavy footfalls. Then the bed shifted, and in complete reflex she opened her mouth and screamed. Her eyes popped and she pulled the blanket over her, pouncing to her feet she crouched on the pillow scrambling for a weapon.

A door opened, and a light went on, then someone else screamed, so she screamed again.

'Nick! Do something!'

'Jesus! Shut it the pair of you!'

Darcy saw Nick in the bedroom door pushing his thumb knuckles into his eyes; he wore only dark boxers. Bella was standing half behind him, in what had to be one of his shirts. Bella gave Nick another shove.

'I'm phoning the police,' Bella exclaimed and pointed past Nick. 'You stay there.'

Nick grabbed her wrist, and pressed her hand to his bare chest, although she stayed behind him.

'Did you see what you did there?' Nick asked over his shoulder. 'You hid behind me. Me man, protect woman.'

'Oh, shut up,' Bella grumbled. 'You did nothing.'

'No one is calling the police…' Nick said, kissing Bella's fist, and looking past Darcy. 'You couldn't have knocked, or used the telephone?'

Darcy had forgotten about the other party, only now did she take the time to turn, and why wasn't she surprised? 'You,' she growled through grit teeth and crawled over the bed to hit him, not just once, but over and over.

'Darc, fuck,' he said but she kept hitting.

'Where have you been? What have you been doing? You left me! You abandoned me! You!'

'Babe,' Nick's calm voice didn't stop Darcy's onslaught. 'Meet Johnny Sloan, Sloan, this is Bella.'

'Oh,' Bella said.

Then a light went off, and a door closed. Johnny grabbed Darcy's wrists and squeezed them into one of his hands. 'I missed you,' he murmured, and kissed her.

Her body relaxed, and she shifted into the ecstasy of those lips on hers soft, warm, secure—'No,' she said, pulling her mouth away. 'How did you find me?'

'Nick phoned when you got here,' Sloan said, kicking off his boots, and standing to pull his tee shirt over his head.

'I've been here for hours,' she said, darting her attention for a clock, but she came up with nothing.

'It's about three,' Sloan said. 'Closer to four.'

'What did he tell you?' she asked.

'Nick said you were talking to Bella… how did that happen?'

'You don't get to ask the questions,' Darcy said. 'I ask the questions. What are you doing here?'

'You need me,' he said, shirking his jeans, and only now did she realise he was getting naked.

'What are you doing?'

'It's late,' he said, bodily lifting her to the side of the sofa bed closest to Nick and Bella's room. Then he stretched out on the bed beside her. 'Any chance of some sugar?'

'Some sugar?' she gasped and began slapping at his now naked torso. 'We split up, remember? We're not together! You're a narrow-minded bastard who hates everything, and everyone remember?'

'Oh yeah, that's right,' he said, throwing an arm around her and pulling her body against his.

She squirmed but couldn't get out of his grip. If she screamed, she'd have Nick and Bella up again, and that wasn't fair. Either that or they would assume it was a different kind of scream and would ignore her.

'I quit the show,' she said, submitting to his embrace. Only to herself did she admit how comforting his hard chest was under her soft cheek. 'They're going to sue me for everything. I'll be ruined and desperate.'

'Not on my watch,' he said and boosted her up, so she was now lying on top of him. The bulge against her belly brought a sigh from her lips.

'I've missed him,' she admitted, wriggling against him. 'You I haven't missed.'

His mouth pressed against the top of her head. 'I have no problem with you being nice to him, and nasty to me. I can live with that. I'm willing to suffer.'

In spite of herself she managed a laugh. 'I needed you this week.'

'I'm here now,' he said. 'I didn't know. It'll never happen again.'

'You weren't at home,' she said.

'No.'

'Do you have a girlfriend now?'

'You could say that,' Sloan said, relaxing his grip to slide his broad hands down her back. 'I'm sort of living with someone.'

Darcy was about to object when his hands gripped her hips and shifted her whole body up causing her to whoop. Her head bumped his chin, her hands dropped to the pillow either side of his head, and her core was brought to his solid ridge.

Her nose touched his, her hair was all over the place around them, and with the heat of their breath the humidity jumped twenty points. Neither said a word, both just looked at what had once been so familiar.

A door opened, and they turned to see an arm appear out of the bedroom door, it tossed something to the bed, and the door slammed again.

'Thanks!' Sloan shouted.

'Welcome,' came the masculine reply from the bedroom.

Darcy's jaw fell when she realised a box of condoms now lay neatly on her side of the bed facing them as if in invitation or warning.

'Are you pregnant?' Sloan asked her.

She still hadn't torn her attention from the condoms, but when she replayed his words, she popped her eyes back to him. 'What? Why would I be—'

'Someone asked me and I—'

'Who would ask you a question like that? No, I'm not, of course I'm not. We were careful.'

'We were,' he said, and his hand left her body to pick up the condom box.

'What are you doing?' she asked.

'Carrying on the tradition.'

'I don't think so,' she said, pressing her hands to his chest for distance, instead he flipped her to her back and his hands moved up her waist to her chest sheltered only by the straining satin of the nightie Bella had given her. The poor fabric did a meagre job, and stretched taut, which pulled up the hem, although now it was somewhere bunched around her waist.

'I've missed you,' he said, pressing a kiss to the swell of one breast then the other. Her breasts were the only thing on her body that fit his hands. Everywhere else she was measly, pathetic in comparison.

Pressing her breasts together he kissed one peak through the fabric, then the other. Nothing between them was the same, nothing was resolved, they weren't together, they wanted different things, except her body shivered in revolt to her mind. Her gut squeezed, tugging the pleasure of his mouth to her centre at his sound of satisfaction, a quiver in her thighs brought hot moisture seeping from within her.

'We're not together,' she whispered but the words lost weight. Somewhere around her thinking about their wanting different things he'd pulled the nightie up over her breasts, and was in her cleavage, kissing toward her naval, his hands covering the mounds of her breasts, massaging the nipples between is long fingers, while his thumbs drew lazy lines on the sensitive undersides.

'I've had a horrible week,' she said. Her words might be trying to deter him, but her hips came off the bed forcing his head away from her stomach, so when they came back down his mouth was in her curls.

Hot breath cascaded her centre, and a whimper left her lips as the first shudder of orgasm touched her. It didn't matter that he hadn't touched her intimately yet, her swollen dampness begged for release.

'I'll make it better,' he said, the words vibrations on her inner thigh. 'I'm here now. I'll make everything better.'

'Kiss it better,' she said, arching her hips up again forcing his hands from the back of her thighs round to her hips.

'You sure?' he asked, she could feel his smile on the seam of her leg.

'God, please, Sloan, don't make me beg.'

And he didn't… he didn't even make her ask twice.

FOURTEEN

'UH! SOMEONE'S PHONE!' Nick shouted.

Sloan knew it could only be Darcy's because it wasn't his, and Nick would know his and Bella's. The men were watching the sports news when Darcy ran out of Bella's room in a pencil skirt, and a bra, nothing else.

'Hell-o!' Nick said, holding up Darcy's bag.

'Hey,' Sloan said, shoving his friend, but if there was a man in the world less of a threat than Nick Bracken, Sloan would never meet him. Nick's teasing was as good natured as Sloan's had been when he'd caught Bella coming out of the bathroom that morning in nothing but a tiny towel.

Nick was watching the news again, and drinking his coffee, the bedroom door lay open, and Darcy wandered in and out of it, without an ounce of embarrassment. The good parts were covered, just, Nick might be able to watch the news without a care in the world, but Sloan remembered how that flesh felt in his hands, how it gave, and urged for more. He'd had his head buried in there many a time, both of them, but it still didn't lessen his reaction to her.

'Damn,' he grumbled and made himself watch the news.

'She's a great girl,' Nick said. 'You did good last night.'

'Have you got a webcam in here or something?' Sloan asked.

Nick laughed. 'No, it's usually my sister out here, and that is not an image I need. I get all the live-action I want from Bella. I meant showing up. She needed you.'

'If I'd known it, I'd have been here sooner.'

'He wants to see me,' Darcy announced to everyone, and Bella appeared in the bedroom door.

'Did you tell him where to get off?' Bella asked.

'Not Terry,' Darcy said, flattening her palms to her forehead. 'Hayes, Paulie Hayes wants to see me today.'

'Oh,' Bella said, resting back on the bedroom doorframe. 'What time?'

Darcy drew in a long breath, which expanded her chest. 'Two,' Darcy exhaled.

'I can go to the hotel for you,' Bella said. 'If anyone asks, I'm just visiting old friends.'

Darcy nodded. 'What if you run into Terry? Everyone's there.'

'Uh…' Bella thought. 'I can get security to go with me.'

'But he'll know,' Darcy said. 'He'll know.'

'So tell him,' Bella said. 'If he wants to start a fight that's his problem, and somehow I doubt he will when Hayes name enters the conversation.'

'Okay,' Darcy said to Bella then turned to Sloan. 'Give me a tee shirt.'

'You want the one I'm wearing?' he asked, which made her try to seek out his luggage. 'I have nothing with me.'

'What's the problem?' Nick asked.

'Nothing that fits me,' Bella said, cupping her breasts. 'Fits Darcy… unless she's looking for a job with a stripper pole.'

'Wear what you had on last night,' Nick said. 'I washed everything that…'

'Yes,' Bella said as comprehension struck Nick. 'Your initiative would have been delightful had you read any of the labels.'

'Babe, even if I'd read them, I wouldn't have understood them.'

'There's no shame in asking for help, isn't that what you say to me?' Bella said.

'This is another wool incident, isn't it?' he asked Bella, then looked to Darcy. 'Sorry.'

'It's okay,' Darcy said. 'Although Bella did say you were good at everything, she forgot the washing disclaimer.'

'I'm good at everything?' he asked Bella with an arch of his eyebrow.

Sloan laughed. 'Women know each other five minutes, and they're best buddies, don't feel bad,' he said with a punch of Nick's shoulder.

'Don't know what you're smiling at,' Darcy said. 'We were comparing notes.'

Sloan stopped laughing and Nick started. 'She got you there, that's my specialist subject.'

Bella cleared her throat, and Nick stopped laughing immediately. The women high-fived and disappeared into the bedroom again.

'Is nothing sacred?' Sloan asked.

Nick held up his coffee cup in silent salutation, Sloan joined with his cup. 'Let's just sit and watch the sports. They'll tell us if we're needed for anything…' Nick said. 'I'd forgotten we had this channel.'

'A girlfriend, and a sister,' Sloan said. 'I don't

envy you.'

'I used to live alone… it was a long time ago,' Nick said.

The words hung in solemn understanding around them as they stared at the TV waiting to be required.

Just as the peace settled the bedroom door opened again. 'Ta-da!' Bella said, and the men turned to see Darcy.

'Good,' Nick said.

'It's a wrap shirt,' Darcy said.

'I can see what it's trying to do, but it's not doing it very well,' Sloan said. 'You're going out like that?'

'I'll be wearing a coat,' Darcy said tugging at the bottom of the shirt, but it left an inch of naked flesh no matter how hard she tried.

'She'll be fine with a safety-pin,' Bella said.

Nick tilted his head to the side. 'I've never taken that off you. It could offer an interesting peepshow.'

'It's not mine,' Bella said. 'We raided Fiona's clothes.'

Nick leaned back a little. 'Any comment I make at this point is going to make me sound like a perv.'

'More so,' Sloan said.

'I need to get my sister out of here,' Nick said, watching the TV again, and slurping his coffee, but he scowled down at it. 'And I need something stronger.'

'It's not ten in the morning,' Sloan said.

'Do you have a sister?' Nick asked, and Sloan shook his head. 'Then you couldn't possibly understand.'

A knock at the door had everyone turning to it. In reflex, Darcy crouched to the floor behind the arm of the couch between Nick, and the bedroom door.

'Fear not, Beautiful, your salvation is here,' Doug exclaimed on entry but stopped when he saw Sloan was in the room. 'My Fiona you're looking more and more masculine every day.'

'Aren't you just hilarious,' Bella said.

'Thought you'd been abducted, Sloan,' Doug said. 'Thanks for telling me about the flat.'

Darcy popped up from her hiding crouch. 'What about the flat?'

'Wow,' Doug said, noticing her conspicuous cleavage. 'What else have you got down the side of that couch, Nick? I didn't you know your furniture did that. Is there a button? Gorgeous… miss me?'

'What flat?' Darcy asked.

'No,' Doug said, zipping his own lips. 'I've made all my meddling mistakes… I brought you something.' Doug tossed a long box to Bella. She caught it and tore off the tissue paper.

'These are Godiva chocolates,' Bella said to him. 'What did you do?'

'Ah,' Doug said, holding up an admonishing finger. 'I have done nothing… I'm about to do something.' He looked to Nick. 'I need a favour.'

'What favour?' Nick asked.

Doug squinted slightly. 'One I maybe shouldn't ask you in front of your girlfriend.'

'Who do you want him to sleep with?' Bella sighed and handed the chocolates to Darcy.

Sloan watched Darcy laugh and unwrap the chocolates. Bella shoved Doug back and plopped onto the couch between him and Nick. Darcy selected a chocolate, then handed it to Bella who put it in her mouth. Darcy selected another and handed it to Nick who did just as Bella had.

'Can I use your oven?' Darcy asked the couple who both nodded and waved her away because Doug was on a long story that didn't appear to be letting up soon.

Darcy bundled up the chocolates, and

disappeared to the back of the flat, and into the kitchen. Sloan couldn't watch the TV and he wasn't interested in Doug's story. What did interest him was the woman who had just left the room. Taking the chance that they could talk in private, he left the other three, and joined Darcy in the kitchen. Already the oven was on, and she was searching the cupboards while singing to herself.

'Things that bad?' he asked her.

Lifting what appeared to be sugar from the cupboard she put it on the counter and faced him. 'They offered me a contract – a proper one.'

'They?'

'Terry,' she said, pushing a fingernail into the worktop.

'You don't want a recording contract,' he said.

'I might,' she said.

Leaving her alone for so long had obviously been a mistake, this woman loved her home, had vowed to be back as soon as she could be. He'd laughed in Glo's face when she had said that Darcy might choose to go onto the high life.

'Is that what you want?' he managed to ask.

His life revolved around her. She might not realise it, but she'd just thrown it in the mixer, and turned it up to melee.

'I might.'

He nodded and swaggered further into the room. 'Why don't you tell me it, from the top?'

'It?'

'What happened to the little Darcy Holmes who left me in Inverquay, with Aerosmith and a smile.'

'She… I don't know that she left the dark wings of that stage. Maybe she's still there… she's not here.'

'Is that right?' he asked, lifting her onto the kitchen counter beside the sugar. 'Tell me who you are then. I'd hate to think I had sex with the wrong woman.'

'So much is different,' she said. 'I might even owe you an apology.'

'For?'

'You were right to get out of town when you did,' she said. 'You were right to run, and I should never have made you go back.'

The woman he knew was so sure of everything. This woman here, now, had no resolve. If she had gone so far as to agree with his boneheaded teenage antics, then there could be serious trouble. Darcy had lost Darcy… everyone was telling him that she'd needed him this week. From what he observed she had needed him for a lot longer than that.

'I left you here alone,' he said, realising she had no rock.

During her time in the city, he had been her touchstone to the Quay even if neither of them had realised it. Weeks had passed, and she'd had no one, nothing. Darcy alone in the big, bad world, he dreaded to think what she'd been through – how could he have been so ignorant to her needs? Darcy was strong, sure, resolute, that's why she took him on, gave him a slap, and straightened him up. He'd believed she could take on the world, that nothing would make her abandon her morals, her ideas. Somehow, he had forgotten about that grateful kitten he'd wrapped in his duvet on night one. How could he have forgotten?

'I'm a big girl,' she said.

'No, you're not,' he said and she faltered. Lottie was Darcy's contemporary, and she still lived with her mother, and traipsed around town like a teenager knocking boots with any boy who smiled her way. 'I'm sorry, Tyke.'

Whether it was his words, or his sentiment that caused her tears he wouldn't have taken either back, if she needed him he would be there, and nothing would get in the way of that again. She pulled herself against him hanging her arms around his neck. Then, her legs locked around him too, and she sobbed into his chest like a lost, frightened child in need of comfort, of support… of love.

'I'm here now,' he said into the top of her head while he stroked her hair. 'I'm here, Tyke; no one hurts what's mine. We're in this together.'

On a long sniff, she pulled back slightly. 'Do you mean that?'

The corner of his mouth curled upward. 'I've never meant anything more,' he said.

Her hand slid from his shoulder, and her thumb grazed his dimple as she sang a couple of lines.

'You're not running from me,' he said, moving to take her lips.

She resisted. 'What about you? Are you going to run?'

'Only in the direction of you.'

Conflict warred in her, but too much of her needed stability. For whatever reason, she chose him to steady her. Internally he vowed he couldn't let her down again; he wouldn't.

'Break it up, break it up.' Nick strode in, making himself instantly known. 'If I'm not getting mine in here, neither is he,' he said to Darcy who ducked her head under Sloan's chin.

'Bella made a promise, she'll come good,' Darcy said.

'She'll come great and repeatedly… if I can get rid of my sister,' Nick said. 'I'm making more coffee, you should get through there, you need an action plan.'

'I appreciate everything you're doing,' Darcy said leaning on Sloan to jump off the counter. 'All of you.'

'Don't appreciate it in my kitchen, that's all I'm saying,' Nick said.

Darcy took Sloan's hand and guided him back to the living room. 'What's with the kitchen?' Sloan asked, his breath warming her ear.

'It's a long story,' Darcy said.

'What's a long story,' Doug asked without a break in his TV viewing.

'None of your business I'm sure,' Bella said and shut off the TV. 'You have a TV in your own home.'

'I don't have a home, Beautiful,' Doug said. 'Not for another two weeks.'

'It's your own fault,' Bella said. 'He burned his flat down.'

'Now that's an exaggeration,' Doug said.

'No one is listening to you today,' Bella said. 'You can leave.'

'Am I going to be forgiven?' Doug asked.

'Not today,' Bella said. 'We're discussing sensitive information that isn't your business.'

'There's a story here,' Doug said, leaping off the couch to seek Darcy out. 'What is it? What is there?'

'Do not say a word,' Bella said. 'This man has a flare for the dramatic the likes of which you've never seen. If you don't want to see it in print, blown up to ten times its proportion then don't tell Doug.'

'Don't tell Doug,' he muttered and sat back on the couch.

'I wasn't joking,' Bella said shoving his knee. 'Go away.'

'What? You talked to me at the National—'

'I wasn't annoyed with you then,' Bella said.

'He licked you,' Darcy said.

In a very short space of time, Sloan had managed to miss a lot.

'It's not the first time,' Bella explained.

Doug leaned in close to her. 'And it won't be the last.'

'If you think about it again, I'll stick a pencil in your eye,' Bella said to him. Doug stuck out his tongue. 'Nick, get me a pencil!' Bella hollered. 'I'm going to blind Doug!'

'They're in the table drawer,' Nick shouted from the kitchen without an ounce of concern in his tone.

Darcy laughed and guided Sloan around to the chair Fiona had used last night. She sat him down, then propped herself on the arm, but he pulled her into his lap.

'Should we be worried?' Sloan asked.

'I don't think so,' Darcy laughed. 'They're good friends… I think.'

Bella shoved Doug away, and he snapped his mouth shut. 'It's okay I'll come around later,' Doug said to Bella. He gestured for Darcy's hand, which she provided he bent to kiss the back of it. 'Til we meet again.'

Darcy nodded, and Doug headed for the front door. 'Phone me when you've talked her into it!' Doug shouted presumably to Nick. Then with a flourish he snatched his coat. 'B, you phone me when you're bored of lover boy.'

Doug opened the door and stepped out.

Before it closed, Bella replied. 'Why don't you hold your breath until then!' Laughter carried from the hall, which made Bella smile and shake her head. 'I'm sorry you must think we're all crazy.'

'Of course not,' Darcy said.

'I do,' Sloan said.

'He doesn't understand, ignore him.'

'It's a wonder our species survived,' Bella said.

'You kicked him out?' Nick asked, bringing a coffee pot through to the table, and filling up the cups that were there.

'Darcy has decisions to make, and I don't trust

Doug not to sniff the story.'

'He takes pictures,' Nick said.

'You know he's always looking for the angle, especially when there's a woman involved. If he offered me page three, can you imagine what he'd offer Darcy?'

Nick had to look at Darcy's chest now that Bella had mentioned it. 'Good point.'

'So what are you going to do?' Bella asked Darcy.

'I'll have to go to the hotel myself to get my things,' Darcy said.

'You don't have to go alone,' Bella said. 'I'll go with you.'

'We talked about this,' Darcy said. 'You're not going to scare Terry away.'

'You know he's going to try and corner you again. Just imagine standing in that bedroom when he starts crowding you.'

'Hold on,' Sloan said. 'Are you telling me this guy touched you? That he…'

Thrusting Darcy from his lap Sloan found his feet. 'What are you—'

Sloan was already at the door. 'Stay here, do not leave this house, do you hear me?'

Darcy dashed across the room. 'You can't go over there. You'll get in trouble. You'll get hurt.'

'I'm not the one who'll be getting hurt,' Sloan growled.

'Stop it,' she insisted, watching him don his boots and jacket. 'Would you stop reacting in anger! Has anything about you changed in the last thirteen years?'

That question stopped him. 'I've had about enough of everyone's judgements this week.'

'I'm not judging you,' Darcy said. 'Think it through. If you go over there, they'll see you, the press, your colleagues, it's what we've been trying to avoid. I don't want to push you into that position—'

'You haven't told her?' Nick asked.

'Told who what?' Bella asked.

Nick and Bella were furthest from his mind when he looked at Darcy's round eyes, full of doubt, and concern.

'I don't work at the National anymore,' he told her.

'Why didn't you tell us that?' Bella asked pinching Nick's arm.

'Ouch! I thought he would have mentioned it.'

'No, he was a typical man, more interested in getting his end away than allaying our worries,' Bella said.

'I didn't do anything,' Nick gaped at Bella. 'I did absolutely nothing.'

'You didn't tell us you'd phoned him when you went out for the wine either, you're a sneak.'

'Now hold on a minute,' Nick carried on, but Darcy touched Sloan, and everything else faded to grey.

'You quit? Or did something happen?' Darcy asked.

'I quit.'

'Why did you do that? I thought—'

'I didn't want to do it anymore,' he said. 'My priorities are different now.'

'But I—' He kissed her words and stole her hands.

'No more hiding, I'll do whatever you need me to.'

'What will you do?' Darcy asked. 'Without your work—'

'Let's concentrate on you,' he said. 'We have to get your things from the hotel. You have a meeting with Hayes, and you have to decide what you want to do tonight.'

'What I want to do?' she asked.

'If I know you at all you don't want to back out

of a commitment, and not just to the show. What about the centre?'

'It's not only my responsibility—'

'No, it's not. But you took this on. I'll support anything you do,' he said. 'But I want to see you happy, don't let anybody stop you, not me, not Terry, not anyone. You don't have to make a decision now, but you will have to soon.'

'I'll feel better in my own clothes,' she said, squirming in the borrowed wardrobe.

'Then we have a step one. Let's get to the hotel.'

***

GETTING TO THE HOTEL was the easy part. Darcy had never been one to get up to mischief so walking through the lobby the prickle of awareness that heated her skin was foreign to her. Constantly alert for anyone who might recognise them, or for Terry who could happen on them at any moment Darcy found herself happy to be led by Sloan to the front desk to retrieve the new key card for her room. Bella had phoned ahead to her ex-colleagues and explained when she and Sloan would be here for it. Darting her attention left to right Darcy didn't like having her back to the majority of the space so she let Sloan do the talking. After that he took her to the elevator and pressed the button for her floor.

'You can relax,' Sloan said. 'This is the easy part.'

'Don't tell me that or we'll never get to the tough part. I think I'm about to have a heart attack.'

'I'm here, you're fine now,' he said.

But she didn't take much relief in that because her mental song seeped out. 'To the comfort of the strangers slipping out before they say so long…'

Taking her shoulders in his hands Darcy found herself facing Sloan's determination. 'Nothing bad is going to happen here. You're not alone.'

'Okay,' she said but couldn't really admit that she didn't have his confidence.

The elevator doors opened, and his hand locked around hers again to lead her up the corridor to the room. It didn't seem to matter that Sloan had never been there with her before. He strode up the carpet like he owned the joint. If she hadn't been so nervous, she would have been impressed.

Sticking the key card into the lock his hand shifted to her lower back and he guided her into the room in front of him. Luckily, everything appeared to be where she had left it, and she wasted no time in gathering her things into her suitcase.

'Don't panic,' Sloan said. 'Take your time.' Another song gave her nerves some comfort. 'You'd be awful on the run; all they'd have to do was follow the singing.'

Choosing not to rise to his bait she bypassed him to dump her toiletries into her case. The lock snicked which froze her to the spot, if panic had been in her before it rose now when Terry moved into the room.

'I heard you were back,' Terry said. Sloan lounged on the wall just out of Terry's view. 'Over your tantrum now I hope.'

'I came here to get my things,' she said.

'And apologise I hope,' Terry said. 'That diva shit gets old easy, Doll-face.'

While she hadn't meant to look at Sloan she must have because Terry swaggered further into the room to spy what she had.

'Well, well,' Terry mocked. 'What's this? Are you scared of me, Doll-face?'

'I'm not scared.'

Sloan dragged his disinterest over Terry's form, then managed to look indifferent and disgusted all at the same time though Darcy wasn't quite sure how he managed it.

'She's got nothing to be afraid of,' Sloan said. 'Not anymore.'

Terry visibly wasn't comfortable with Sloan's presence, but that fact didn't stop him from sniggering at her. 'You hired security? That's entertaining, do you think you're that important that I couldn't pay this guy off and do with you whatever I wanted?'

Sloan moved and her panic ratcheted to terror. 'Don't,' she exclaimed, halting Sloan, then talking to Terry. 'He's not security. He's my boyfriend.'

Taking the time to observe Sloan then her Terry certainly wasn't convinced. 'You mean the boyfriend who hasn't shown up for you once?'

'He shows up when it counts,' she said. 'And I'd be careful what you say because there are no witnesses in this room to corroborate any version of events you could dream up.'

'Are you threatening me?' Terry demanded.

'No,' Sloan said. 'That's why I'm here.'

'You're pushing it, girl,' Terry said, addressing her because Sloan made his nervous.

Seeing Terry uneasy was satisfying and she'd never been one for schadenfreude… until now. Having Sloan at her back straightened her spine, now she could understand and appreciate Sloan's confidence. Terry was nothing more than a bug on the windshield of their story, and Sloan could swipe him away with as little effort as flicking on a wiper blade.

'It's not nice to threaten women,' she said. 'You're lucky that I'm feeling charitable. I kept the secret of how you were treating me, and that was a mistake. Being nice gets you so much further in life. Asking politely, with a smile will reap greater results. Unfortunately for you I've seen your true colours, and there isn't a thing in the world that would make me want to work with you through choice… and my boyfriend facilitates that choice for me nicely, don't you think?'

Being in a position of authority had soured any goodness that might ever have been in Terry Hamlin but that wasn't her problem anymore. When she went to gather the rest of her clothes from a drawer Sloan moseyed toward Terry.

'You don't think about her,' Sloan warned. 'You don't come near her. You don't speak to her unless spoken to. Do you understand me? Your wellbeing is going to rely very much on my mood, if I think you've crossed a line with her, or any other woman we'll meet again… and, if I were you, I'd pray that never happens because it will only happen once.'

'We better go,' she said, zipping her case with the poise Sloan had afforded her. 'We have a meeting.'

'A meeting,' Terry asked though he didn't take his focus away from Sloan. This wasn't a man warring for power; this was a man watching the hungry dog that could pounce at any moment.

'Yes,' she said.

'You are coming tonight,' Terry said. 'You have to come.'

'I haven't decided yet,' Darcy said. 'That will depend a lot on my meeting. I've heard Paulie Hayes can be quite persuasive when he wants to be.'

His fear faltered at the mention of that name. 'What?'

Dragging her case off the bed she skirted it to take Sloan's hand. Linking his fingers in hers Sloan took her luggage in his other hand and urged her toward the door. 'Hold your breath,' Sloan said. 'Maybe she'll show up tonight, maybe she won't. You'll know all about it when the sexual harassment charge hits your mat. Have a good one.'

The words weren't said with any pleasance, but she enjoyed hearing them probably as much as Sloan did saying them. Giving a bully their comeuppance always held satisfaction, but she'd never experienced it until now. Johnny Sloan sure knew how to show a girl a good time, and somehow, he still surprised her with his conviction. The Original Badboy used his powers for good now, and a tiny part of her wanted to believe that she'd contributed to some of that conversion. Whether she was or not didn't matter, she still owed him far more than she could repay.

FIFTEEN

'I INSISTED ON COMING to your flat because we can't take over Bella and Nick's lives, it's not fair. He does still work for the National, and from what Bella said to me Doug got a dressing down from his boss after sneaking his way into my place even with the story Doug gave about me throwing him straight back out again, and him having to plead with me not to call the police on him for trespass. Doug kept our secret which I don't think you gave him credit for.'

Sloan took his key from his jacket and put it into the lock steeling himself for her reaction when they got into his flat. Swinging the door open he held it for her, and she strode in only to come up short.

'Where are all your things?' she asked twirling in the empty space.

'In storage,' he said. 'The vast majority of my stuff anyway.'

'Why?' she asked. 'Why would you put your furniture into storage? Was this what Doug was talking about this morning?'

'No,' Sloan said. 'He was talking about the flat for rent I set him up with.'

'Okay,' she said. 'So where is your stuff?'

'In storage.'

Dropping her handbag to the floor was the equivalent of throwing down the gauntlet. 'You're being deliberately evasive,' she said.

'I'm not,' he said.

With everything that had transpired that morning, and would transpire at the meeting with Hayes, and her decision on tonight's show Sloan didn't think lumping on his life changes would be well received right now. Of all the decisions she had to make today Sloan wasn't about to take the risk that this would be one too many.

'You are.'

'I sold it,' he shrugged and went to the kitchen to then be reminded there was no fridge, or kettle, or anything.

'You sold it?' she said. 'Why would you do that?'

'Didn't need it anymore,' he said, planting his hands on the counter to levy himself up to sit on it. 'Come over here, we can find something to do in this empty space, I'm sure.'

'Our meeting with Hayes is in less than an hour.'

'I can be quick,' he teased. 'Really quick, time me if you want.'

'Johnny, talk to me, tell me why you would…' From the way her words trailed off he knew she'd come to a conclusion – and probably not a complimentary one. 'Did you have trouble paying your bills?'

The note of hope in her tone intrigued him but his mobile sung out interrupting his question before he asked it.

Pressing receive he slunk off the counter to talk. 'Hi, are you okay?'

'Me?' Glo asked down the phone line. 'Your father phoned here this morning. He said you ran away last night. What happened? I've been out of my mind! Do you know the last time JS phoned me? I can't remember the last time that's how long ago it was.'

'I'm fine,' he said.

Over the years he'd had friends who cared but wouldn't follow up on odd behaviour. He'd had girlfriends who followed up on odd behaviour too much. What he'd never had was this – a concerned relative, genuinely worried about him.

'I'm not,' Glo said. 'Where are you? No one's seen you in the village.'

'I'll be back soon,' he said, passing Darcy's curious expression to head for the far living room wall, he couldn't have his aunt blowing the big surprise.

'Back? You just got here.'

'Everything is fine, nothing has changed,' he said. 'This is just a blip.'

'A blip? Is it Darcy? JS said—'

'Everything's okay.'

'Don't be cagey now,' Glo said. 'I'm worried.'

'I can't talk now,' he said.

Glo paused. 'She's there? Is Darcy there with you?'

'Yes,' Sloan said.

'So you're back in the city?'

'Yes, for now.'

'But you are coming home again? You're going to bring her back?'

'We haven't gotten that far yet,' Sloan said.

'You haven't told her, have you?'

'Not yet.'

'You know, you shouldn't run away like that. It's not nice to scare people.'

'I'll sit on the naughty step when I'm back, okay?'

'Aye, you will.'

'I have to go.'

When he hung up, he tried to think of what to say to Darcy.

Rightfully, when he caught sight of her, she was definitely wary.

'Why did you sell your flat?' Darcy asked him. 'Why is it empty?'

'We don't exchange for another couple of weeks,' he said, which was true but not what she wanted to know.

His phone rang again, and when he glanced at the screen hope flared in him. 'Hang on,' he said to Darcy holding up a silencing finger. 'Hello.'

'Hello, Sloan. I tried to get hold of you first thing—'

'Yes, I had some unexpected business. Sorry about that.'

He'd left things in the air with Nancy and the community at the last meeting because none of them were interested in committing to anything presumably until they knew he was for real. The fact that she was phoning now, when the community meeting wasn't until the end of next week, had to be a good sign.

'That's okay,' Nancy said with an air of joviality he convinced himself was also a good sign. 'I have to be honest, when you came to the meeting, and presented in the way you did…'

'You weren't sure if I was for real,' he said.

'You do have a reputation,' Nancy said.

'I'm all too aware of that,' Sloan said. 'Have you had a chance to think about my proposal?'

'We have,' Nancy said. 'Some of the details were a bit sketchy though, and I wanted to go over your presentation with you again before the next meeting if that's at all possible?'

'Yes,' he said. 'Yes, that's definitely possible.'

'Are you free this evening?' Nancy asked.

'I'm not,' he said, wincing at the cliché he was projecting of being unreliable the last thing he wanted to do was prove to the town that he hadn't matured but Nancy laughed apparently sensing his defeat.

'Don't worry,' she said. 'Notice is short. When are you available this week? What about Tuesday morning?'

'Yes,' he jumped on it. 'That is great for me.'

'Come over to the schoolhouse, I'll pull together a few bodies and we can go over the barriers that we're going to face. This is going to be a big project and it might not go smoothly. But I have to say that more than a few of us were impressed with your ideas… and your attitude.'

'Given the history I can understand that,' Sloan said. 'But I'm in this for the long-haul. Don't mistake that. I'm determined.'

'Yes.' Her smile carried down the line. 'I think we can all see that.'

This time when he signed off the call Darcy's curiosity had become horror, which instantly set him on alert. 'What?' he asked, fearing he'd been discovered. 'What is it?'

'You're living with someone,' she whispered. 'That's what you said last night. Oh God.'

Her hands leapt to her mouth, and tears were on the agenda from what he could tell.

'No,' he said, bounding toward her but the phone went in his hand again. 'Damnit!'

The timing might have been terrible but when he read the name, he wasn't surprised.

'I should leave you alone,' Darcy said.

'No. Wait there, don't go anywhere, this will take one second.' He answered the call. 'What?'

'Glo said she just spoke to you,' Lottie's voice sailed down the connection.

'She did. What is it?'

'Are you okay?'

'Yes,' he said.

'Do you know that little guy, Rodney?'

Sloan closed his eyes to search his memory bank. 'The little guy with the lisp and the lazy eye?'

'He does not have a lisp,' Lottie asserted.

'What about him?' Sloan asked, enjoying the rise Lottie never failed to deliver. 'He asked me to the Halloween party in the community hall.'

'So?'

'He's really cute, and I know that at least two of the girls in—'

'Do not have sex with him,' Sloan asserted, his eyes popped open to see Darcy clearly taken aback.

Though he knew it wouldn't make any difference to her audio he flipped around to face the wall again. The last thing he wanted to do was pique Darcy's interest more by leaving the room.

'But I was just thinking that—'

'I don't care,' Sloan said. 'We've had this conversation about your thoughts. I mean it. Don't do it.'

'But—'

'No,' he said. 'Be strong, and it will be worth it.'

'You're very sure,' Lottie said.

'Aye,' Sloan said. 'I told you I would help you, didn't I? You have to let me help you.'

'Okay,' Lottie sighed. 'But if you're wrong, you owe me sex.'

'You got it. I'll find someone to deliver,' he laughed.

'You better,' she sulked and hung up the phone.

'Was that your girlfriend?' Darcy asked.

Tucking the phone back into his pocket, he removed the distance between them, which seemed all the greater in the hollow room. 'You're my girlfriend for as long as you'll have me.'

'But you said—'

'Everything will become clear,' he said. 'You have to trust me. Do you trust me?'

'I suppose,' she said without a shred of conviction.

'Great,' he said, sticking a kiss to her forehead. 'Let me take you to lunch before your meeting.'

'You mean outside?' she said. 'Us? Outside? Together?'

'We'll go for broke, Tyke,' he said.

They left the flat together, he still carried her suitcase, but he welcomed her arm around him, and tucked his over her shoulder holding her close. Maybe naive Darcy hadn't gone too far because she had just accepted his request for faith. Not many women would after witnessing those calls. When he left the city, the calls had been constant, which led to him shutting off his phone entirely. Despite the witness Sloan hadn't wanted to duck any of those calls that had just come through. A life was forming for him in a place far from here, with people he hadn't thought about for years, people he'd given no substance to. From everything he had learned he couldn't have been more wrong about the town he'd claimed not so long ago to hate. Now he could see what Darcy loved about the community spirit. Calls from the city were for information, but calls from the village made his life better, richer, people showed they cared, and looked out for each other, and that was something he could get used to.

***

THE TAXI DRIVER had asked three times about the address when they'd got into the car outside the restaurant Sloan had taken her to eat. Having a break from the situation she found herself in was welcome, and he filled the lunch with jokes, and observations, keeping the conversation rich and warm until they finished, then he'd slipped onto her side of the booth and kissed her. The kiss was chaste enough for public consumption, but he followed it by pulling her against his chest, holding her so completely that for that minute she understood the meaning of life. When they couldn't put it off any longer, he'd led her onto the street, and into this cab.

They stopped outside a large wooden gate, and Sloan paid the driver, but Darcy wasn't sure they were in the right place. The journey had taken so long that the possibility the taxi driver had taken them around the houses did occur to her. Sloan hadn't said anything, so she didn't either.

Sloan had no hesitation in going to the buzzer next to the gate, and he kept hold of her hand offering a silent reassurance that she appreciated. As soon as they were identified the gate opened, and they hadn't got ten feet up the drive when a uniformed man buzzed up in a golf cart and took the suitcase from Sloan. The porter then seated them both and drove up to the most magnificent three-storey Edwardian style mansion with more windows, and therefore more rooms than she could count. Her head still spun when she and Sloan upped the stairs and found themselves in a sumptuous, cavernous lobby flanked by dark marble pillars.

When another uniformed man greeted them, he spoke of Mr Hayes gratitude for the visit, and took them to a room at the back of the house. He knocked and opened the door to show a vast office space dominated by a large oak desk, behind which sat Paulie Hayes himself.

'Ah, my saviour, Miss Holmes,' Paulie Hayes said, opening his arms and rising from his desk to meet her.

'Please, there's no need for…'

Sloan enjoyed her discomfort at having this man embrace her, but his amusement didn't last long.

'That will be all,' Hayes said, taking Darcy's hand from Sloan's.

'Excuse me?' Sloan said.

Hayes own man scurried away apparently used to the mogul's brisk commands. Sloan wouldn't go down that easily. 'I'm assuming that you're some sort of…' Hayes looked Sloan over, and while Sloan seemed ready to deck the guy Darcy got her own back on his previous entertainment. 'You're some sort of employee, a moocher… or perhaps you call yourself a manager?'

'No,' Darcy said, placing her hand on Sloan's forearm. 'This is Johnny Sloan, he's my boyfriend.'

'Ah,' Hayes said but didn't seem to have moved any on his opinion. 'You have to be careful of men such as this, young Darcy.'

'No,' she said. 'No, it's not like that. Johnny and I have known each other for a long time. He's not a hanger on. I promise. He's not after money… it's sex he likes.'

Hayes laughed at her frankness. Although Sloan frowned, she could see a twitch of a smile in his expression. 'Have you been together for a long time?' Hayes asked, gesturing to the two tub chairs on the guest side of the desk.

'Uh…' Darcy started but didn't say anything else until they'd all sat down, and Sloan had taken her hand again.

Her hesitation concerned Hayes. 'If you would prefer him to leave—'

'No,' Darcy said, tightening her grip until she

scored Sloan's hand with her nails. 'He goes where I go. I need him here.'

'If you're sure, because it wouldn't be a problem to—'

'No,' she said again this time with a strength intended to humble. 'Without him there's no me. I go where he goes.'

Sloan kissed the back of her hand. If she hadn't wanted him here, she would have told Sloan herself to his face, and he would have accepted it. This meeting was important, and she could need Hayes help, but if Sloan was disrespected, she wouldn't accept it.

'As you wish,' Hayes said. 'I merely wish you to understand that your desire here is law.'

'That's very gracious of you,' she said. 'We've known each other for a long time but… I was only reluctant to confess I had a crush on him long before he even knew who was.'

'Childhood sweethearts,' Hayes beamed.

'You could say that,' Darcy said, squirming at the inaccurate moniker.

'You saved my life, young Darcy. I'm sure you've seen in the press—'

'I have,' she said. 'But I only did what any number of people would have done. I just got there first I suppose.'

'I disagree,' Hayes said. 'I owe you a great deal.'

'I didn't do what I did for any payment. If I'm completely honest I didn't know who you were. It didn't occur to me.'

'I don't have children,' Hayes said. 'When something like that happens… I was close to death, several times, my money doesn't guarantee life as I found out perhaps to my detriment because I am still on a strict diet and exercise regime. I have a lot of work to do to rebuild my body, and indeed my spirit. But you… what you did for me cannot be repaid in any monetary way, though of course if you want—'

'No,' Darcy said. 'I don't want any money. To be honest, I'm not sure why you requested my visit.'

'You deserve recognition for what you did.'

'I don't.'

'You do,' Hayes said. 'I understand that you are still a part of the Hidden Talent show, the final is this evening.'

'Yes,' she said. 'It's supposed to be anyway.'

'Supposed to be?' Hayes prompted.

'Darcy has had some trouble with the agent assigned to her,' Sloan said.

'Trouble?' Hayes asked. 'What kind of trouble?'

'It's not a big deal,' she said. 'But I'm not sure that I'll be competing this evening.'

'Why is that?' Hayes asked. 'Do you have your contract?'

'No,' she said. 'I signed it at the beginning of the process, and I haven't seen it since. I'm sure that I am required to sing tonight, I'm just not very sure that Terry will be accommodating after recent events.'

'Terry Hamlin,' Hayes said. 'Yes, I've heard of him. He has had trouble in the past. Can you describe to me the nature of his misconduct?'

'How do you know he was the one in the wrong?' she asked.

A smile flitted to the mogul lips. 'You have a good heart, and from everything I've heard Terry Hamlin is a toad.'

Hayes had come across as strict with his staff, perhaps dismissive, but he'd been nice to her. It seemed wrong to judge him on that one factor. His dark hair and his skin were flawless, and his wardrobe understated but he was tired, his eyes were a little too heavy, and his spirit somewhat squashed. But he smiled at her with a gratitude that was overwhelming.

'We shouldn't have come,' she said, leaving her seat to the confusion of the men.

'Why not?' Hayes asked. 'What is the matter?'

'You want to leave?' Sloan asked.

'Yes,' she said. 'We should.'

Sloan didn't hesitate in moving for the door.

Hayes spoke again. 'Please, tell me what your trouble is?'

'You are not indebted to me,' Darcy said. 'I wouldn't want you to think… for anyone to think…'

'We are friends,' Hayes said. 'At least allow me the liberty of that relationship with you. I can see that you do not take compliments well, and you are an honestly good person. You would have to be after what you did, but I see that gratitude makes you uncomfortable. But understand my burden too, young Darcy. I have been given the gift of life, a gift that you gave me. Please, imagine yourself in my position and realise that I want to be of help to you, in any way I can.'

When Hayes put it in that way she could understand where he came from. Her nature didn't give her the leeway to accept his attention, but if she had been the one saved, she too would feel it necessary extend the hand of friendship to her rescuer. She sat down again. Sloan took a moment, ready for her to change her mind again, then when she didn't, he sat.

So Darcy took a deep breath and told Hayes about Terry's behaviour, about how he pressured her to sign a contract that she didn't want, and how he treated Jet so abominably when there had been no call for it. Hayes listened intently and interrupted to reiterate her words so that there was no confusion. Throughout the discussion Sloan said nothing, and more than once she feared he would explode into action. Terry hadn't forcibly touched her, which Darcy made sure to be completely clear about, but Hayes insisted the intimidation was as bad, and had to be stopped.

'I'll get a copy of your contract,' Hayes said. 'If you do not wish to continue with the competition my lawyers will defend your position. Is that what you want?'

'I don't know,' she said. 'I don't like to quit. I like to see things through. But after today's developments I'm not sure I'd be welcome.'

'Nonsense,' Hayes said. 'If you want to compete then you shall. I respect your determination. You have to stand up to bullies, or you let them win.'

From his dismissive attitude towards the staff and some of the things she'd read of his behaviour in the press Darcy was sure Hayes could take a leaf from his own book. Still, the man was helping her, paying a debt as he saw it, and his gratitude gave her the opportunity to finish what she came here to do. As it stood it didn't matter whether she won or not, what mattered was doing what was right. Her signature on the contract showed her intention, and with the help now offered she could follow through.

Hayes pressed a button and called in a member of staff whom he then spoke with quietly.

She took the opportunity to delve into her bag. 'I'm going to phone Bella,' Darcy said. 'Just to let her know that we're okay.'

Taking herself out of the way she rang Bella's number.

Nick answered. 'How are you getting on?'

'We're okay,' she said. 'I wanted to thank you for taking pity on me last night.'

'Sloan's a friend… sort of.'

'I know, and I hope I won't get you into trouble at work.'

'What Toby doesn't know won't hurt him,' Nick said. 'Are you with Hayes?'

'Yes,' she said, noticing that the staff member had scurried from the room, and Sloan currently leant over Hayes desk and the two were intent in their whispers.

'Are you okay?'

Nick might have been talking but Darcy hadn't been aware of it. 'Yes. Sorry. We're both okay. I got my things from the hotel. Will you tell Bella thank you for me?'

'I'll try,' he said. 'I'm not in the flat right now but I'll tell her when I get home. She'll call you herself.'

'Oh, that's not necessary, I wouldn't want to impose—'

'You're not imposing,' Nick said. 'You're too nice for your own good. You probably hear that all the time. Sloan's a lucky guy.'

'He puts up with a lot,' she said. 'The truth is until last night we were sort of broken up.'

'All's well that ends well,' Nick said.

'Yeah.' She tried to be enthusiastic, but this wasn't the end, not yet. 'I have still have a show to put on tonight.'

'You're going?'

'Yes,' she said. 'I think so. It doesn't seem right to have gone through all the weeks only to give up now.'

'Fair point,' Nick said. 'Good luck from us, and I'll make sure that Bella doesn't phone while you're on stage.'

'Thanks,' she said and terminated the call.

Hayes had just left the room, and Sloan crossed to her. 'He's putting us up in a flash hotel.'

'Who?'

'Hayes,' Sloan said. 'Are you okay? What did Bella say?'

'I phoned Nick,' she said, tucking her phone back into her handbag.

'Why?'

'I have his number,' she said. 'What were you and Hayes talking about?'

'This and that,' Sloan said.

'You wouldn't tell me what all those phone calls were about at your flat, or why you sold your flat. Now you won't tell me about your conversation with Paulie Hayes?'

'Aye,' he said without an ounce of shame. 'That about sums it up.'

He took her hand but instead of trotting out with him she stayed put. 'I don't know what's going to happen tonight.'

'You have nothing to worry about,' he said. 'I'll be there, and Hayes has assured me that there will be security everywhere you go.'

'I'm not worried about Terry. I mean I am but… I mean tonight.'

'I'm not following you,' he said.

Tonight was the final, whether she won or not the ride would be over. Time closed in on her from all sides. The bubble she'd travelled in since leaving home got smaller every week, and now it was like a second skin. If she didn't win, then a contract would probably be the best way to raise money fast for the emergency incident centre. But she missed home despite her wish that she didn't. Perhaps the turmoil of the last few weeks was getting to her more than she'd realised, except scurrying home to Inverquay probably wouldn't solve a thing. After all of her work she would go home in exactly the same position she'd been before this competition.

If she did win then she could fund the centre, at least enough to get the project off the ground, but things were different now, and she wondered if the centre was enough. Sloan. Tying herself in knots about ifs and buts was easier than facing the fact that after tonight it would be over between them. They had lost weeks while apart that she now wished she could live over again to suck every morsel of her time with him into herself, to keep in her heart, to keep her warm when she was all alone again.

'Never mind,' Darcy said when she realised that Sloan still stood in front of her expecting an answer, an elaboration on her statement. 'A hotel?'

'Yeah,' Sloan said. 'He's going to get a driver to take us over there now. He said we should order room service, pay-per-view, whatever we want.'

'He didn't really say pay-per-view,' she said, letting him take the lead again.

'No, I added that one in,' he said.

'Right now, I'd be happy with a bath and a change of clothes. I'll have to get to the venue for sound checks. Normally Terry would—'

'I'll take care of it,' Sloan said.

'You and Terry are not best of friends.'

'Neither are you and he,' Sloan rightfully said. 'I'll run it by Hayes, he gave me a direct number.'

Enough of her day had been spent fighting, pushing against a seemingly immovable force so she nodded, and gratefully leaned on him while they waited for Hayes car on the front steps. Tonight was the night – win, lose, or draw.

SIXTEEN

FROM WHAT THEY SAW of the hotel it was beautiful, and certainly beyond their pay grade. The car had stopped, and the door opened half a second later being held by a porter who had been expecting them. He'd escorted them through the lobby giving commentary on all of the available services in the hotel and reminded them that they were at liberty to take advantage of any, or all of them, at Mr Hayes urging and expense. Their room wasn't a room at all, it was a suite. When the porter ushered them, in she spied her suitcase, which she had forgotten all about. Somehow, it had made its way here before them. The porter bent over backwards to be pleasant and reminded them to enjoy their stay. When he'd eventually left Darcy was spinning, but Sloan was gone.

Before she had the chance to worry about him, he called for her. Of course she found him sprawled out on the bed. Tempting as he was, she had to refrain from joining him. She had a show to perform tonight, and she hadn't been at rehearsals today. Granted, all of the run through that they'd done this week were flawless, and the technical rehearsals had ironed out all of the kinks. But that didn't stop her from wanting to get there and remind herself. The day had been fraught, her nerves were frayed, and she needed time to get into the zone. Though she'd said all of this to Sloan then retired to the bathroom the truth of their union coming to an end slipped back into her consciousness. Just as she was sure her tears would win, he'd shocked her by leaping into the shower behind her. Keeping a physical distance had been part of her plan to ease him out of her life, or rather ease herself out of his. Yet when he swept her wet hair aside and kissed her, she'd been powerless to stop him from giving her exactly what she needed.

Allowing herself to be swept into his enthusiasm gave her a chance to relax. Being with Sloan, close to him, a part of his world made her world seem more secure, more stable. Just his presence awarded her joy, and the knots of tension ebbed further away with each moment they were together. They'd showered, made love there against the tile then slithered out together taking the time to dry each other, only to dampen their skin with a shower of kisses. When she couldn't put it off anymore, they got dressed and Sloan called for a car to take them to the venue.

The high life certainly wasn't for her. Having people wait on your every whim made her feel awkward and uncomfortable. Though it did serve a useful purpose, especially when she was so drastically over scheduled. And, of course, sex hadn't been in her original schedule, but Sloan had slipped it in there.

The driver took care of security, or at least Darcy assumed that he did. When the door was next opened, they were outside the open stage door and right enough two men dressed all in black flanked her. She could only assume that this was Hayes security.

'This is sexy,' Sloan whispered above her ear. 'Sneaking in the back door with the star of the show.'

'I'm not the star,' she said.

'Could've fooled me,' he said, glancing back at the security men. 'Can we have sex in your dressing room?'

'I'm here to work,' she said but her throat tickled in a laugh.

'Sure,' Sloan said, giving her derriere a squeeze. 'But we can have a little fun, can't we?'

'Probably not,' she said, slipping out of her coat.

'Spoil sport,' he grumbled.

'I share a dressing room with Jet, so unless you want us to have an audience.'

'I'm sure I could come up with something,' Sloan said.

'Stay here,' Darcy said when they reached said dressing room. 'All of you.'

Pushing through the black door she expected to see Jet in some stage of preparation for the last run through that they should manage to shoehorn in before the main show began. Instead, Terry sat at a table in the corner, pouring over some paperwork, but her entry disturbed him.

'Decided to show up then, did you?' Terry snarled.

'I don't want to argue,' Darcy said. 'We're both here to do a job.'

'Yeah, but you've fucked mine haven't you,' he exclaimed, bolting up from the table. 'You had to go telling tales, didn't you?'

'I don't—'

'Sure you don't, Doll-face,' he snapped. 'You and Hayes thick as thieves I'll bet – you fucking him and that goon you had with you today? You're handing it out all over town, but you couldn't—'

A draft on her neck explained his sudden silence, the door had opened at her back, and from the way Terry paled she didn't need to ask who the newest entrant was.

'I have to get changed,' she said to Terry.

The bottle of frustration in the agent must have shot up in pressure because he literally fumed. But he was smart enough to huff and puff, and grind his teeth then make a sharp exit – straight past Hayes' hired security she hoped.

'What the hell is he doing in the changing room?' Sloan demanded but she just dumped her bag and hung up her coat.

'I only have to deal with him for a few more hours,' she said. 'I'm not going to sweat it anymore. After tonight he won't be a part of my life anymore.'

The same could be said of Sloan, but she tried not to think about that.

'This place looks empty to me,' he said, scanning the room but didn't get a step in Darcy's direction when the door opened.

'Oh, you're here! I was so worried!' Jet came up short when she noticed Sloan. 'Do I know you? Are you with the pair outside?'

'Jet this is Sloan, Johnny Sloan.'

Clarity seeped to Jet's expression. 'This is your fella!'

Sloan tensed when Jet grabbed him into her arms, but Jet didn't notice because she was already on the way to Darcy, whom she took clean off the floor.

'You're excitable tonight,' Darcy laughed finding that Jet's exuberance was contagious.

'Tonight's the night!' Jet exclaimed. 'The final, can you believe that we're here? We were the best from the start, everybody knew that, but the time has just flown by, don't you think? Oh, I'll be so sad not to see you every day. We'll have to call all the time, and write –

email I mean, no one writes on paper anymore. Oh, Diva! We're nearly through! We're both winners, both of us. We're going to be a success. I just know it.'

Jet carried on blethering about the night, and headed for wardrobe as she did. Sloan took a step away telling Darcy with his expression how proud of her and happy for her that he was. He thrust a thumb towards the door, and she nodded. She had work to do now, and like she had pointed out this rollercoaster would come to its end soon, this was a time to keep her head in the game, to keep her focus, because there were too many questions about what came next, and where they were going. If she thought about saying that final goodbye to Sloan, all she could accomplish would be curling into a ball and melting into tears. Bella, Nick, and even Doug had helped to get her here, so had her family, and Simon, and other Quayers but her main thrust had been Sloan, and she wouldn't let him down now, she couldn't let any of them down. Her all was what they expected and that was exactly what she planned to give.

***

SLOAN LOITERED OUTSIDE with the security guys for a while, but neither were great conversationalists, so he went exploring in the backstage area, and observed the tasks the crew completed. While he was sure everyone's job was important the sheer number of people was surprising. At this time, before the show he would have thought not too many people were required, but the prep it appeared was as important as the show — much like in a restaurant kitchen.

'She pulled you out of her hat.'

Sloan turned to see Terry in the shadows not far from him. 'I really don't give a shit what you think.'

'I get loyalty, and she's paying you, right? It could

be worthwhile…'

'What?' Sloan asked though he didn't really care what this cretin had to say.

'You and I, we could talk, sort something out.'

'I don't swing your way, pal, sorry.'

Terry's breezy laugh made Sloan's skin crawl, but that was only half as bad as when Terry had the cheek to pat Sloan's shoulder in a friendly way. 'She's going to be worth a pretty penny.'

'Are you trying to be my friend? Do you think I'm your buddy?'

'There's nothing wrong with talking,' Terry said. 'All I'm doing is talking. I get that she's gorgeous, and I'm not exactly god's gift. But she doesn't know anything about the industry, about money, about her potential. I can help her. I can help both of you.'

'So you offer me fifty per-cent exploitation fee and I tell her to perform like a good girl wherever we roll her up to?'

'It doesn't have to be like that. She'll get the hang of it. We just need to show her what's out there and give her the chance to make the most of what she's got. She's hot property, and it doesn't exactly hurt that she's hot property if you get me.' Terry's leery laugh curled Sloan's lip.

'What you are is scum,' Sloan said, getting in Terry's face. 'You don't deserve any success you've had off the back of exploiting women like my Darcy. After tonight you'll be lucky to sign up the z-list beauty pageant dropouts. You've made an enemy of Darcy, which means you've made an enemy of me… and of Paulie Hayes.' Sloan readied to leave but wanted one more thing straight. 'She didn't shop you to Hayes. I did. She might have told the story, but I filled in the details. So if you want to make a complaint, I suggest you put it in writing, then shove it up your arse.'

If the guy didn't get the message now, then he was beyond hope. Sloan strode away noticing that more than a few of the crew members were smiling in his direction. Terry made enemies all on his own, but Sloan certainly wasn't sorry he'd helped the process with Hayes. People would come to learn that Sloan could be a good guy, he wasn't all bad boy, but the latter came in handy when protecting his woman, and that was an area of his life that he eagerly anticipated for his future, because nothing would come before Darcy. He might not have filled her in on the details yet, but he'd quit his job, sold his home, made in-roads into mending relations with his father. No doubt existed in Sloan that he and his father would always have their issues but if they could take baby steps, a little at a time, eventually they would get to civil, and maybe they could learn to tolerate each other. All Sloan was sure of was that if it mattered to Darcy then it mattered to him, and he'd make damn sure his father understood Darcy's importance in the equation. Sloan wouldn't have anyone starting a fight in Darcy's home, or her business, and he certainly wouldn't let her be drawn into the game herself.

Her wholesome background pretty much guaranteed that she would want to spend holidays, or events like Christmas as a family unit. Glo would relish it, and he had more than enough cousins to fill seats, but Darcy would expect all immediate family, which would most probably include his father. Having acknowledged all of those things he also knew that if he gave it his best, and his father faltered Darcy would stand at his side as fiercely as he would hers. All he had to do now was tell her that they lived together, and he planned to spend every moment of his existence complimenting hers in any way he could.

'Are you okay?'

Being lost in his thoughts he hadn't seen her

approach but looking at her now he wondered how he'd missed her. Her hair was high, and fluffed out, the gaudy make-up wasn't much to his taste though he had to admit she was gorgeous with it – he still preferred his pure, perfect shower sprite as he'd dubbed her earlier. The body was better naked too but right now in the stilettos and glittering red number that hung around her neck by the tiniest strap he'd ever seen he accepted that this was half a step behind naked. His expression must have betrayed this because she held her hands up in surrender.

'You've got that big, bad wolf look on your face, Johnny, do not touch me.'

'How does that thing stay on?' he asked, reaching for her but she dodged his hand.

'You don't want to know how it stays on. You want to know how to take it off.'

'You're like a mind reader,' he said, knowing that the flash of his dimple would soften her – it did. 'Come here and let me try it.'

'No,' she laughed. 'It's tit tape, if you pull at me it'll hurt.'

'It'll hurt?' he said. 'Not letting me have a go is hurting me.' Her focus dropped to his groin. 'That's right, Tyke.'

'Stop flirting with me.'

But her words didn't marry with her expression and when he finally got a hold of her, she met his mouth with her own.

Music had been blaring out from somewhere, but he hadn't watched her perform so tonight would be a first for him, and he'd be the only one in the room that had experience with this dress… this night was guaranteed to be top notch.

'I have to go,' she laughed pushing out of his arms, but he managed to trap her against the wall. 'Marla will go insane that you've smudged my make-up.'

'You don't need makeup,' he said. 'You're the most beautiful woman I've ever seen.'

'Not on camera,' she said. 'They have to be able to see me from the back row.'

'Who cares about the back row,' he said. 'Here's me, right up front.'

'You get to enjoy me in a way others don't.'

'Damn right I do.'

'So they can't possibly understand me like you do,' she said. Her smile made him want to sneak her into the closest private space. 'Johnny, I don't have time.'

'I know that,' he said, reluctantly backing away from her. 'I can't help myself around you.'

Something flitted over her face, but she tried to smile through it. 'I have to sing tonight. I have to be… professional.'

'Okay,' he said. 'Why are you telling me?'

'Things between us are… I'm really happy that you're going to be in the audience tonight… You are going to stay, aren't you? I mean if you're not that's okay—I've done it again, haven't I? I've made assumptions, and been selfish, and—'

He took hold of her arms. 'I'm going to put all of those insecurities down to your nerves about tonight. It's okay to be nervous. But don't doubt yourself. Hayes was right that you are too good. Be selfish tonight, Tyke, be selfish on lots of nights because what you call selfish the rest of us call compassion. You have to look out for number one. Look out for what's important to you, not to anyone else. Think about yourself, think about what you want, and why you're doing this, and you'll realise what the rest of us have known all along. You're an angel, Darcy – a God given angel here on earth walking amongst us mere mortals. You see the good in everyone, but for some reason see yourself as a burden. We're lucky, every person who has stood with you, spoken with you, existed with you is lucky. I certainly count myself it when you land that smile on me.'

'You are one smooth talker,' she said, reducing the push in her hands. 'I'm lucky to have you… even if we are approaching our expiry date.'

He couldn't exactly turn her away when she threaded her fingers through his hair and relaxed her body against his, so he returned the embrace. Now he understood that fleeting expression and her timidity in the hotel that afternoon. By not landing his life decisions on her he'd thought he was saving her an added load in the midst of a frantic day. What he hadn't seen was that by not telling her he'd lumped on a load of a different sort.

'I have to get back,' she said. 'They'll be opening the doors for the audience in a few minutes.'

'Okay. I can go to my seat, and let you be… professional.'

'Thank you,' she said but he wasn't quite ready to let her go yet.

'Darc,' he said. 'Good luck. Whatever happens tonight I'm proud of you, and you're going to be great.'

'There's still a chance I'll fall on my face. Have you seen these heels?'

'You won't fall,' he said. 'And if you get nervous picture the audience in their underwear.'

She slunk closer, her body coming up flush when his, tilting her head back her teeth sunk into that plump lower lip, dragging against the flesh making him want to kiss it all better.

'When I see you in your underwear all I want to do is take it off,' she hummed, batting those long lashes.

Without waiting for a response, she sashayed away leaving him panting for more. Forget dragging her into a private room, if she wasn't available, he might have to find that room just for himself.

***

THE SHOW WAS OVER in a flash, for her as a performer anyway. The audience had been great, and those who had tuned into the live TV feed of the show had made the final phone calls to decide who would triumph. Stand-up comics had filled the transitions, but she'd sung for her life, just as Jet had, and no matter what happened they could both be proud. The lights were so bright that they couldn't make out individual audience members, but Sloan was out there somewhere, just for her, and that made this whole experience easier. But it also ratcheted up the pressure because she didn't want to let anyone down, least of all the man who had kept her sane for most of this journey. Yet, she knew that no matter what happened he would be there for her tonight, and if she was honest then she would be happy to see the back of Hidden Talent. That did leave one other glaring fact though, the end of Hidden Talent meant the end of her relationship with Sloan. From the beginning she'd asserted her desire to get home, and now that she'd made it here, she did need home. But she needed Sloan too.

The dramatic music hit its crescendo, and the spotlights bathed her and Jet. 'And the winner is...'

Darcy didn't hear a thing because her ears were ringing, with a thud the light to her right went off, and she couldn't see Jet anymore. Then the music was on, and the glitter began to fall from above as the pyrotechnics went crazy. Handed a masked metal figure, and a bunch of flowers she was pulled into the arms of the man who had read out the results. The crowd were going wild, and her head thrummed with the disorienting activity. She'd won. Lord, almighty after everything she'd put up with, everything she'd experienced, this was the end, and more than the money, and prospect of the centre that realisation blurred her eyes and smeared her make-up. People came at her from every which way, and she was dragged into one hug and then another. Still the audience were cheering, and the lights were flashing, the music blasted, and then she was pushed to the front of the stage and handed a microphone.

'I… I don't know what to say. Thank you to everyone who voted, and to all of you for your support over these last few weeks. Where's Jet?'

Darcy turned to see Jet emerge from the crowd clapping just as exuberantly as the rest of the people crowding the stage – though she had to admit she couldn't identify any of them.

'You did it, Little Diva,' Jet said hugging her again.

'Will you sing with me? I'm not sure I can… that I'll…'

'You got it,' Jet said. 'Where's your fella? Shouldn't he be up here?'

'Oh, I don't think—'

The crowd began to chant for her fella but there was no need because in a flash he was there at the front of the stage running up the stairs. He came straight to her sweeping her completely off her feet and swallowing her mouth in a consuming kiss more suited to the bedroom, but that only made the crowd cheer louder, with more than a few wolf whistles mixed in.

'I have to sing,' she said, appreciating the stability Sloan gave her.

'I'm so proud of you, Tyke. I knew you would do it.'

'Yeah,' she said. 'You're this happy because your bet's going to pay out.'

He kissed her again, then the stage manager was calling for the stage to be cleared while the music cued up. Darcy grabbed Jet's hand, not willing to let her friend sneak off because Sloan's strength had to wait in the wings. Watching him go he didn't take his attention away from her, and though he merged into shadow she knew he was still there, and that only encouraged her to get the song over with faster to get into his arms again.

'Are you ready?' Jet asked springing behind Darcy and forcing her shoulders back. 'Think Diva. Be Diva.'

And for all this experience had sucked out of them both, she and Jet gave their all once more, together, and had the happiest performance of her career by far. Things couldn't get much better than this, she'd fulfilled her goal, and she had her man within reach. For now, she vowed not to think about tomorrow, tonight she had to live in the now.

SEVENTEEN

THE QUESTIONS HAD BEEN coming thick and fast for more than an hour. Sitting between Terry and one of his lackey's Darcy had answered as best she could but with her own future so uncertain in her heart she couldn't exactly go into details. Hayes had come up in conversation and Terry bristled at the reminder. As she felt was proper, she'd promised print exclusive to the National. Surprised their on-site reporter, but Darcy wasn't going into details.

On an apology Terry whisked her off stage demanding that she change for the party that was apparently taking place in a function room in a hotel somewhere. Happy to oblige she headed for the dressing room but searched every face on the way wondering where Sloan had hidden himself away. The only thing to perfect this whole whirlwind would be him at her side. By the time she changed, and got herself back out into the melee of people, she was carried along on a tide of congratulations until she drifted out onto the pavement. People were crowded around barriers looking for autographs, and she had no idea where to start with something like that. The adoration was nice but the only person she wanted to be the focus of was nowhere in sight.

'Where's Sloan?' she asked one of the security men who remained at her side outside.

People continued to call her name but drowning them out with her frantic thoughts she searched the group for Sloan. The night was unexpected and magical, but panic dissolved the pleasure when she considered what could have happened. Their ride was over, and he knew that as well as she did. Could he have left? Gone away to be with the woman he alluded to? Her rapture on stage might have displayed intent to an onlooker, so the possibility circled her consciousness that Sloan had gone to do damage control with one of the mysterious callers from that afternoon.

'Where is he?' she asked again when she got no response.

Someone took her arm and ushered her toward the car, but she wrenched her arm out of the grip that had her and searched for her inner diva. 'No!' she asserted. 'I am not going anywhere until I know exactly where Sloan is!'

The noise around her was deafening so her shout didn't have quite the effect she'd banked on. With nothing behind her except the car she hadn't expected a hand her thigh, though it didn't take long for her to seek out the aggressor.

'Sloan's in the car,' Sloan said, peeking through the lowered limo window. 'It's cold out there. I'm getting things warmed up in here.' The window began to ascend in the same moment Sloan opened the door from the inside. 'Care to join me?'

Her diva outburst was out of character, but effective all the same. 'Can you believe any of this?' she asked, sliding onto the leather beside him.

Sloan leaned over her to pull the car door closed, and the vehicle began to move despite the crowds that still hung outside the glass, complete with paparazzi flashing their bulbs through the tinted window.

'That you won?' he asked, pouring champagne into two flutes then dumping the bottle back in the ice bucket. 'Damn right I believe it.'

'Johnny,' she said and took the glass he gave her.

'To you,' he said, tinging his glass on hers.

'Not to me,' she said.

Sloan drank, but for her the adrenaline intensified the reality. Here they were in the most ludicrous situation, the fact that it was surreal only added to its dreamlike quality. Tomorrow she would wake up — alone. They'd spend the night physically with each other but her already fraught emotions had to face the truth. By the look on Sloan's face, he didn't struggle with the same demon.

'Drink up,' he said, putting his own glass aside.

'I'm not really in the mood,' she said.

He took her flute away and cast it aside with his. 'Let's see if we can change that.'

Jarring her contemplation Sloan scooped her from her seat and straddled her across his lap. 'What are you doing?'

'Do you want me on top?'

Sighing, she flattened her hands to his cheeks. That he was happy for her was an understatement. The look on his face was of pure adulation, he was proud of her, he was happy for her… she wanted to go back to the beginning and live their time together all over again.

He draped her hair over his forearm to push it back over her shoulders, his mouth followed heading for her neck, but she took his shoulders and urged him back.

'I want it hard,' she said.

'It is,' he grinned, pushing his hips upward but she wasn't interested in playing with him, not until she'd made herself perfectly clear.

'I'm going to sign the contract,' she said.

His own playful exterior evaporated. 'What?'

'I'm going to take the deal.'

'With Terry?'

'No,' she said. 'Bella said Nick would put the feelers out, and I'm sure Hayes could point me in the direction of—'

'You're going to record an album?' he asked. She nodded. 'But why? You told me that you weren't interested in fame. The prize money was your goal – you've achieved that.'

'That was my goal in joining the competition,' she said. 'But I don't need to be in the village to donate that money to the cause.'

'And who will fight to make sure the cause is actioned?'

'I wasn't the only one who realised the need for the emergency centre,' she said. 'Plenty of people in the village want to see it built. This way I can make more money and donate it to the centre. I can probably make at least enough to cover overheads for a while. The fundraising will have to continue to keep the place running.'

'Why?' he asked.

'Costs will be—'

'No,' he said. 'Why do you want to sign the contract? What's brought about the change of heart?'

'Going back was the safe path, the easy path,' she said. 'The town doesn't need me.'

'I think there are more than a few people who would argue with that,' he said.

'Nothing is worse because I'm not there,' she said. 'I can do this. I can stay here in the city and record the album.'

'Then what?' he asked. 'You go on tour? You record another album?'

She shrugged. 'I don't know,' she said. 'I suppose I have to take it one step at a time.'

'I don't believe this,' he muttered.

His joy had become confusion. He lifted her off his lap and put her back in her seat. Something in him warred with the turmoil she had inadvertently caused. Much as she hadn't exactly expected him to jump for joy, she hadn't expected him to be so bereft.

'Johnny.' When she touched his forearm, he snatched it back. 'What's the matter?'

'Nothing,' he said and carefully took her hand to kiss her knuckles. 'Nothing.' He pressed her hand down against his thigh, and kept it covered with his own. 'Okay…' He nodded seemingly to himself. 'Okay. I can… I'll figure something out.'

'Johnny, I don't understand why—'

The limo lurched to a stop and the door opened within a couple of beats. Sloan practically leapt from the vehicle and was already in the lobby when the doorman closed the car door behind her.

Another man rushed toward her – shorter but slicker than the door attendant. 'I am Raymond Andrews, and I am the manager here. I would like to congratulate you on behalf of myself, and of all the staff here.'

'Thank you,' she said.

A group had formed behind a barrier she was sure hadn't been here earlier. Sloan was in the hotel, at the reception desk, leaning over to talk to the beaming receptionist. Still Sloan didn't look happy, and when he didn't look happy, he looked terrifying. His whole body was tense, and Darcy couldn't figure out what this change in demeanour meant.

Taking the time to talk to the small group, she signed a few autographs then was ushered into the hotel by Mr Andrews the manager. Sloan was no longer in sight so when Mr Andrews took her to the elevator she didn't object. Mr Andrews offered her every service the hotel offered, and she didn't want to tell him that his colleague had done so already that afternoon. Now that she had won this competition, she imagined that her life would change in various ways. None of that pomp interested her, and she was sure she wouldn't get used to people gathering in groups to talk to her but if she had to do it to stay with Sloan she would.

As politely as she could muster, she thanked Mr Andrews, and was careful not to imply any sort of invitation into the suite because she had someone else to face, and he wouldn't want an audience.

'Thanks.'

Sloan's said the single word into the phone he had at his ear. When she closed the suite door, he ended the call and tossed the phone to the couch in their lush living room filled with expensive, designer furniture – none of which was particularly comfortable.

'I thought this was what you wanted,' she said, his frown landed on her. 'If you don't want to be with me—'

'Don't be ridiculous,' he said, driving his fingers through his hair.

'I don't need the town,' she said. 'Inverquay will always be there. I can make a go of this, there is no harm in trying, and it would be silly of me to throw this opportunity away. I can help Inverquay, and all of my friends, if I have an income to support a vital service that is needed there. It makes sense I suppose. I was talking to Bella about it, and… I've been so attached to the town because I'm scared. Life in Inverquay is easy for me but it's all I know. I can't very well dismiss this chance just because I'm afraid of the unknown.'

'You love the Quay,' he said.

'Yes, and I always will. I can't change who I am, and I'm sorry that the town I love can't find a place in your heart. But you're in my heart too Sloan. Maybe this wasn't meant to be, I doubt we were supposed to meet again after all these years, but it has happened, and I can't erase that just because it's easier to run home, to run back to the simple, safe answer and ignore how I feel about you. But I can't. I can't do it, Johnny. I'm terrified. I'd be lying if I told you that I wanted a contract, or that I was comfortable with people gathering in the street to talk to me but if it's what we need to do to make a go of this then I'll do it.'

'Make a go of this, you mean us?'

'I can't say goodbye to you, Johnny,' she said, moisture pricked her tear ducts, the very notion of turning away from him permanently flushed ice through her veins. 'Every second we spent together today was a second closer to saying goodbye. I can't enjoy this. I can't enjoy you when this is hanging over us. I'm not out of line. I know you feel something for me. I know you do.'

'Yes,' he said. 'I do but—'

'You're not making me do this,' she said. 'It's my choice, and I will live with it. I love my town, but I won't resent you if things don't work out because this is my choice, and there is nothing to stop me going back to the Quay in future. The Quay will always be there. But you might not always be here for me. If I go back now, you'll move on, and I'll eventually realise that leaving you was a huge mistake, but by that time you'll be with another woman, and I couldn't bear to think—'

'You need to stop,' he said, approaching her and taking hold of her hands.

'But I—'

'Stop, Tyke,'

'This can't be it. Please, Johnny, don't let this be the last moment in time we share.'

'This isn't it,' he said.

Some of the tension had left him, which she was glad of, but she didn't understand how he could smile while she shredded her heart with the uncertainty. A tear escaped and his smile only widened, which made her prickle, but she was glad of the anger that erased some of her sorrow.

She sang as he brushed the tear from her cheek.

'You don't have to be nervous,' he reassured.

'I'll take Hayes offer for you,' she said.

'Tyke, I don't want you to do that.'

'Why not? I'll stay here. You don't ever have to think about the Quay again. I promise.'

'The thing is,' he said drawing out each word. She tried to take her hand back, but he kept hold of her. 'I live there now.'

'What?'

'I live in the Quay,' he said. 'What do you think took me so long to get to you last night?'

'You... you...'

'Surprise,' he said with a faltering smile.

Each of the words made sense individually but she was having a difficult time putting them together in a way she could comprehend. Since they'd met, he'd made no secret about how much he hated the town she loved vowing never to return. That night in the woods he'd been only minutes away from blazing a trail out of there. When he'd come back to the Quay for her, they'd broken up. How could she now believe that he'd somehow found a way to live there when everything about him screamed of his discomfort about being in their hometown?

'You sold your flat,' she said putting the pieces together. 'And those phone calls...'

'My new neighbours.'

'What about your father?'

'I'm working on that,' he said with half a shrug.

Stumbling away from him, she couldn't blink for fear this aberration would vaporise. 'You're working on that? You…? You're… you're working on that?' He nodded. 'But you hate your father, you two don't… I mean you never… all the stories.'

'My parents had marital problems from the beginning, he was distant, and liked the attention of other women. My mother was fragile at the best of times; her side of the family have a history with alcoholism, so it's no surprise she was driven to it.'

'You're talking to me about this?' she exhaled. 'You're… you're telling me about your family?'

'Anything you want to know,' he said. 'The point of no return between my father and I was my mother's suicide. Neither of us handled it very well. It was easier to attack each other than to face our own participation in exacerbating the situation.'

'You're talking now? You and your father are talking?'

'I'm not sure,' Sloan said. 'We argued when I went to visit him but… I was with him last night when Nick phoned.'

'You're fixing it,' she whispered.

'That's not completely up to me,' Sloan said. 'But I'm trying my best for you, Tyke.'

'Johnny,' she exhaled and rushed toward him. Flinging her arms around his neck she pulled herself as close as she could get.

'You were right,' he said into her hair. 'I had to try something, the anger wasn't healthy.'

'I have some things to tie up tomorrow,' she said. 'Then I have the morning shows on Monday.'

'Tuesday then,' he said, taking her from their

embrace. 'On Tuesday, we go home.'

'Together?'

'Together,' he said.

He couldn't have given her a gift that she could value more, and she had to admire his courage. They hadn't discussed moving, but he'd already sold his flat and done it. If she'd gone back to the Quay, he would have been there for her. For the first time since they'd been together there were more answers than questions. Details were unimportant because the most important thing had been dealt with – they'd figure out the rest – together.

***

SAYING GOODBYE had been one of the most difficult things he had ever done, and it was only for a night. After her whirlwind of TV and radio interviews on the Sunday and Monday, they'd said goodbye on the Monday night. Darcy had enough clothes to fill a big-rig, but he only had his bike. He'd rode home after hiring her a car for the following day. Hayes had offered her a driver, but Sloan could see how uncomfortable Darcy was with the attention, and with help recommended to her at every turn. The thought of her driving up alone didn't sit easily with him. But there was nothing he could do about it because she'd rejected his offer of help too. Hidden Talent and its entanglements in Darcy's life would need some recovery time but he was glad now that he could be there to experience it with her.

The bunting-decorated street was bustling when he walked down to the bakery on the Tuesday afternoon. Every single person he saw had to stop and talk to him – apparently, their kiss on stage at the finale hadn't gone unnoticed by the locals. One person he had still to speak to was his father but Sloan was in no hurry to rush that, and he didn't want anything to taint Darcy's arrival. She'd phoned him half an hour ago, and he'd reamed her for phoning while driving, to which she hung up and facetimed him to show she was actually parked in a layby. He told her to take her shirt off and she hung up on him again. Now she would be due to rock into town at any minute, and with this amount of local and media attention he had to hope she hadn't fulfilled his request – not this publicly anyway.

The bakery was as busy as the street, but mostly with the older folk who wouldn't want to be outside in the cold. Glo stood at the counter with Lottie, and both women lit at the sight of him.

'Where is she?' Lottie asked applauding his arrival.

'I left her in my other jeans,' he said and smiled at Lottie's perplexed frown. 'She's on her way.'

'Did you tell her?' Glo asked.

'Tell her what?' Lottie asked.

'Not exactly,' Sloan said. 'We'll get to that. She doesn't need the details. There have been other things going on. We'll get to it.'

'She's coming home today,' Glo said. 'A home that you're living in.'

'What does it matter?' Sloan asked. 'It's not like we've never spent the night together.'

'The night is way different to living together,' Lottie said. 'That's what guys always tell me.'

'Where's Rodney?' Sloan asked.

'We're going to the party tonight,' Lottie said. 'He's picking me up.'

'Have you had sex with him yet?' Sloan asked, Glo hit the back of his head though it was quite a reach for his aunt. 'What?'

'No,' Lottie said. 'You told me not to.'

'Good for you,' he said.

'You told her not to have sex with someone?' Glo asked. 'Why did you do that?'

'He's helping me,' Lottie said.

'Helping you what?'

'Find a man,' Lottie said.

'Finding them isn't the trouble,' Sloan said. 'She's a pretty girl.'

The make-up was gone, and her sleeveless top didn't even hint at cleavage. 'You do look good Lottie, the tables in here have been talking about it,' Glo said. 'You're more relaxed too.'

'We'll get you to that altar, Lots,' Sloan said hooking an arm around her, and then his aunt. 'Stick with me, kid.'

'Yes,' Glo said. 'If his coaching doesn't work, he can always scare a man into marrying you.'

'Who would ever be scared of Johnny Sloan?' Lottie asked appreciating her own joke.

Hubbub in the street had Sloan leading the women toward the door. 'Think that might be Darc?'

The cheering got louder on the street and when the three of them got outside and through the row of people between the bakery and the road Sloan saw the little hire car chugging up the street. While everyone else stayed on the side-lines out of her way Sloan broke ranks and approached, which made her slow to a stop. Resting his forearm on the roof he leaned into the electric window she buzzed down.

'Give us a kiss,' he said.

'Have you got an exhibitionist streak I've not been made aware of?' Darcy asked, complying with his request.

'Now get out,' he said, stepping away to open the car door.

'What? I've been driving for hours—'

'The masses want their satisfaction. I'll take the

car up.'

'You're going to send me out there alone,' she said.

He leaned over and unclicked her seatbelt then took her hands to draw her out onto the street. Darcy stumbled back against him when the cheering went into overdrive.

'You're right,' he said, closing the car door. 'I'll get it later.'

The crowd might want her, but he wanted her in one piece, and she'd need some sort of protection to ensure that. He did his best to keep her in the cocoon of his protection but so many people wanted to speak to her, to touch her, that it took them almost fifteen minutes just to get the platform that had been temporarily erected beside the bakery. Still the crowd continued to shout for her until she lifted her hands off the makeshift podium and everyone began to quiet.

'Thank you,' she said to the crowd. 'You are all very kind, too kind, this is a welcome that I could never have dreamed of. A lot of you are locals who I've known and loved, but a lot of you are not from these parts and I have to say welcome on behalf of Inverquay and all of us lucky enough to hail from these parts. You have all been very generous to come here, and to welcome me home.

'When I left, I didn't tell any of you where I was going, or why, but I feel it's safe to say now that the cat is out of the bag.' The crowd laughed politely. 'I didn't do this for myself, and I didn't do it for vanity. I know a lot of you will be surprised to see me back here in my hometown so soon after the finale of Hidden Talent. I went on the show not because I was interested in fame and fortune but because my town is in need. The need might not be immediately apparent to the visitors because our town is beautiful as it is. But it does need something, it needs a safety net, something it has lacked to the detriment of some of our Inverquay family. For more than a year we've endeavoured to raise money for our emergency response centre, and we haven't come close to what we need to get it up and running. We lacked the exposure, the knowledge… the capital. The money that I won by being a part of Hidden Talent I'm proud to say will get us moving in the right direction. Every penny of those winnings will be put into the ERC fund, and our town will get what it needs to keep us all safe. Thank you.'

For a moment the crowd did nothing, but each face betrayed a mass-awe, and Sloan had never been prouder of her. After the shock wore off the group began to cheer and applaud for her. But Darcy only waved then came down from the platform and into his arms. She'd done what she set out to do, and now the truth was out so the town could appreciate her for what she had done for the collective good. He'd never known anyone so selfless, who would give over that amount of money without a second thought. But by now he didn't need to be told how special Darcy Holmes was, he was her number one fan.

***

'THAT WAS INSANE!' Darcy exclaimed almost two hours later when she finally got to her own house.

Some of the villagers had followed her but they'd left her alone at the end of the street. Sloan was currently taking her luggage from the hire car that he'd driven to the house. Darcy dumped her bag on the kitchen table and stretched her back a little. Fruit in the fruit bowl was fresh, when she thought she'd left it empty. Her lips curled upward when she saw the kettle on the stove.

Sloan came in with her suitcase and took it

straight through to take it up the stairs. The fridge was full. She was surprised to see a half-used block of cheese, and the tossed salad in Tupperware beside it.

'How can weight-less clothes weigh so much?' he asked, dropping an elbow to the fridge. 'What do you want to do now? There's a party tonight in the hall for you but you'll be tired after your journey so—'

'Where did the food come from?' she asked.

'The shop.'

'You bought used things from the shop?'

'I used them,' he said and crossed the room to turn on the heat under the kettle.

'In my house?'

'Yeah,' he said. 'Everyone is so proud of you; the tourist season is going to be in manic this year. Colin says they're already fully booked March to October.'

'Why would you use food in my house?' she asked. 'I thought you'd bought things to ease me back home, thought about something so I didn't have to.'

'I did,' he said, grabbing an apple from the bowl. 'Do you want me to cook you something?'

'In my own kitchen?'

'Are you tired?'

'Johnny, what is going on here?'

Her phone inside her bag on the table chirped to life sparing him from answering the questions. It took her so long to unearth the thing that she caught it on the last ring. 'Hello?'

'Is this Darcy Holmes?' a male voice on the other end of the phone asked.

'Yes,' she answered.

'I am calling on behalf of the Hidden Talent legal department.'

'Okay,' she said. 'Is there a problem?'

'Yes,' he said. 'The money cannot be released to you.'

'What?' she gasped. 'Why not?'

'There has been a breach of your contract.'

'I don't believe that—'

'I am merely advising you of the situation,' the male said. 'If you want to pursue this matter, I suggest you get yourself legal representation.'

The line cut off, but she didn't lower the phone immediately. Sloan came to her side and took the phone. He read it but it had already disconnected so he cast it aside.

'What's wrong?' Sloan asked.

'They… they're not going to release the money,' she said, trying to find reason. The wind was gone from her sails and nausea overwhelmed her. 'What am I going to do?'

'Why not?' Sloan demanded. 'What did they say?'

'That I should get legal representation,' she said her hands flattened on her stomach. 'What am I going to do? I just told everyone that… they'll think I was lying, or that I've kept it for myself.'

'We're going to sort this out,' Sloan said, pulling out one of the dining chairs to seat her in it. 'We'll call Hayes.'

'What is he going to do?' she asked. 'He can't do anything. This is because of Terry, or maybe the whole thing was a hoax all along, it wasn't on one of the mainstream channels maybe they—'

'You won that money, and everyone in the venue, in the TV audience saw that, the Quay saw that. I saw it, and we're not going to let them get away with paying any less than every single penny. Stay here.'

When he left her side, the nausea increased. Terry would find a way to make sure she didn't see a penny. She could imagine that he was that vindictive. Darcy clambered to the door in need of air, the fresh, free air of Inverquay that she had so desperately missed. But as soon as she was on the lawn her neighbours began to approach, and she knew they would want a show. People wanted to congratulate her and yet she could still let them all down. Making for the hire car she got in and slammed the door, luckily the key was still in the ignition. But the fact that she was surprised made tears threaten, she'd been in the city too long because in this town no one locked doors, or took their keys from their car, everyone here was good, and she had failed to remember that. And now without that money, she had failed the townsfolk too.

EIGHTEEN

'AREN'T YOU THAT FAMOUS singer doohickey,' Ritchie said when he opened the cabin door, but she wasn't in the mood to be reminded. 'What's wrong?'

'Everything's fallen apart,' she said, slumping in past him. Nudging Rocky out the way she fell onto the couch.

'What happened? Where's Sloan?'

'I think he's been invaded by body snatchers,' she said. Ritchie closed the door and crossed to his armchair by the fire. Rocky circled him then settled on the floor. 'You should've seen him today,

'Aye,' Ritchie said. 'So?'

'I think he's living in my house,' she said.

'He's suffocating you?' Ritchie said. 'I thought you were into the guy.'

'I am into him,' she said.

'You came all the way over here to tell me that Sloan's suffocating you but you're into him. Don't you have other things to do today? You can't have got into town more than an hour ago.'

'Two,' she said, grabbing a cushion and pressing it into her gut. 'I told everyone why I did it.'

'The ERC.'

'I never told you that,' she said, piqued by suspicion.

'What other reason would you have?' Ritchie asked. 'Every time you were over here you talked about it. What would you need a hundred grand for? You're not exactly the type for fame and fortune.'

'It doesn't matter now,' she said. 'It's gone.'

'What's gone?'

'The money,' she said.

'What?' Ritchie exclaimed, sliding to the front of his seat. 'How could it be gone?'

'They won't give it to me,' she said. 'Some legal wrangle.'

'They can't back out of giving you your winnings, the press would go berserk.'

'Fighting them will probably cost more than the cash they owe,' she said.

'So they'll give in. It won't be cheap for them either.'

'I announced to everyone what the money was for,' she said, cringing at her own eagerness to get the news out before she actually had the cash. 'Now they'll all think I'm a flake.'

'The town is thrilled that you won.'

'How do you know? You're a hermit.'

'We've got the radio,' he said. 'You're a popular feature at the minute.'

'Until it turns out I've conned them all. I should've known that Terry wouldn't be crossed, he'll have the last laugh.'

'What about the Hayes guy? He'll help you.'

'Sloan said that,' Darcy said.

'Smart man.'

'I had to get out of there,' she said. 'I think I ran away from him. Not him but… a few months ago I sat in my kitchen, on my own, in a quiet street, with a completely unremarkable life. Now look at it.'

'This was all for a good cause. You did what you did for a reason, and Sloan is a good guy.'

'How do you know?' she asked.

'I don't,' he said. 'But you do, and I trust your judgement. After Josie left me, I had nothing, and no one. She got the rumours out in force, and she got them out fast. By the time I realised what she'd unleashed everyone in town believed her, and no one was interested in hearing my story – except you.'

'Ritch—'

'Actually, you didn't care about my story, and you didn't care about hers. You didn't want to hear the gossip and tittle-tattle that enraptured everyone else. You took me in and looked after me when I had nowhere else to go. I know what that cost you in reputation-capital.'

'I didn't—'

'I know you didn't want anything in return,' Ritchie said. 'You're a good person, and you cared that I was alone. If it hadn't been for you, I don't know where I would've ended up. She took everything from me, every last penny, and enjoyed doing it. I was too in love to notice how she took advantage of her access to my savings, and she was the one that convinced the town I'd begged her to take the money for her silence on how awfully I'd treated her, like what she had confessed wasn't the half of it.'

'The way that she treated you—'

'She taught me a lesson,' Ritchie continued. 'And she did me a favour.'

Darcy didn't believe that. 'Friends that you'd had for years crossed the road to get away from you. You didn't deserve that.'

'They weren't really friends in the first place then, were they? You and I said hello, but we'd never been close enough to consider each other friends. You showed kindness to a stranger that you had every right to fear based on Josie's lies. When the town started talking about us you held your head high and let them draw their own conclusions. You never made me feel like charity, and never wanted me to display gratitude, or grovel for the favour you gave.

'I owe everything to you, Darc, and I wouldn't change my life now for anything. I've never been happier, and I wouldn't have got here if it wasn't for you.'

'Are you trying to make me cry?' she asked cuddling the cushion closer.

'No,' he said. 'I'm telling you that you're the strongest person I know. If they want a fight, you better stand up for yourself, Darcy, you're more than capable of it.'

'I don't know if I have any fight left.'

'You do,' he said. 'And if you don't then let Sloan fight it for you, I heard that was a speciality of his once.'

'I think he's moved in,' she whispered.

'You deserve it, Darcy, don't second guess your feelings now. You're in love with him, and he moved his life to a place that he left in hate. He's in love with you too… I can't say I blame him.'

'I'm scared.'

'You're supposed to be,' he said.

'What if I lose him?'

'What if you don't?' he asked. 'Sloan wouldn't have come back here for you if he wasn't ready to make it work.'

'How do you know he came back for me?' she asked.

'Because I did,' he said. 'When you found me on that roadside, in the rain, in the middle of the night, I was ready to walk into the loch and never come back to dry land. You convinced me to come back into the Quay, and I did. I hated the place; it had forsaken me I didn't see why I should do anything but the same in return. In thirteen years, Sloan never came back, you changed that in him. The fact that he did this after avoiding it for so long proves the depth of his feeling; you have to see that, don't you?'

'What if I can't live up to what he expects?'

'Darcy,' Ritchie smiled. 'You're enough. The reality of you is enough. He doesn't want an illusion, he wants you.'

'He moved his life.'

'Aye,' Ritchie said, leaving his armchair. 'Clearly, he's as crazy as you. I'll feed you but once you've had a hot meal you're going back there, and you're going to fight for what's rightfully yours, the money, and the man.'

Ritchie had been a voice of wisdom that she couldn't imagine her life without. She had a feeling that when Sloan saw how caring and subdued Ritchie was, the two men would become friends.

'Do you want to come into town for my party?'

Ritchie laughed. 'Not on your life, but thanks for the offer.'

Helping Ritchie through a bad time in his life had meant as much to her as it had to him, he trusted her, and he protected her now probably because of her actions. In his heart he was good and pure but his experience with Josie still haunted him, and all of his relationships suffered for it. Closing himself off out here gave him a protection against the world and its evil tongue, and Darcy doubted there was anything that would tempt him from his sanctuary.

***

'SHE WOULDN'T DO ANYTHING silly,' Glo said, taking Sloan's hand from his knee to clasp it in her own. 'You have to calm down.'

'Calm?' Sloan demanded. 'How can I calm down? She left.'

'She didn't leave you,' Glo said to her nephew who occupied his space centre-couch in her front room. 'This whole thing must be very overwhelming for her.'

'I was there. I was with her. I could've helped… underwhelm her.'

'You're not thinking straight,' Glo said. 'The party tonight will—'

'The party starts in less than an hour,' he said, pointing needlessly to his own watch. 'I don't think she'll be early.'

'She won't let everyone down.'

'Who cares about everyone?' he said, flying from the couch. 'I don't care about what folk say. I care about where the hell she is, and if she's safe!'

'The care home won't be open this late,' Glo said. 'Perhaps her father—'

'I drove by there, but I didn't see the car. She'll be with him; I know she will.'

'With who?' Glo watched him pace the width of the rug.

'Ritchie what's-his-name.'

'McHugh,' Glo said. 'You could be right.'

Sloan stopped pacing. 'She's in love with him, isn't she? You might have slipped that into conversation before I contracted myself to the deposit on the land.'

'If she loves another man, you're going to withdraw your donation to the ERC?'

'I'm donating the money from the sale of my flat; I now have nowhere to live.'

'You're overreacting,' Glo said. 'She doesn't love

Ritchie McHugh.'

'How do you know that?'

'Because if she did, the pair of them would have acted on it years ago. He lived in her house months before he started building the lodge he's in now.'

'Great, that's just great, so he's an ex? I sent the woman I love into the arms of another man. They don't love each other; they're just having sex. Great, what am I worried about?'

He flopped into the chair closest to him. Thinking of Darcy with another man made him want to put his fist through something, and the smirk on his aunt's face did nothing to alleviate that.

'Her world doesn't look the same as it did when she left. It's no surprise that she wants something, someone familiar to help orient her. Darcy is a good girl.'

'I know,' he said. 'You keep saying that, but—'

'Do you trust her?'

'What kind of—'

'Do you trust her?' Glo asked again.

A creak from the kitchen lifted his attention then her figure came into view. Darcy, right there in his aunt's living room.

'Where have you been?' he asked, clambering from the chair to skirt the couch and get to her.

'I saw your bike outside,' Darcy said, touching his jaw with her fingertips. 'Were you worried?'

'Was I worried?' he mumbled. 'No, I wasn't worried. I'm just great over here.'

'I'm sorry,' she said, sliding an arm around his waist. 'Hello, Gloria.'

'Darcy,' Glo smiled. 'You've had quite a time of it.'

'Things will be back to normal soon,' Darcy said.

'You're both pretending nothing happened, where did you go?' Sloan demanded.

'Maybe we could go home,' Darcy said. 'We have a party to go to.'

'I'm not going to any party,' Sloan said. 'Why did you disappear?'

'I was… I didn't disappear, but it doesn't matter now because I'm back.'

'It doesn't matter now?' he said. 'I've been frantic.'

'And I promise never to make you so again. We're in the Quay, nothing bad happens here.'

'I've told him that,' Glo said.

'He's been in the city too long,' Darcy said.

'Did you have sex with him?'

Darcy's smile flickered, but she caught it in place. 'I'm going to go home now. It was nice to see you, Glo, and I hope I'll see you tonight at the party.'

She didn't offer him any words of comfort, but Sloan wasn't surprised after his offensive question. Darcy left the way she had come in, and as quickly, and quietly.

'Did you have sex with him?' Glo hissed and threw a cushion at his head. 'Go and apologise to her. She came in here because she saw your bike, she was looking for you, and your question is – did you have sex with him? I'd be surprised if she lets you back into her house at all. I wouldn't. You didn't tell her about your conversation with Hayes, that worry must be playing on her mind, and you ask her—'

'I get it,' he said, dipping down to kiss his aunt's cheek. 'I'll tell her I'm sorry.'

Glo grabbed his hand. 'She loves you. You have to realise that love should come with trust. Don't let your parents' relationship be a model for how you conduct yours. Don't drive her away; Darcy is about love, not anger.'

Sloan had been the way he was for as long as he

could remember but his aunt's words played on his mind. He started his bike and pulled on his helmet, Darcy's lights were long gone but he'd catch her up, and he'd apologise, then he'd spend the rest of his life trying not to drive her away.

***

THE RENTAL CAR would be picked up in the morning, so Darcy left it on the street and took the empty paper coffee cup from the holder she'd left it in and gave the car a once over to make sure she hadn't left anything. The roar of Sloan's bike came from the back of her property so at least she knew he was here. His question had hurt her feelings, but she must have hurt his by running away at the first sign of trouble.

In the same second that she entered the front of the house he entered the back, and they met at the kitchen door.

'I'm sorry,' he said, stroking her hair. 'I was wound up. I shouldn't have—'

'I've never had sex with Ritchie,' she said. 'I think there were one or two times when it might have happened, but he's a friend. I don't want anything more from him, and he doesn't want anything more from me. I want to be your girlfriend.'

'My wife?'

'Maybe,' she shrugged.

'Mother of my children?' he asked.

'One day,' she said.

This ease was what she needed from him, the gentle teasing, the heat of his gaze, the tenderness of his otherwise heavy fingers.

'I panicked when I saw you had gone,' he said. 'I've never been scared like that. I wanted to be with you, and I lost you.'

'I wasn't leaving you,' she said. 'I was ashamed that I'd promised my winnings to a good cause only to be told I wouldn't get them.'

'I spoke to Hayes,' Sloan said. 'The Hidden Talent lawyers were working from Terry Hamlin's direction, the exclusive you offered to the National, that's what they're trying to attribute the breach to. Hayes isn't worried. He has his legal team on it and has promised his own donation to match.'

'Match?'

'Your winnings,' Sloan said. 'And he'll fund the centre for the first three years. As soon as the money from the sale of my flat clears through we'll have the deposit, and Hayes money will get the ball rolling while we wait for your winnings – if they make us wait.'

'You've got it all figured out,' she said.

'You're not the only one who cares about this,' he said. 'I had a meeting this morning with Nancy and the other community members. They're impressed by your proposal.'

'My proposal?'

'I might have put it on to paper,' he said. 'But it's yours.'

'I didn't—the committee have been talking about the centre, and we've tried to raise funds…'

'Getting serious about something helps to move it along,' he said. 'You have to take the bull by the horns and not be complacent.'

'You really know your stuff,' she smiled. 'Is that what you've been doing here while I was in the city?'

'That and converting your garage into a garage.'

'What?'

'Out the back,' he said. 'I can tinker around with machines, I used to do it a lot.'

'Chop shop?' she asked.

'I wouldn't ask too many questions,' he stage

whispered from the corner of his mouth. Nudging his chest, he took the chance to bundle her into his arms. 'There isn't a mechanic for fifty miles around here. If people need help in a pinch, I can help out.'

'In a pinch?'

'I'm writing too,' he said.

'About what?'

'I've got a few pots on the boil,' he said, tapping his temple. 'But it's progressing.'

'Sounds like you have a wonderful life ahead of you. Two business ventures, a novel or two, a great relationship with your aunt, and a developing one with your father.'

'I'm going to get Lottie married too,' he said.

'Lottie?' she asked unsure how her friend and colleague had got involved. 'Are you responsible for the toning down of the make-up, the clothes?'

'I offered a couple of pointers.'

'You are a man of many talents.'

'One thing's missing though,' he said. 'I think I pissed off my roommate.'

'Oh…? You didn't piss her off, you surprised her… or maybe shock is a better word,' she relented.

'If she needs me to clear out, I will. I won't do anything to upset, or to rush her… anything more than I already have I mean.'

Darcy slowly shook her head. 'You're not going anywhere,' she said. 'You were always supposed to be here Johnny, and now you're here with me.'

'Aye,' he said. 'Maybe if I'd spent a little more time listening instead of reacting, I wouldn't have left you alone in the woods the night I left town.'

'I'm glad you did,' she said. 'You went into the world, and it's only after you've been out there, away from here that you can truly appreciate what home is. It never mattered where we were Johnny, what mattered was that we were together, we make each other better.'

'You're the wholesome one in this relationship.'

'I know it,' she said sliding her hands up his chest to drape them over his shoulders. 'I had you pegged the night we met.'

The question was in his expression. She pushed up to her tiptoes bringing their mouths to within breathing distance and whispered the same lyric she'd sang to him that night.

He laughed. 'Yeah, Tyke, I guess you did.'

Thank you for reading this tale!
If you can, please take the time to review.

~

Ask your local library for more Scarlett Finn novels!

~

For all things Scarlett Finn
check out:

www.scarlettfinn.com

CHECK OUT

OUT NOW!

www.ingramcontent.com/pod-product-compliance
Lightning Source LLC
Chambersburg PA
CBHW060759190726
48285CB00002B/486